CW00550145

THE MERSEY GIRLS

SHEILA RILEY

Boldwood

First published in Great Britain in 2020 by Boldwood Books Ltd.

Copyright © Sheila Riley, 2020

Cover Design by The Brewster Project

Cover Photography: Shutterstock

A CIP catalogue record for this book is available from the British Library.

Paperback ISBN 978-1-83889-324-8

Large Print ISBN 978-1-83889-669-0

Ebook ISBN 978-1-83889-325-5

Kindle ISBN 978-1-83889-329-3

Audio CD ISBN 978-1-83889-322-4

MP3 CD ISBN 978-1-83889-667-6

Digital audio download ISBN 978-1-83889-323-1

Boldwood Books Ltd
23 Bowerdean Street
London SW6 3TN
www.boldwoodbooks.com

I dedicate this book to my agent Felicity Trew, my rock.

The Boldwood team, so supportive and understanding. Special thanks to Caroline Ridding, editor extraordinaire, who keeps me on my toes, to Jade and Nia and all the team who work so hard to bring our stories to you, dear reader.

But, in these uncertain times, I also want to thank the nurses who have attended my son morning and night, rain, hail, snow and sunshine:

Christine

Anne

Terri-Anne

Caroline

Kate

Jenny

Amanda

Tony

Bless

Mark

There are more in this heroic band of caregivers, and I apologise if your name has slipped my mind, but I will never forget your face or the professional care, dedication and support you have given Alan. Thank you for all that you have done and all you continue to do.

Love,

Sheila xx

PROLOGUE

'Ten... Nine... Eight...'

Twenty-five-year-old Grace Harris lifted her finely sculptured chin, allowing her dark curls to caress her sun-kissed shoulders as her outstretched arm took in the audience of first-class passengers, before striding with ultimate confidence across the spot lit stage prominently situated in the chandelier-lit state ballroom of the *Marine Spirit.* The D'Angelo line's newest cruise ship was embarking on a cruise that left Grace's hometown of Liverpool on the first day of December, heading to tropical waters and visiting islands off the Caribbean before docking in New York on Valentine's Day.

A far cry from her hometown – the dockside streets of her beloved Liverpool, where the legacy of the Second World War was still visible in the vacant bombsites, broken houses, temporary prefabs and gardens turned into allotments for those lucky enough to have a garden, Although back in Reckoner's Row there were no such things as gardens.

'Three... Two... One...! Happy New Decade!'

The elite passengers on board were either famous, royal, or

incredibly wealthy. Celebrity guests such as Queen Elizabeth and Walt Disney cruised among many of Hollywood's top stars.

From her lofty perch on stage, Grace watched the party people rise as one and join hands to make a huge circle, merging together for a rousing chorus of 'Auld Lang Syne' to welcome the new decade of 1950, and a sea of emotional faces sang out a decade of war, destruction, austerity and want, which she had been lucky enough to avoid, since joining the ship two years ago and mixing with the richest of the rich.

Grace knew her singing afforded her a luxurious lifestyle that others envied, especially now she had reached the coveted position of headlining act. But her smile froze when she caught sight of something that made her heart skip a beat and caused the stirring words of the old song to stick in her throat. Clifford, the entertainment director, was bringing in his New Year locked in a passionate clinch with one of the dancing girls. And Grace realised the onboard gossip could be true after all.

She had reached the dizzy height of headline performer through hard work, determination and talent and had not slept her way to the top like some. So when Clifford had said he loved her at the start of the trip, and proved it by asking her to marry him on Christmas Eve, she felt like the luckiest woman in the world.

However, aware of scurrilous rumours regarding Clifford from some on-board staff, she put their gossip down to jealousy. A handsome man, he schmoozed the rich and famous clientele as part of his job, so speculation, like meat and drink to some crew members, had been rife.

Although Grace tried to ignore it, letting nobody see the hearsay hurt her, reassuring herself that his dashing good looks and devastating charm was bound to feed the gossip. Part of England's social elite, Clifford had served with distinction in the Royal Air

Force during the war and blended perfectly with the high society passenger list.

She was thrilled even though he swore her to secrecy regarding their engagement. Apart from the ruling that fraternising between the staff was not allowed, Clifford told her that being engaged to marry may harm his standing with the well-to-do big tippers, and they needed all the money they could get to save for a place of their own. Grace believed him, knowing every female on board had their eye on Clifford.

From this height, she could clearly see Clifford and the girl moving to the area behind 'the staff bar'. Hidden away from the passengers, the small room had walls of optics containing every alcohol, where the waiters fulfilled the table orders without having to queue with passengers. Making sure the coast was clear, Clifford locked the door behind them.

Every muscle in her body was taut and Grace wanted to storm off the stage and interrupt their fun. But to make a scene would be tantamount to career suicide for both of them.

When Clifford had asked her to marry him on Christmas Eve, slipping a pink diamond ring onto her finger, she marvelled at the perfect fit, thrilled. And he told her she must only wear the ring when she was performing, that way there would be no embarrassing questions to answer.

Her throat tightened and Grace felt crushed. The betrayal was as sharp as a slap in the face, making her realise she could be replaced by any of the on-board hopefuls hungry for the limelight, or any of the frustrated women with rich husbands who were willing to give more than she had been prepared to part with.

Her brain scrambled to find a logical solution. A brand-new decade dawned. The horrors of war were behind them. The whole world looked with renewed hope to a better future. But none of those things excused Clifford's scandalous behaviour.

As the singing ebbed, Grace caught the dazzle of her engagement ring in the spotlight and when she left the stage with applause still ringing in her ears, she eased the ring from her finger and vowed never to wear it again.

The glittering diamond had been a symbol of their love for each other. But like the sparkling stone, she knew her relationship with Clifford was phony. It looked fabulous, but as far as she was concerned, neither had any worth whatsoever.

1

FEBRUARY 1950

Grace Harris believed she was going to be a star without Clifford Brack's help. His promise to marry her a month ago was meaningless when she discovered he had been cheating on her with a host of women. The betrayal steeling her determination to succeed without him.

Thank God only her family knew she and Clifford had been engaged. She would never have been able to hold her head up again if the crew had got wind of it.

Her soulful voice had taken on a gutsy edge after a week in sickbay, feigning laryngitis. Her stunning smile dazzled the elite audience on her first show of the New Year, and hid her inner humiliation of Clifford's sleazy assignations with any woman to whom he snapped his fingers.

The truth came out after a blazing row, when the New Year show ended, and was the real reason for her sore throat on New Year's Day. Fortunately for her, the on-board doctor said she must rest her voice; the ensuing days in sickbay gave her plenty of time to contemplate.

When Grace tried to give Clifford back his engagement ring, he said with a sneer, 'Keep the damn thing. After all, it's only sparkle and has no worth. I can always get another if I want one.' Grace believed he wasn't just talking about the ring.

Her climb from the chorus line had been a long one; she had learned her craft from the bottom rung before Clifford noticed her, unlike chorus girls who hung on to every flattering lie he uttered, and offered themselves up to him so readily. Although, she too had been ensnared by his fine words and empty promises when he told her he had contacts who would put her name in lights. But he never introduced her to any of them.

'*You're going to be a star. You* are *not just a girl from the backstreets of Liverpool! Everybody is going to love you.*' Eager for the limelight, she believed every flattering word he uttered, which was a far cry from the stinging putdown that brought their fleeting engagement to a sudden halt. '*You came from the gutter and I can put you back there,*' he sneered. '*Don't ever forget that.*' His throwaway remark was branded on her heart and grew over the sickbay days into an invisible shell of armour that made her determined to be the woman she wanted to be. Not the tramp he expected her to be.

Onstage, she felt naked, imagining everybody could see her self-loathing, but night after night she forced herself to go and sing her heart out, and become someone she no longer recognised. Clifford's charm and sophistication had blinded her and she had been in awe of his joie de vivre. But not any more. When she realised how naïve she had been, she wanted to run and hide. But soon realised she couldn't run far on a ship.

Now, the girl in the spotlight was confident, fun-loving and had the audience eating out of her hand. But her inner demons were never far away, especially when, at the back of the stage, Clifford Brack was watching her. His face showing no expression whatsoever.

He was wrong about one thing, though. She was not *just a girl from the backstreets of Liverpool.* There was no such person. Liverpool girls were wired in a different way. Not just in their own family, but in the whole city. She was remarkable. She would go far. She was going to be *someone.*

Another performance ended with a standing ovation and the thunderous applause rang in her ears as, straightening her spine, Grace stood taller, flicked back her abundance of chestnut curls, and dipped a curtsey before leaving the stage. She would take a walk round the deck before turning in for an early night, but first she must feel the balmy breeze waft through her hair, let her thoughts wander...

'Going somewhere?'

Grace gave a small gasp of surprise. She hadn't seen the figure sitting alone at a nearby table. She felt her heart flip when she recognised Bruce D'Angelo, the son and heir of the man who owned the shipping line, was speaking to her.

'It's such a wonderful night I thought I'd take in the sights.' Grace smiled, professionally friendly, like an air hostess, or an assistant in a high-class store.

'Such a wonderful night for a beautiful lady,' he said, rising from the chair.

'I bet you say that to all the girls, you smooth talker,' she replied, noticing he stood with the aid of a barley-twist walking stick in one hand, and held out his other hand towards her.

'Bruce D'Angelo,' he said, as if needing to introduce himself, and Grace realised she was staring when he explained, 'war wound, shrapnel hit my leg and broke my thigh bone in three places, the doc said I was lucky to walk again.'

'So, you're quite determined, then?' The words slipped effortlessly from her lips and his smile was somewhat apologetic. 'Why are you sitting here, alone, with just a book for company? Everyone else is having a good time.'

'I might ask you the same thing,' Bruce said, as the smile in his voice matched the twinkle in his chocolate-brown eyes. 'I'm just a guy who likes reading more than partying. What's your excuse?'

'I'm just a girl who likes her own company sometimes.' Realising she may have overstepped the mark, she said, 'Sorry, my mouth opens without engaging my brain. Sometimes, even I don't know what's going to come out of it.'

His laugh was an easy-going rumble that made her glad he hadn't taken offence.

'You were terrific tonight, as always.' His accent was Ivy League with a touch of Southern charm and Grace began to relax. 'I was here, listening.' His friendliness gave Grace the confidence to jest.

'Don't tell me you're stuck out here 'cause you've got no mates?' she said in the broad Liverpool dialect that she had trained herself to lose over the years and was amused when his brow furrowed.

'I have not got the faintest idea what you just said.' Bruce laughed, and Grace laughed too. 'Champagne?' he asked, nodding to summon a waiter, and pulled out a chair for her to join him. The crew would be eager to know what it was like drinking the finest, most expensive champagne with Bruce D'Angelo.

'That would be lovely,' Grace said, sitting opposite him and wondering why such a powerful, important man chose to sit alone reading *The Great Gatsby*.

Dressed in a Saville Row suit, his black tie hung loose round his neck. 'It's lovely to finally meet you,' he said, and Grace wondered if he was being facetious. 'Are you comfortable?' Bruce seemed genuinely concerned as a warm breeze ran through her hair.

'Yes, thank you, Mr D'Angelo,' Grace said, and for some unfathomable reason, she felt sorry for him sitting here, all alone.

'Please, call me Bruce,' he replied, handing her a long-stemmed wide-rimmed glass. 'I don't stand on ceremony.' She imagined he was not a man who had heard the word 'no' very often either. Although it was the other passengers that made her feel overawed. 'Don't mind them,' Bruce gave a reassuring smile, noticing her restraint, 'they don't bite.' Neighbouring tables were peopled with famous faces she recognised from going to the pictures. All personal friends of the D'Angelo family, yet Bruce had been alone until she came along.

They chatted easily over a few glasses of champagne and she enjoyed his company more than she would have expected. Bruce was not a bit snooty, as she thought, in fact he seemed a bit shy, unlike most men she had met.

'Are you cold?' Bruce asked. 'Shall I get you a rug?' He was eager for her to feel comfortable, but Grace shook her head, reassuring him she was fine. He stood head and shoulders above Clifford, and his impeccable manners, a world away from the off-hand way Clifford had behaved, very quickly made her feel like she was worth something after all. Secretly, Grace hoped Clifford was watching every move from a few tables behind them.

As she had performed the early show, the evening was her own. And a beautiful evening it was turning out to be too, she thought, luxuriating in the tropical breeze wafting across the deck. They had been at sea for two months and in the heat of the Southern Caribbean, Grace felt more calm than she had done for a long time.

'We are crossing the line tomorrow,' she said, referring to the ceremony of crossing the equator, which was performed by members of the crew. A rite of passage for some who were crossing for the first time and something the passengers looked forward to with much delight.

'I know,' said Bruce with a smile. 'I'm King Neptune,' he lowered his voice as if taking her into his confidence, nodding to somebody behind her, 'and I have it on good authority that Clifford Brack has never involved himself in the ceremony.'

'Really?' Grace was surprised and turned to see Clifford sitting with a group of people, knowing all sailors, male and female, went through the ancient initiation rite. Her suspicions that he still bore her ill will for breaking off their engagement was assured when the grim expression on Clifford's face caused a cold shiver down her spine.

Grace was glad he could see she wasn't heartbroken, and hoped he understood that their relationship was not the be-all and end-all for her. 'Do you think he should be initiated on this trip?'

'Most definitely,' Bruce said with a smile that made the corner of his dark eyes crinkle and made Grace feel they were somehow partners in crime. She giggled, feeling she had unexpectedly met someone out of the ordinary – but in a good way.

The more she thought about how quickly Clifford had wanted to seal their relationship with an engagement ring, the more she realised he was as phony as the pink *so-called diamond*. But why was Clifford so eager to give her a ring? And why had he forbidden her to tell anybody about their engagement? And why, when she tried to give him back the ring, had he told her to keep it? The whole thing was a bit of a mystery.

'Would you like to cut a rug?' Bruce asked in that gentle drawl that sounded almost apologetic, like a boy at his first dance, yet she was flattered that a man of his stature was paying her so much attention when he had a whole ship full of people to choose from.

'That would be lovely,' Grace said politely, feeling a little giddy when he held out his hand and led her into the ballroom. Grace wasn't the kind of girl who jumped out of one relationship and straight into another, but there was no harm in a dance.

Bruce was an excellent dancer and deftly moved her round the floor to the mellow sound of the orchestra, and Grace was floating on air. But instinct warned her nothing good lasted forever.

Bruce whispered something she couldn't quite hear as she inhaled the fragrance of his expensive cologne. Where she came from, men smelled of toil and carbolic soap and she was fully aware that all eyes were on both of them.

Pulling away slightly, she saw Bruce looking mildly surprised, until she gave him a dazzling smile and pointed to her ear, shaking her head. He nodded, realising she had not heard him, and leaned closer.

Turning her head to listen, Grace caught sight of Clifford stroking the face of another young dancer whose hungry expression proved to Grace he went for easy targets. Under normal circumstances, she would warn the dancer what Clifford was really like, although she doubted the young starlet would listen, knowing she would not have listened either.

Watching how smoothly he ingratiated himself was like seeing her past playing out before her eyes. The showgirl, so naïve, so gullible, was the kind of girl she had once been. She looked away, silently thanking her lucky stars she found out what a deceitful, two-timing fake Clifford Brack truly was, before she married him.

The wedding! A thought suddenly struck her as Bruce guided Grace round the dance floor. She would have to write to her mother and tell her she didn't need to buy that new hat after all.

'You look fabulous,' Bruce D'Angelo, totally charming, crooned into her hair, interrupting her thoughts as he moved with the ease of a professional dancer.

'Thank you.' She felt as if she had known him for much longer than the hour they had spent together, and when the upbeat samba rhythm struck up, Grace felt her hips snake into a life of their own.

'You can certainly move, Grace,' Bruce whispered as they danced so naturally together. She did not give a second thought to the fact that she was dancing in the arms of the most important man on board. Nor that this, the heady stuff of her dreams, was the lifestyle she had once strived for. 'I want to kiss you, right here on the dance floor.' Bruce said when the music stopped.

Grace gave him a look of mock surprise and said in the voice of a southern belle, 'Why, sir, we have only just met!'

They were still laughing when he steered her past Clifford and his cohorts, off the dance floor to a table on deck, where it was a little cooler.

Grace didn't have a care in the world, smitten by the magnetic pull of Bruce D'Angelo, whose dark Mediterranean looks would always be a draw, even if he weren't heir to one of the world's finest shipping lines. A purser brought more champagne in a silver ice bucket to refill their glasses.

'So, tell me everything about you,' Bruce said as if it was the most natural thing in the world.

'You first,' Grace replied, knowing she could not possibly tell him about the muddle of characters that made up her family. Although, when he told her that he lost his mother in a car accident when he was seven years old and was sent to boarding school, she wondered what it must be like not to have a loving family to call on when the need arose.

'Dad and I don't see eye to eye on much,' Bruce explained. 'He loves the cut and thrust of the business world, whereas I prefer to be quiet and read a book.' He gave an endearing half-laugh, 'You're never lonely with a book to read.'

'Tell me about your mother,' Grace said and immediately his dark eyes softened.

'She was the most beautiful woman in the world.' He gently touched her hand and Grace, feeling moved by the simple gesture, gave him a reassuring smile. 'My world is a poorer place without her in it.'

Grace spotted the deep sadness in his eyes and wondered what it must be like for such a young boy to lose his most precious treasure. The woman who had given him life and nurtured him for his first seven years.

'I'm so sorry,' he said brightening, 'you must think me a bore...'

'Not at all!' Grace insisted, she loved listening to him talk.

'That's the first time I've ever spoken about Mom,' he said. 'I didn't want to share my precious memories of her with anybody, in case talking would somehow dilute my remembrance of her, but since talking to you, Grace, I feel... stronger.'

'I'm glad it helped,' Grace said.

When he urged her to tell him about her home life, she gave him the well-rehearsed tale of a middle-class girl from one of the better-off districts of Liverpool and she was thrilled when he wanted to hear more about her family.

'Well, our Danny was a sergeant in the army before he went to work for our uncle, who has his own haulage business.' Grace had no intentions of telling Bruce that Uncle Henry was a carter, who plied his trade along the dock road of Liverpool. 'Then there's our Bobby, who is still in education.' Nor was she going to tell him the little bugger spent as many days sagging school as he did in it. Bobby tried every trick in the book to get a day off school. 'Da... My father was severely injured when smugglers broke into his warehouse.' Not the truth her father was a night-watchman on the docks.

'How severely injured?' Bruce gripped her hand across the table.

'Very,' she said, keeping the news that her dad had lost his toes in the Somme to herself. 'He has not been able to work since, and is barely able to walk far, needing someone to help him.' *Especially when he's kale-eyed coming out of the Tram Tavern.* She hoped her downcast eyes hid her daughterly disparagement. The old bugger had never done a proper day's work in his life, and if it hadn't been for her sainted mother, they would have starved many a day.

'And your mom?' Bruce asked, urging her to continue.

What could she say about Mam?

'She does a lot of work for the church.' *Washing the alter cloths and vestments.* 'And she is involved in many local charities.' Feeding the pockets of local spivs, or donating to Da's daily contribution to bookies runners were as close to charity as her ma was ever going to get.

'Your family sound delightful,' Bruce said, and Grace lowered her head. She had embellished her clan's credentials to the point of sainthood, embroidering a family who were too perfect to be true, instead of the bewildering muddle who got by as best they could.

'I'm just a girl from Liverpool who happens to be able to sing.' She had never told anybody where she truly came from, not even Clifford. He found out for himself from the ship's records.

'You are not *just* anything,' Bruce said, 'you are talented, unique and absolutely gorgeous.'

'Stop it,' Grace laughed, and said, 'I'll never get my head through the door with all these compliments.' She was thrilled, especially when he roared with laughter so loud it cut off the conversation of people nearby.

'You are a breath of fresh air,' he said. 'Everybody is so careful what they say around me, they forget to be themselves.'

'I only know how to be me,' she replied. She hadn't told lies; she had embroidered the truth. There was a difference. A Mersey girl, she knew how to look after herself from an early age, had learned how to answer a question with a question so as not to give away useful information.

Something Clifford Brack hadn't reckoned on when she reminded him that fraternising between staff was robustly discouraged and threatened to let it be known he flouted company rules for his own benefit. Seeing her in close conversation with Bruce, she suspected Clifford got the message loud and clear. They were over. Done with.

'What a charming necklace,' Bruce said, looking at the rope of pink diamonds that matched the engagement ring she didn't wear any more but kept locked away in her jewellery box in her cabin.

'Paste, I'm afraid.' Her words carried to Clifford, who was coming on deck from the ballroom and fixed her with a piercing glare. 'Cheap costume jewellery.'

'Oh, honey, I do adore your candour.' Bruce reached for her hand, wiping Clifford from her thoughts. He lowered his voice, so only she could hear. 'I can see we are going to have a wonderful time.'

However, their intimate moment was interrupted when Clifford approached the table, his assured demeanour in complete contrast to his glowering expression only moments before. His male ego obviously dented. His masculinity challenged by a man who outranked him in stature, respect and was an absolute gentleman.

'I came over to say goodnight. Mr D'Angelo, I trust you have had a wonderful evening?'

'The entertainment was a resounding success, Clifford. Congratulations.'

Clifford shook his boss's hand, ignoring Grace. It was as if she wasn't even there. Invisible. Of no consequence whatsoever. And that was just the way she liked it.

2

APRIL 1950

'You bloody lunatic, you nearly ran me over!' Evie Kilgaren was holding her foot when Danny Harris's truck screeched to a halt and he jumped out of his cab straight into a puddle of April rain that splashed her beautiful face and coat. A spring deluge had drenched the busy Liverpool street, causing puddles in the cobbles, but did not deter well-dressed clerks in their bowler hats to hurry from their place of work and rush to Evie's aid.

'I'll see to her,' Danny said, a defensive rush flooding his body as he pushed his way through the crowd of onlookers. His heart was racing. If he had done her some serious damage, he would never forgive himself. '...I did a left turn, swung round the corner... You stepped off the kerb, then bam! You were flying through the air like a paper bag in a gale-force wind.' Every detail of that awful moment filled his head. Evie looked up at him and that flash of fury turned her beautiful eyes a mesmerising shade of blue that sent his pulse racing. 'Evie, I am so sorry.'

'I'm glad to hear it, you bloody road hog!' Evie answered, sitting in the midst of the clerical group rubbing her ankle. Amid the questions and enquiries, she began to feel a bit sorry for Danny. He was as white as a sheet and obviously believed it was his fault. But it wasn't, she was the one who had not been paying attention while waiting to cross the road.

'Here, let me get you up out of that puddle.' Danny stooped down but decided against pushing his luck when he caught sight of the murderous look in her eyes and knew the idea wasn't one of his best. Evie, like a feral cat, was feisty when cornered. 'I am so sorry, one minute you were on the kerb and the next...' Danny sitting on the heel of his army-issue boots tried to reassure her as some of the murmuring onlookers began to disperse, realising she was not an ambulance case.

'...I was flying through the air like a paper bag. Yes, you said.'

Danny suppressed another apology, he had always had a soft spot for Evie, who lived at the top end of Reckoner's Row next to the Tram Tavern. She had been the backbone of her little family all her life, not just since her ma was killed and her da arrested for murder.

She had to be mother and father to her seventeen-year-old brother Jack, who worked in the hauliers' yard, and her thirteen-year-old sister, Lucy, who was also a friend of his younger brother Bobby. Danny had never met a more courageous girl in his life.

'Let me help you up, are you hurt?' Danny held out two big, strong, work-hardened hands and pulled her out of a puddle that had collected in the dip of the road. Looking over the heads of gathered bystanders, he spied a policeman getting off his bicycle and advancing like an avenging angel in his black waterproof cape and domed helmet, galvanising the diehard stragglers who had stayed to see the event until the end.

'He ran her over, I saw everythin'!' A drayman, in a blended mixture of Irish, Welsh and catarrh offered his opinion and Danny gave a low groan.

'No, she stepped off the kerb and tripped, I saw it, plain as day,' said a woman in a waterproof pixie hood and Danny opened his mouth to protest.

'Came round dat corner like a whirling dervish, Missus...' said the carter while office workers edged closer, and Danny's dreams of owning his own haulage yard began to dissolve, knowing he could lose the heavy-goods licence he got as a soldier in the army.

'Are you sure you can walk?' Danny asked Evie. 'If I lose my licence, Henry will sack me.'

'I doubt it, your uncle owns the business, but it's good to know you're not just thinking of yourself.' Burning with mortification and hobbling on one foot, Evie knew the only thing that was truly hurting was her pride. She could think of nothing worse than being the centre of attention, her mortification made worse by a gaggle of opinionated nosy pokes.

Wobbling on her one good leg, Evie gained her balance when Danny's strong hand tentatively circled her waist. He now recognised her piercing glare as embarrassment rather than anger, knowing from experience how feisty she was, which wasn't surprising – given the life she had led, and the misfortune she had faced, she had to be. But she had a good heart and would help anybody out.

'You need to go to hospital,' Danny said, worried she had done some damage to that ankle, which was turning a worrying shade of purple. 'You might have damaged something.'

'I have,' Evie answered, stooping to retrieve her squashed handbag, which had cushioned her fall. Although she suspected the bag had not been strong enough to prevent a huge bruise forming on her backside, if the pain was anything to go by. 'I have to get home.'

Mister Walton, the stoic office manager had asked her to stay behind to do a bit of overtime on the monthly accounts for the D'Angelo Shipping Line and Evie could not pass up the chance to earn a few bob more, determined to keep the hunger of bygone days at bay, and also to be seen as a keen and competent employee, but now she was going to be late home.

'What's happened here, then?' asked the police constable who parted the crowd of Onlookers milling around who freely gave their own contradictory versions of what they thought they saw; while Evie wished she could shrivel up and blow away on a gust you could lean into blasting off the River Mersey.

'I'll never be able to show my face round here again,' Evie said to nobody in particular.

'You've got to,' Danny grinned, 'you work in that office over there.' He pointed up to the arched first-floor window overlooking one of Liverpool's oldest streets.

'Not for much longer after this mortification.' Evie would have liked to storm off, but as she could hardly put her weight on her bruised ankle there was no point in trying.

'I think you should see a doctor.' Danny's voice was full of concern.

'Think what you like, but I'm not going, I'm late enough as it is.'

'Then you've got to let me take you home.' Danny's eyes were full of concern and Evie felt a bit sorry for him. He'd had a shock too. It wasn't every day you almost ran your neighbour down with a ten-tonne flat-back wagon.

'Do you make a habit of rescuing a girl from...' The gutter? She only just stopped herself from mentioning her other humiliation. *Bloody hell. Not again.* Evie cringed when she recalled that day, three years ago, when Leo Darnel attacked her in the street and Danny came to her aid. 'I'm fine.' She slumped at the enormity of what could have happened.

'Are you sure about that, Miss?' The constable asked and Evie nodded.

'You are not fine, and I'd like to help'. Danny was so relieved his wagon hadn't touched her. Realising what could have happened in that split second when he turned the corner, heading straight for her, he had never stopped the wagon so fast in all the time he had been driving.

'I think my ankle gave way as I stepped off the kerb,' Evie said to the black-caped bobby, explaining the moment that sent her tumbling. 'It wasn't Danny's fault, he's an exceptionally good driver... His wagon didn't touch me.'

The constable accepted her explanation and dispersed the crowd when he saw she was up and talking.

'Are you sure you don't need an ambulance?' Danny sounded repentant. 'Or maybe it'd be quicker if I carry you over to Saint Paul's Hospital.'

'That's the eye hospital, you twit,' Evie said impatiently, 'there's nothing wrong with my eyes, although you might want to get yours checked out.' That wasn't a fair thing to say, she knew. It wasn't his fault. If he hadn't been such a skilled driver, there could have been a very nasty accident on the busy road.

'I could put you in the truck and have you round to the Royal Infirmary in no time.'

'You will not take me to the Infirmary, Danny Harris,' Evie said stiffly. 'There's nothing wrong with me... I tripped... I'm freezing, and my drawers are soaking wet.' He didn't need to know that, she thought. And rolling her eyes, she noticed her laddered stockings. 'Oh they're ruined beyond repair, and I've only had them six months.'

'But you tripped ever so gracefully, so there is a silver lining,' Danny told her, taking hold of her cold hands and giving them a good rub as the April breeze eddying off the River Mersey was fiercely nippy. 'I imagined all kinds of horrors, losing my licence, my job...'

'Don't mind me, like!' Evie's biting remark was softened by the ghost of a smile as she pictured herself flying through the air and had to bite her lips together to stop herself from laughing. 'And you can take that smug look off your face. I'm not going to be the cause of you losing your job.'

'You're a good sort, Evie.' Danny knew she'd been through more than most. Her father strangling her mother and dumping her body in the canal during the 'big freeze', three years ago was just one of the things that made Evie one of life's fighters. She had come through the ordeal much better than some people would. Caring for her brother and sister while studying for her bookkeeping examinations and getting a good job... And, she was lovely to look at.

'C'mon, I'll take you home, it's the least I can do.'

'You owe me a pair of silks, don't forget,' Evie said, looking down at her tattered stockings and giving Danny's hand a sharp slap when he dusted down her coat.

'Sorry!' he apologised when Evie gave him a look that said, *no trespassing*. Turning to a straggler who was determined to see the rumpus to the end, Danny waved and said, 'Nothing to see here, the show's over.'

'All you're short of is a red coat, and taking a rescuing-hero bow,' Evie said, allowing Danny to help her towards the wagon.

'Shall I carry you?' he asked, ignoring her last remark.

'Over my cold dead body,' Evie exclaimed, remembering that hot summer day, three years ago, when Danny all but carried her over to Connie McCrea, the landlady of the Tram Tavern. She'd never felt so ashamed.

'What about a hot cup of tea, for the shock?' Danny asked, nodding towards the little cafe on the pier.

'I'm late as it is. Lucy will be worrying where I've got to.' Lucy had spent the war years in Ireland and although she was very independent, babysitting the son of the Tavern landlady after school, she had a fierce imagination. 'She'll have me dead and buried.'

Evie would have liked to go for a cup of tea with Danny, who, at twenty-five, was four years older, but it wouldn't be right, not when he was rumoured to be courting Susie Blackthorn. But Danny had always been a kind and friendly face to her. He had grown in strength and stature in the army, reaching the rank of sergeant after serving in the war. He was good-natured, good-looking, and good... simply good right through.

But she had no right to think those things, especially when Danny was courting. Susie Blackthorn was a nasty piece of work and she couldn't understand what a bloke like Danny would see in her. Susie had made her life a misery when they worked together at Beamers Electricals with her snide remarks and constant put-downs. Susie thought herself many rungs up the ladder from Evie when she was the office clerk and Evie was the office cleaner and made no secret of her intention to marry Danny Harris one day. However, that was a few years ago, and Evie still hadn't seen a ring on her finger.

'I think you're making a habit of this rescuing lark.' Evie remembered there was also that time when she slipped and fell during the big freeze, her arms windmilling in mid-air before landing in the deep snow.

'Hardly a habit.' A wide smile caused his eyes to twinkle and her heart to do daft jumping jerks.

'Well, whatever it is, you can stop doing it now.' Evie, soaked to the skin with her golden curls plastered to her head, tried to avoid his gaze. 'Three rescues in one lifetime is enough for any girl, thank you very much.'

Danny helped her into the cab and hopped in beside her. 'What d'you say to a night at the pictures, to say sorry.'

'No thank you,' she said without hesitation. 'I'm far too busy looking after my family. I can't go galivanting.' *More's the pity.* 'I've got to think of Jack and Lucy. There's too much work and not enough day.' Evie felt her heart was being run through a mangle. She would have enjoyed a night at the pictures. But with a ready-made family to care for and a pile of ironing waiting for her, she did not have time to waltz off to the pictures like any other girl of twenty-one. 'And you should be ashamed of yourself for asking,' she scolded, causing a look of confusion in the pleat of Danny's brow. She had no intentions of stealing another girl's fella, even if that girl was Susie Blackthorn.

'Here we go again,' Danny let out a sigh of irritation when the truck wouldn't start, knowing Evie had to get home. 'Sorry about this. Old Gladys plays up in the rain, she doesn't like it at all.' He opened the creaking cab door and jumped down onto the busy dock road before going to the front of the cab and lifting the right-hand side of the bonnet.

Looking up at one of the four clocks under the Liver Birds, Evie saw it was almost seven and the sky was turning to cloudy dusk. Lucy would be starting to worry by now, she might even have Jack scouring the dock road looking for her. They all had a dread of their father being released and coming back to torment them.

Taking a slow shuddering breath, she reached for the door handle and decided to walk, but as the pain shot through her ankle, Evie realised she would not get further than a few yards even before she opened the passenger door.

Danny popped his head through the driver's window. 'If we're going to get back to Reckoner's Row before dark,' he said matter-of-factly, 'you'll have to take your stockings off.'

'I beg your pardon!' Evie's jaw dropped and her eyes became as wide as side plates. She was sure she had heard properly, but if he said what she thought he'd said, she was going to land him a fourpenny one right between those optimistic blue eyes.

'Your stockings,' Danny said, nodding to her slim, bleeding legs.

'I'll knock your bloody block off, Danny Harris!' Her voice sounded like a strangled mouse, and as her face grew hotter, the lion in her refused to be silenced. 'You take one step towards my stockings and you will be walking with a limp.'

'The fan belt's snapped.' Danny was obviously unaware of the unsettling effect his innocent remark had created. Nodding to her legs, he explained, 'I need your stockings to use as a fan belt – so we can get back home.'

'Oh.' Evie felt her flash of indignity putter and die, and to cover her confusion, she said, 'Very inventive, I must say, but I've got no intentions of stripping off at the Pier Head.' She shuffled indignantly in her seat. 'If you think I'm going to part with my undergarments in front of half of Liverpool, you are sadly mistaken.' A defiant nod of her head ended her diatribe.

'Come on, Evie, be a sport,' Danny said, realising he must try to persuade her. 'After all, your stockings are already ruined. Otherwise we'll be here all night.'

'I'm not having you hanging through the window gawping at me.' Just saying the words caused her face to burn.

'Sorry, Evie, I'll wait out here. While you... erm... You know... Sort of...' He nodded to her legs, while Evie nodded to the windscreen, her eyes thunderous.

'What do you propose to do with that? It's glass. See-through glass.'

'Oh, yes, right.' Danny quickly removed his jacket and stretched it under the windscreen wipers. 'How's that?' he called.

But Evie didn't hear him over the drumming rain on the roof of the broken-down wagon. 'I can't believe I'm doing this,' she muttered. 'Taking part in this unrespectable act, in a public place an' all.' She had never felt so mortified in her whole life.

Unclipping the aspirin that was holding her stocking to the suspender belt, then, rolling her stocking down her leg, she straightened her black skirt firmly over her cut knees before winding down the window. Her face glowed and she looked both ways before discreetly sloping the warm laddered stocking into Danny's hand. What a day this had turned out to be.

A few minutes later, Danny slipped behind the steering wheel looking like someone had thrown a bucket of water over him, soaked right through. However, he didn't seem in the least bit troubled by it when he banged the steering wheel with delight as the engine purred into life like a newborn kitten.

Given that cheeky grin on his gob, Evie knew a man like Sergeant Danny Harris, who had spent the war years in the service of his country, would know all about fixing engines with a woman's nylons. Not that she was in any way concerned what he got up to when he was not driving busy girls home in his clapped-out wagon.

She had seen first-hand what ignorance and desperation could do to a woman. It turned them into slaves at best. And, at worst, it killed them. That same ignorance and desperation was sometimes mistaken for love... Evie knew what her mother's life had been like and vowed to make her own way independently in the world, that was why she had scrimped and saved. She wanted more for herself and Jack and Lucy.

So-called love turned some men, like her father, into monsters. What he felt had been twisted into a jealous obsession that ultimately turned to hate so strong it had the power to kill the only woman he supposedly adored. Evie had no intention of getting mixed-up in that caper called love. Not now. Not ever.

'Comfy?' Danny asked and Evie jumped a little at the sound of his voice that still held that hint of army discipline.

'Yes, thank you.' Her words were clipped, and winding down the window, a stiff breeze blew in from the River Mersey and cooled her flaming cheeks.

'I suppose Jack's told you about the Mayday Parade?' Danny said, breaking the oppressive silence, 'we won't be entering this year.'

Evie nodded. The Mayday Parade was a symbol of the coming of spring but was also combined with International Labour Day when workers withheld a day's labour in protest of better working conditions.

'Uncle Henry is concentrating on the big one. The Netherford Cup.' The August fete, which was held in the small village of Netherford, ten miles outside Liverpool in the Lancashire country-side, hosted the prestigious Heavy Horse Competition. 'Uncle Henry got second place for best Shire horse and Clydesdale last year, but it was a bitter disappointment to him. He has no intention of repeating the result this year.'

Evie knew, through Jack, that horses came from all over the country, although she had never joined the annual beano to see Carters showing off their finest working horses.

'It's a point of honour,' Danny explained. 'A chance for Skinner to show off his impeccable equine husbandry. He saw last year's second place as failure, "nobody remembers an also-ran, Lad,"' Danny did a perfect imitation of his uncle and Evie was impressed.

'He's determined to lift the prestigious Netherford Cup this year,' he added. 'The winner doesn't only win a thousand pounds. First place brings in big money in stud fees and other lucrative work. And Uncle Henry's business needs all the help it can get,' Danny did not elaborate. And the lengthening silence was broken when Evie realised he was going to say no more on the subject of his uncle's firm.

'Jack and Lucy spend most nights at the table polishing the horse brasses.' She said proudly.

'Jack's a natural with the horses,' Danny said, 'and a good worker, Uncle Henry has high hopes for him.'

'He tips his money onto the table come Friday night, which was more than Da ever did.' Evie had no idea why she had just told Danny that bit of private family information. But it was out now so she couldn't take it back. 'How's your empire-building going?' Evie asked, quickly changing the subject back to Danny before realising that what he did was none of her business. He probably couldn't even recall the conversation they had, when he told her he was going to have a business of his own one day.

'I'm saving hard,' Danny didn't seem in the least perturbed when he answered, pulling into the busy traffic of wagons and horses and carts and cars, 'but you know what it's like... taking over the world takes a bit of time.'

'I'm sure it does,' Evie replied, she had ambitions of her own and knew that it took more than determination to get what you want in life, 'but it must be hard trying to save when you've got a wedding to plan for too?'

'Whoa! Who mentioned a wedding?' Danny felt the road tilt.

'Your Bobby told our Lucy that Susie told him you two are getting engaged.'

Danny shook his head as if trying to figure it all out. 'I don't think so,' he said emphatically. 'Susie's a nice girl, well... sometimes... but I've got no intentions of marrying her now, next week, or in this lifetime. She is just a friend of my sister's and we are certainly not courting.'

'I didn't mean to pry.' Evie was secretly thrilled to hear Danny was not dating Susie. Her brother, Jack, told her Danny was highly thought of in the haulage yard where they both worked for Mister Skinner, and she had no doubt whatsoever that he would achieve everything he set out to do. Then, aware of the lengthening silence, she said, 'I hear your Grace is doing well.'

'She's having a fine old time, according to her letters,' Danny answered. Grace was his younger sister by ten months. And, though his father, Bert, had not done a tap of work since he was attacked in a warehouse robbery on the docks three years ago, he must have been a fast worker at one time. But he and Bert had never got on, and the least he thought about him the better. No woman deserved a husband like Bert Harris, Danny thought.

'Grace likes going away to sea, then?' Evie asked, recalling their Lucy telling her Grace sang on board one of America's finest passenger cruisers after the ship had been demobilised.

'It certainly looks that way,' Danny said, keeping his eyes on the road. 'The ship's director is Clifford Brack, ever heard of him?' Danny, obviously proud of his sister, didn't wait for Evie's reply. 'Apparently he's a big noise at the BBC. Well, in with all the top executives. He's going to get her a contract to make a record. There's even talk of a show on television.'

'Fancy' Evie said with a non-committal shrug, not knowing what a big deal it was to have a show on television. They, along with every other family round the dock road, did not own a television set, so there wasn't much chance of seeing Grace sing. The pragmatic women of Reckoner's Row weren't easily impressed by *maybe's* and *going to's*. 'That's a bit of all right, Guv,' she said, tugging an imaginary forelock and he laughed.

She was all right, was Evie, Danny thought. No sides to her, straight as they come, what you see is what you get. He liked that. 'Did I tell you she's engaged? We got a letter. She's coming home early May and we're going to meet him. Ma will be outside Costigan's before the doors are even opened, demanding their best boiled ham.'

Evie was quiet for a moment, wondering what it must be like for

Grace to sail the oceans to far-off lands with no family around her, and she sighed. Danny might be right. Ada, his mother, could be overbearing when she had a mind.

Evie, beginning to relax, could well believe it. Danny seemed unimpressed by his mother's constant fussing and everybody knew Ada believed she was a cut above the rest of the street, having the biggest house.

3

'That's never your Evie being helped out of his wagon by Danny Harris!' There was a giggle in Connie McRae's voice and Lucy put the brake on the pushchair with her foot while little Fergus was sleeping inside. She went over to one of the bay windows in the living room above the Tram Tavern, overlooking Reckoner's Row.

'It is, you know.' Lucy had returned from the park where after school she took three-year-old Fergus now the warmer weather was here. The little treat gave Connie, who was having her second baby in the summer, a bit of a rest. 'Evie looks mortified, and I bet every curtain in the row is twitching.'

'Oh, I hope Susie Blackthorn sees this,' Connie could not contain the glee in her voice, 'she'll have a fit of conniptions.' There was no love lost between Evie and Susie Blackthorn, a haughty piece who thought she was better than everybody else in Reckoner's Row.

'Why?' Lucy asked, opening the starched nets to get a better view. 'Are Susie and Danny courting?'

'No,' Connie answered, 'but it's not for the want of trying on Susie's part. She's been trying to get Danny to take her out for the last three years, but he's having none of it. Although if he's not careful, Susie will have him.'

'I don't think our Evie's that bothered about courting either,' Lucy said. 'She always says she's too busy for romance. All she does is work and keep the house clean. When Danny asked her last time, her cheeks went bright red, and she said she didn't have time to go gallivanting.'

'It might do her the world of good to have a night out with someone like Danny,' Connie said, and Lucy agreed. 'He's got a good head on his shoulders and he's got ambitions, which is more than I can say about that idle father of his. Bert Harris will neither work nor want, propping up the bar every night, and poor Ada has to find the money to pay for it.'

'She hasn't had it easy, that's for sure.' Lucy, fourteen in September, liked the fact that Connie treated her more grown up than their Evie did. But she had to admit, Evie had a lot more to put up with than Connie. She worried every day that their father would come out of the institution and return to Reckoner's Row, and no amount of reassurance from their brother Jack could persuade her otherwise.

'You don't mind looking after the nipper for a while, Lucy? He's a bit of a handful for Mim.'

'No, I don't mind at all.' Lucy was being paid five bob a week to look after young Fergus while Connie and Angus, her husband, worked behind the bar, and the arrangement suited her fine.

'Since Angus has taken over the pub full-time and given up the police work, Mim goes gallivanting all over the place, she goes out more than the gas!'

Lucy knew Connie's mother, Mim, and Danny's mother, Ada, had been best friends for donkey's years, and neither had a good word to say about each other, especially when Ada dropped their

Grace's name every chance she got, telling everybody her daughter would be famous one day.

'I'd better see what's happened, our Evie's limping,' Lucy said, dropping the net curtain when she heard the door close downstairs. 'That must be why she is late; I was beginning to worry.'

'Is that young Evie Kilgaren I've just seen with no stockings on and a wet behind?' Mim called as she climbed the stairs to the living room. 'I wonder what she's been up to. Oh, hello Lucy, I forgot you'd be here.'

'So I gathered,' Lucy said under her breath.

'But I suppose you gathered that already,' Mim smiled; she had heard every word.

But Lucy didn't have time to stop and apologise for unwittingly cheeking Connie's mam as she took the stairs two at a time, hurrying home next door. She was closely followed by Connie who left her sleeping son with her mother. A trained nurse Connie worked abroad during the war and was always on hand if needed.

* * *

Picking up the unmistakable aroma of engine oil and the woodbine cigarette wedged behind his ear, Evie hung her head, 'I'll be the laughing stock of the Row.'

Instead of lowering her to the pavement, this eejit held her in his arms like a newborn lamb, kicking open their wooden gate and carrying her up the narrow path to the ever-open front door, followed by Skinner's dog, Max, who made himself at home in anybody's house.

'Oh, I've never felt so humiliated in all my life,' Evie gasped. 'Picking me up in the street and carrying me in like a bundle of washing.' And, to make things worse, the street was full of gawping kids, who stopped their football and hopscotch to watch Danny being the local hero – again. Wasn't it enough that he had earned a chest-full of medals during the war? He did not need to add her to his list of heroic deeds.

'Jack, come and tell this fella I don't need carrying, like some invalid who's broke her leg,' Evie called up the lobby to her brother.

'Hello there, Dan,' thirteen-year-old Lucy said in a chirpy voice, ruffling Max's ears, 'why are you carrying our Evie into the house like that?'

'She's had a bit of a fall,' Danny told her good-naturedly as he stopped to give Max a brief pat on the back and Evie let out a slight squeal of fright in case he dropped her.

'You ran over me, you mean,' she said, knowing a cut knee and swollen foot did not render her helpless. She had suffered far worse when she was on her hands and knees scrubbing the offices of Beamers Electricals.

These days she was a respectable auditor in a major shipping office, and she did not appreciate being shown up in front of the entire street.

'Flippin' heck. I wondered why she was late. I peeled the spuds for our tea when I got back from the park with Fergus.' Lucy stood to one side to let them in the kitchen. 'I'll cook too if she's helpless.'

'Well that told me,' Evie said with an indignant sigh. 'Now I've lost my job as chief cook and bottle-washer too.'

'She fell over and hurt her leg,' Lucy told seventeen-year-old Jack who had appeared in the kitchen from upstairs, and a wide grin spread across his face when he saw his older sister in the arms of his workmate. And judging by the thundery expression on Evie's face, she was not happy

'Evie, are you all right?' Connie approached the front door, resplendent in a blue-flowered smock over her black skirt and white blouse.

'I've hurt my ankle,' Evie called over Danny's shoulder, 'and my dignity. This fella's taking liberties because I'm in pain.'

'Do you want me to have a look at it?' Connie looked concerned as Evie nodded, rolling her eyes.

'Make way for the invalid,' Danny called. 'Mind your backs please, mind your backs.'

'Oh, very droll,' Evie said deadpan. She had heard Mr Walton say the word *droll* in the office when one of the office juniors had made a funny remark, and, impressed, she had been looking for an excuse to use it ever since.

'I'm sure it's nothing,' Evie said when Connie followed. 'I think Danny's overreacting.'

'It'll still need looking at,' Connie said, taking charge. 'Oh, and Danny, I've left your dad propped up by the bar talking to my Angus.' She led the way into the kitchen.

'He's been propping up the bar since I was born.' Danny did not look pleased, which didn't surprise anybody. Danny was the bread-winner in that family. Why Ada put up with Bert's idleness for all these years was a mystery, Connie thought. Thank goodness Danny didn't take after him.

'Danny banjaxed our Evie's leg,' Lucy's sing-song Celtic lilt had diminished little since she came home from evacuation in Ireland

'He did not!' Evie's irritation startled Lucy, and given her shocked expression Evie went on to explain, 'Well, Danny came hurtling round the corner...'

'Terrifying the Bejaysus out of our Evie' Lucy cut in, 'and caused her to fall over.'

'That's a different matter,' Jack said. 'You can't blame a bloke for your clumsiness.'

'I was not clumsy. He came round the corner like a blue-arsed fly! It startled me, the kerb was broken, and the next thing I know,

I'm sitting in a puddle of water with soaking draws and laddered stockings.'

'So, where are your stockings?' There was a hint of censure in Jack's tone, and Evie felt her face burn. 'You had them on when you went to work this morning.'

'Well, that's another story.' Evie felt sheepish. No longer wearing her dark stockings, she could only imagine what the situation must look like. 'And you can take that expression off your face, our Jack.' Evie felt she was being judged before they aired the facts, and the injustice steeled her words. 'The truck wouldn't go. The fan belt broke. And Danny needed something to fix the engine.'

'Genius,' Jack's voice, laced with admiration which he did nothing to hide, forgot his sister's modesty, 'that's why auld man Skinner depends on him so much.'

'Oh it was nothing,' Danny said in mock restraint as he blew on his fingernails and polished them on the upper arm of his wet jacket. 'Any genius would have done the same.' Although, he felt bad about poor Evie's stockings, which were now not so easy to come by since the Yanks had all gone home after the war. 'Right,' he said heading towards the table, 'where shall I put her?'

'I'm not a cardboard box, you know,' Evie cried, pulling her coat round her bare legs, her pleading expression summoning Connie over.

'Just on this chair here,' Connie pulled out a straight-back chair from the table and Evie was ever so glad when Danny put her down. Being so close to him, she could hear his heartbeat, which made her own heart do some very peculiar jumps which she had never noticed before.

'Can I get you a cup of tea, Danny?' Lucy asked, not waiting for an answer.

'Danny's got to rush off I expect,' Evie said, 'haven't you, Danny?'

'No rush at all.' Danny knew his father would not drag himself from the Tavern for another half an hour at least. 'Ma doesn't put the tea out til Da gets in; she won't mind if I'm late, seeing it's in a good cause.' His mother would be livid, he knew, but Evie didn't need to know that.

Taking the cup and saucer from Lucy, he sat on the sofa by the door while Connie dabbed Evie's knee with saltwater. Putting his first visit three years ago behind him, Danny didn't like to dwell, given the circumstances of Evie's father being arrested for murdering her mother.

Frank Kilgaren had convinced the jury he had not meant to kill his beloved wife Rene, but they found him insane and they sent him to a lunatic asylum. Danny's heart had gone out to Evie that day, and he wasn't sure he had ever regained full possession of it since.

An involuntary sweep of his eyes took in the cosy room. Evie had made it a lovely, warm, welcoming home. The entire place had a different feel. The atmosphere was light and friendly, and even though Evie was mad at him for humiliating her in front of the kids of Reckoner's Row, he knew she was one of the most sociable people he had ever met.

She reminded him of Aunty Meggie, who also had a heart of gold and would do anything to help anybody if she could. Evie was a friend to everybody. A far cry from the days when her mother was alive and used her like a skivvy.

He could only admire Evie's determination to keep her little family on the straight and narrow. Everything she had set out to do she had accomplished with flying colours... However, he thought, Evie was no soft touch. That gracious exterior hid a rod of pure steel.

'I've put the spuds on, they'll be about half an hour,' Lucy said. 'Would you like to stay for your tea, Danny, there's plenty.'

Evie's marine-coloured eyes fixed on her younger sister and sent stormy signals. She had only bought three scrawny leg chops after standing in the butcher's queue for most of her dinner hour and had been looking forward to that chop all afternoon. If Danny stayed for tea, she would have no choice but to give it to him.

'Thanks for the offer, Lucy, maybe another time,' Danny said.

'I wasn't sure what time you would be home,' Lucy said to her older sister as Connie finished cleaning Evie's leg.

'I stayed behind to finish some work and then I fell and then the fan belt snapped,' Evie explained quickly. 'Obviously if I worked nearer home, I would have been home ages ago.' Her hand flew to her mouth when Evie realised what she had just said. She sounded so ungrateful and Danny was only trying to help. 'Oh Danny I didn't mean...'

'Think no more of it,' Danny said holding up his hand to stop Evie embarrassing herself further. 'Although, I have a solution to that problem, if you're interested,' Danny offered. 'But it's a big ask, compared with the grandeur of River Chambers.' The pokey office in Skinner's yard was a far cry from the Portland stone façade of one of the world's major shipping lines. And then there was Susie... He knew the two girls did not get on at all well. Although, in for a penny... 'Uncle Henry's looking for someone reliable to manage the office, but they need to use discretion.' Danny sounded secretive and Evie turned to face him.

'Discretion is her name,' Lucy answered and then whispered to Connie, 'What does discretion mean?'

'It means minding your own business,' Connie answered, knowing to get to Skinner's haulage yard Evie would only have to walk down to the bottom of Reckoner's Row and turn right, across the waste ground known to the locals as the *debris*.

It might be worth working at Skinner's, Evie thought, if only for peace of mind. She knew their father was securely locked up in an institution, given the severity of his crime, but he was as slippy as melted margarine and she did not feel comfortable being so far from her thirteen-year-old sister all day.

'If you can put up with the smell of horses, and working with Susie Blackthorn again...' Danny said, 'I'll put a word in if the job's any use to you?' He kept his pale blue eyes on the gentle glowing embers, glad she could not hear his heart hammering in his chest.

'I would like to be within shouting distance of home and I like horses. Susie will just have to get used to me, I suppose,' she said, as Danny tugged the peak of his flat cap, covering a mane of thick ebony hair. His easy-going nature, like the silver army dog-tags hugging his strong neck, was all part of who he was.

Danny glanced in her direction. 'So you'll think it over?'

'Tell Mr Skinner I could call in tomorrow,' Evie told Danny.

Fancy Susie Blackthorn thinking she stood a chance with Danny. They were as different as day and night. He was just the friendliest man she had ever met. Kind and helpful to people. Made them feel at ease, while Susie was stuck up and lazy.

'Is Susie leaving?' Evie asked, feeling hope in her heart.

'No,' Danny said, 'what gave you that idea?'

'She manages the office,' Evie told him, recalling vividly the day Susie boasted about her lofty position in the Skinner workforce.

'She can't manage a smile most days, never mind a business,' Danny said, making everybody laugh.

Any misgivings she may have about working with Susie had to be put aside. 'I would be thrilled if you would put a word in for me...' her voice trailed off.

'Don't worry your head, I'll see Uncle Henry when I take the wagon back to the yard, I'll let you know what he says.'

'Thanks a lot, Danny.' His suggestion had taken her by surprise, but she didn't have to think twice about the offer of a job so close to home. Being just down the street would ease her mind. Evie didn't want Lucy to feel the way she once did. Coming home to an empty house was the loneliest feeling in the world.

'I suppose your mam's excited about the wedding?' Connie said conversationally.

'Thrilled to bits,' Danny nodded and rolled his eyes, 'we haven't heard the last of it.'

'If I were in Grace's shoes,' Evie said, wondering why someone with such a glittering lifestyle would contemplate settling down, 'I wouldn't be in any hurry to get married, full stop.'

'No?' Danny's blue eyes twinkled. He was sure she believed every word she said. 'Me neither.'

Evie glanced down at her swollen foot, glad Lucy and Connie did not make any remarks, although it was only a matter of time, she knew.

Her hunger pangs returned because of the delicious smell of Lucy's cooking. She was glad their evening meal was on the go. She didn't want Danny thinking they ate out of the chippy every night.

'You've done an excellent job with the tea, Lucy,' she said, grateful her sister had the wonderful sense to start the meal. 'I'll make it up to you when I get paid. You deserve a bit of pocket money... I don't know what I'd do without you.' Her own words gave her a start. They rolled off her tongue as her mother's used to do. Mam said those very words to her all the time when she was growing up. 'Not that it's your job to look after the house and make sure the meals are ready, while Jack and I are working,' she added. 'I don't want to make a drudge out of you, not at your age... it's just...'

'I don't mind mucking in,' Lucy cut in, her eyes lighting up at the mention of earning more pocket money, 'it makes me feel grown-up.'

'There's plenty of time for you to grow up, Lucy. Don't rush things.'

'Hark at you, Mother Hubbard,' Lucy laughed. 'I'll finish the cooking while you rest your leg.'

'You've sprained your ankle,' Connie said after a thorough but gentle examination, 'so Lucy's on kitchen duty for the foreseeable and you have to rest it until the swelling goes down at least.'

'But I can't take time off work, we need the money.' It wasn't easy looking after a family when she had a full-time job, it meant she would have to depend more and more on Lucy, and she didn't want that. Running the house was something her mother expected her to do from an early age, but she had no intention of making Lucy old before her time like she had been. 'Lucy's got a good brain in her head, we all have, and she's not wasting it looking after me. She will go to school and get the education to make something of herself.' The way she wished she could have done earlier, but she could neither afford the time nor the course until she started working as a cleaner at Beamers and then started typing up the office files for lazy clerks. 'Education and hard work are the quickest route out of the dockside,' she told Lucy.

Connie nodded in agreement, 'You will make a better life for yourself, I'm sure.'

'I've got to get the wagon back to the yard and fix it before tomorrow's deliveries.' Danny's handsome face stretched into a friendly smile and he made his way to the door.

'I'll come over to the yard and give you a hand if you like?' Jack said.

'Thanks, Jack, but I've got to let the old man know what's happened first,' Danny said. 'Oh, and I won't forget that little favour I promised you, Evie.' Danny's mischievous glint in his eye made Evie shake her head.

'Right-o, Dan,' Jack said, 'but give me a shout if you need a hand.'

4

Before Danny set to work on the truck, he popped in to see his Uncle Henry and Aunt Meggie as he did every night, wondering how Evie would get to work now she had sprained her ankle. And he owed her a pair of silks. Aunt Meggie would know about that sort of thing, he thought.

'Poor Evie.' Meggie's dark blue eyes were mellow as always when Danny finished his tale. 'I'll pop into the shops and see if there are any stockings to be had.'

'That's if she'll let you do anything for her,' Danny sighed, his shoulders drooping a little. 'She's stubborn and independent.'

'Pain can cut through the most tenacious temperament,' Meggie said, proving to Danny that anything rarely ruffled her.

'I don't understand how women's minds work, they're a mystery to me. All I know is that when I asked Evie to go to the pictures, as a way of saying sorry – nothing serious – she couldn't say no fast enough.' It surprised Danny at how disappointed he felt.

'She's devoted to her little family,' Aunt Meggie said, pouring strong tea into a white mug.

'Better than a lot of mothers I know,' Danny answered in a dull voice and, noticing the crease in Meggie's brow, he blurted, 'present company excepted, Aunt Meggie. You'd have made a smashing mam.' She was a home port when storm Ada was wreaking havoc.

'Women are a wonder to behold, my boy,' Henry said with a good-natured grin, knowing Danny was a catch, there was no mistake about that, and he was sure the lad would find himself a lovely girl just like his Meggie. 'That wildcat Susie wouldn't take to you asking the lovely Evie to the pictures, not when she's waited so long.' Everybody knew Susie had her eye on Danny.

'What's it got to do with Susie anyway?' Danny's genial tone sounded bruised. 'She knows I only see her as a friend. I've never made her any promises. Not even a hint.'

'I don't think she sees it like that,' Henry answered. 'You're on to a sticky wicket there, my boy, she's got her sights set on you. Women don't like a bloke playing fast with their feelings.' Henry paused for a moment to light his pipe. 'They can make your life a misery if you upset them.' He blew out a cloud of tobacco smoke, pensive before picking up his large mug, draining the remains. 'I've heard many a sad tale from a brow-beaten husband who married the wrong woman.'

'Who mentioned marriage? I came for some moral support, not to be frightened out of me wits.'

'Sorry, son, just thought I'd mention it...'

Danny felt his neck, it was clammy and growing hotter. 'You could give a bloke palpitation with remarks like that.'

'Don't scare the lad, my love,' Meggie smiled to her husband. Having never had the chance to raise any children of her own, she liked to spoil Danny. He was one of life's optimists who had plans and was ambitious for a better life. And something told her that Danny, being determined, would make something of himself, climb out of the backstreets. He would make some lucky girl a wonderful husband, she thought.

'I've got to build an empire before I settle down,' Danny said, 'and empire building takes time.'

'It does,' Meggie said, returning to the dining room, carrying a tray holding three enormous bowls of meaty broth and thick-cut crusty bread, which she had made only this afternoon. 'Tuck into this, it'll cheer you up.'

'Don't tell Ma,' Danny said, his mouth watering at the tasty-looking food Aunt Meggie plied him with every chance she got. She was a smashing cook, much better than his ma, but he would never dare say so.

'Of course not,' Henry answered, 'we would never hear the last.' He would never betray young Danny's confidences to that sour-faced cousin of his.

For the next half an hour, they chatted and ate, and it was the best time of day for all of them.

'Remember when you said someone needed to lick the office into shape?' Danny said tentatively, wiping his bowl clean with a hunk of bread and studied concentration, 'well, I mentioned it to Evie... She needs to be closer to home... And those files are in a terrible state... I just thought...' Danny lifted his head, satiated.

'Tell Evie to pop in when she's ready, I'll always need a good bookkeeper,' Henry said.

'Can I tempt you to another bowl of broth?' Meggie asked.

'We can't have you wasting away, Danny,' Henry laughed, knowing Ada could be frugal at the best of times, 'not if you've got empires to build.'

'There's no danger of that with Aunt Meggie feeding me up,' Danny said, 'but I have to say, if there's any more talk of this marriage lark, I will put me deaf ones on.'

'Come on, I'll give you a hand mending that fan belt on the truck.'

* * *

'Thanks for peeling the spuds, Lucy,' Evie said, trying to dodge awkward questions, but it was no use, Connie and Lucy looked on expectantly.

'Well, how did you manage to get your stockings off without anybody seeing?' Lucy asked and there was a mischievous glint in Connie's eyes.

'I told you both,' Evie answered, feeling her face grow hot, 'he put his jacket under the windscreen wiper, he was a complete gentleman. And you heard as much as me when he asked me if I wanted the job at Skinner's,' she said, not wanting to talk about Danny.

'You'd be practically working on the doorstep,' Connie said, and Lucy looked hopeful. 'I wouldn't let the likes of Susie Blackthorn put me off. You've got much more up top than she has.' Connie tapped the side of her head.

'You could run rings round her, our Evie.' The hope in Lucy's eyes told Evie she must put her younger sister's needs before her own.

'Taking the job would save on bus fare and dinner money, I suppose,' Evie said listening to the chops sizzling in the pan in the back-kitchen. 'Lower the gas down a little bit, otherwise the outside will be like charcoal and the inside raw,'

'She'll soon get the hang of cooking,' Connie said, and Evie frowned.

'That's just it, Connie,' Evie replied, 'I don't want her to get the hang of it. I want her to do more with her life than cook, clean and pop out babies every year.' The sight of young women pushing prams was a common one. This area especially. Most of the inhabitants were descendants of Irish Catholics who came to Liverpool after the potato famine hit Ireland in 1845, looking for work on the docks and had stayed ever since.

'Good for you,' Connie said. She was proud of what Evie had achieved through hard work and determination.

'I could even nip home in my dinner hour,' Evie said knowing Skinner's yard was only in Summer Settle at the back of Reckoner's Row. She could roll out of bed and into work. Not that she would of course. 'Well, we'll soon find out because I've decided, I'm going to take the job if it's offered.'

* * *

The following evening Susie Blackthorn made her way to Auld Skinner's house, separated from the yard by a low wall and a wooden gate, to return the office door keys as she did every night when she had finished her work.

The outer door was open as usual, and as usual she went straight into the narrow hallway. She could hear voices and put her ear to the closed inner door, hoping to catch a bit of juicy gossip. Her hand, bunched ready to knock, stilled in mid-air...

'Henry?' Meggie's gentle lilt held a tentative note as she and Henry sat at the kitchen table. 'Remember that bit of land I bought from that poor chap at the meat market during the war?'

Henry was cutting into the streaky bacon, which Meggie had somehow gained even though meat was still on ration, five years after the war had ended. He looked up from the newspaper propped against the sugar basin and his generous brows puckered at the interruption.

'Aye, I remember,' Henry said, wondering if he wanted to discuss his wife's rebellious decision to use funds that led to her helping some poor bugger out of a penury hole. He knew most women around the dockside did not have the wherewithal to buy the deeds to plots of land on spec when they had only gone out to buy a loaf of bread.

'You remember old Mr and Mrs Appleton, who I worked for in their enormous house on the Isle of Man?'

'We don't have to talk about that now...' A slight cloud of concern crossed Henry's face, 'Not if it brings back painful memories.'

'It doesn't,' Meggie said, stirring her tea, 'not any more...'

Henry patted her hand, 'I understand that when the Appleton's rotter of a son promised to marry you, my love, you believed him. And it still gets my back up when I think how he left you in the lurch. But then it was his loss, and my incredibly lucky gain.'

'Appleton's hush money gave me the chance to buy that land in the first place and there was no use letting the money rot in that old tea caddy at the back of the cupboard...'

Henry waited for his wife to speak again, watching Meggie twist her wedding ring round the third finger of her left hand as if gathering her thoughts.

For the second time, she opened her mouth, her words seeming to fall over themselves to be free. 'As you know that land has just been sitting there, derelict.' Meggie shuffled in her chair opposite and Henry's bacon-laden fork stilled before reaching his lips. 'And, as you also know, I had to put the deeds in your name.'

'I seem to know an awful lot.' Henry gazed across the table to his wife of nigh on twenty- five years. He had put Meggie's impulsive transaction to the back of his mind, and never mentioned it. 'If the truth be told, I'm proud of the fact you are your own woman.' She did not suffer fools after that Appleton fella. Fortunately, he was not one of those. His Meggie had a keen mind – everybody knew that. If she saw an opportunity, she grabbed it with both hands. No shilly-shallying! Nevertheless... Had she done one deal too many in her quest to make sure they did not go without? It was fine to move a bit of this and a bit of that when it was going spare, he thought, and pass it on to some poor sod who had nothing. If only that were the case.

The business was haemorrhaging money. And she knew nothing about it after giving up doing the accounts, but he also knew that blackmailers, once they had you on a hook, rarely set you free.

In a way, he was glad Susie Blackthorn did not have a clue how to run the office like Meggie had. A spot of typing and nail filing was Susie's speciality, she didn't understand much else and seemed to be biding her time, hoping Danny would ask her out. She didn't even open the post most days, so had no clue about the demands for money. More and more money every time.

'What I mean is,' Meggie said, lifting her cup and cradling it in both hands, 'I know we're not dirt-poor like some round here. You've made sure of that.' She reached for his hand and his strong fingers curled round hers.

They were not flush with spare cash either, Henry thought. Much less than they had been when she told him she had bought the land, suspecting the purchase was such a waste of good money. Although he said nothing.

They'd had serviceable stables in the yard, along with horses and flat-backed carts. He employed men who delivered goods to and from the docks and warehouses. The business was doing well. He would even say they were well off in those days. But not any more. The business was limping along now.

Henry sighed, for the first time in his life he felt helpless. He had to get someone who could manage the accounts and chase up the invoices, but he could do nothing to stop the demands for money. Meggie must not know. Blackmail was a dirty word and she would feel responsible. But she wasn't the one to blame.

'Are you listening?' Meggie's question jolted him back to attention.

'Sorry, love, I'm all ears, carry on.' He smiled across the table, determined to give her the best of attention, besotted from the moment he saw her all those years ago.

'Well, it's like this...' Meggie paused, not knowing how Henry would react. Looking down at her untouched meal of two rashers of juicy bacon and a new-laid egg from one of their own chickens, she prodded the delicate, frilly crisp just the way they both liked it and hoped that he would understand when she broke the news. 'That plot of land is right on top of the docks. Prime estate, I've heard it called.'

'Get on with it, love,' he smiled, 'my tea will soon be me supper.' He made quick work of the now cold bacon on the end of his fork.

'Well, that little hut in the middle of the...'

'A little hut!' he interrupted, wondering if he dare relax. 'It's bigger than Saint Paddy's church hall.'

'I was coming to that,' Meggie sighed, laying her knife and fork either side of her plate; she had lost her appetite now. 'I can't eat this, you have it.'

'You can't leave a good meal; you'll get fined for wastage.' Henry reached across to scrape her tea onto his plate. 'But I'll save you, Meggie, love, you can rely on me to keep you out of bother.'

'You're so thoughtful, my love,' Meggie said, giving him a strained smile before she rose from her chair and went over to the sideboard. Opening the drawer, she took out an official-looking envelope, and his fears that her dealings had gone wrong returned. Taking in her worried expression, he took a gulp of tea and got up from his chair.

'Don't worry, love. Whatever happens I'll be beside you....' Henry took the envelope she offered. 'You're not on your own here, whatever it is we can deal with it... I know people... I'll have a word... Get some advice...' His fingers fumbled with the envelope.

'Read it.' Meggie watched him open the letter. 'I will be forever grateful of the fact that whatever I do, you will always be by my side. I love you so much for all you are, a fine upstanding, dependable man who took me on when I came to Liverpool from the Isle of Man – the unmarried mother of another man's child!'

Susie had to stuff her fist in her mouth to stop the gasp of shock leaping from her lips. This information was dynamite, not because Meggie was a landowner, or that she would soon roll in money, but because when she came back to Liverpool after working for a rich family on the Isle of Man, she was already a mother and not even married. Scandalous!

The words, out in the open now, were the ones Meggie had never said aloud more than once, when Henry had encouraged her to confide in him about her predicament, all those years ago. Henry had helped her forget the heartache and promised to marry her if she would have him. He said those same words he was saying now.

'We'll stick together, Meggie, love, we'll muddle through somehow.'

'Look at the papers,' Meggie said and watched Henry's jaw drop.

'All those zeros.' Henry shook his head. 'I'd say I'm in a fortunate state of shock! I thought you'd bought a white elephant during the war, with being so close to the docks and the air raids. No doubt the chap who sold it to you thought so too.' He lifted his head to look at Meggie and then said, 'This is official?' Henry could not believe what he was reading as Meggie wiped happy tears from her face and she nodded. 'The dock board want to pay you all this money for that bit of land by the dock?'

Susie listened and her interest piqued when she heard the Skinners had come into a few bob. It was all right for some, she thought, money goes to money. But if the news got out that Meggie Skinner had a child out of wedlock, it would ruin them for sure. She moved closer to the door and held her breath.

'They said it's prime land,' Meggie replied. 'How can we refuse to cash in now the business is on its uppers.'

'I never said things were that bad,' Henry protested, but Meggie stopped him.

'I know you didn't,' she whispered, 'but you have looked so worried, what with the expense of keeping the wagon on the road and feeding the horses. You need an office manager to take everything in hand. We could buy a new wagon; business will pick up.'

Henry's heart flipped when he saw that twinkle in her eye and the strain left his limbs. 'I've worked with the horses since I was knee-high to a grasshopper, love.'

'But the money will make things easier. I'm going to help you out,' Meggie said, 'the same way you helped me all those years ago.'

They were so engrossed in the enormity of their conversation, neither of them heard creaking floorboards in the next room.

'Marrying you wasn't a noble gesture, Meg. I'm no saint.' He put his arm round her and kissed her. 'I know a wonderful thing when I see it. You are the finest woman I know.' His tender blue eyes were pools of love. 'None better.'

'In that case,' Meggie said in that no-nonsense way she used when she was wavering under his persuasive charm, 'you can do me one more kindness, say you'll come with me to the Port of Liverpool building at the Pier Head?'

'I will,' Henry said, 'but this money is not mine to spend.'

'I knew you'd say that too, and being a stubborn old bugger, I believe you meant it, but so do I.' Meggie wanted to wipe the worry lines from her beloved husband's face, little realising it would take more than a new wagon to fix the mess he was in. 'You have worried long enough,' she said, 'and now, if we at least get a proper book-keeper, it will relieve you of the headache that is Susie.'

'I believe we said for better or worse,' Henry smiled, 'well, we've seen both. So, if I haven't got the strain of an ailing business to worry about, all I need to concentrate on is winning that Netherford Cup.'

'That's what I thought.' Meggie was glad to see the deep-set lines on his forehead smooth a little, knowing the most prestigious trophy in the carting year would be a dream come true for her husband. The reward for years of toil in all weathers.

Henry pushed his new National Health specs halfway up his forehead and pinched the bridge of his nose. He felt relief seep through him for the first time in a long while. Meggie must never know how close they had come to destitution and how much her money would ease his burden. But when he was on his feet he would make it up to her.

'Maybe it's time for you to relax as well,' Henry said as the spread of a still handsome smile stretched his rugged features. 'You've worked so hard helping me all these years.' He was quiet for a moment, thinking. 'How different things could have been if, all those years ago I stood up for you against my mother.'

The pain in Meggie's eyes, the night he took her baby and gave it to another woman, would haunt him to the end of his days.

'Remember when I made you a promise, Meggie, the night I gave away your child. I said I would always keep a roof over your head, and we would earn the money to rear your child.' Meggie nodded again, too full to speak. 'I also promised nobody would ever know your secret. And I meant it.' He loved her more than life itself, and his heart swelled. Without Meggie, he had no life, that was why he must not tell her...

The blackmail demands started years ago, and he believed they would not last. But they continued, and he had paid handsomely to hide Meggie's shame. Henry would never allow his darling Meggie to become a cause for gossipmongers. But nothing, it seemed, could stop the relentless demands for money.

'I suspect meladdo who sold me the land, walked away with a grin on his chops, thinking I was a right mug,' Meggie said, breaking into his thoughts once more, 'and then laughed all the way to the Tram Tavern to spend the money I gave him for the deeds.'

Henry, taking her lead, laughed out loud. He would make things right. For Meggie's sake. 'I was thinking much the same thing myself, love. But serves us both right for doubting your eagle-eyed business acumen.'

'My what?' Meggie's brow furrowed. 'You don't half say some fancy words sometimes.'

'I thought you'd made a colossal mistake,' he said, 'I won't deny it.'

'I know,' Meggie said, the letter ignored for the moment, 'you doubted me.'

'I have never doubted you, my sweet,' he stroked her soft cheek. 'You scare me witless with your madcap schemes sometimes, but how could I doubt you when you have such good taste in your choice of husband.' He grinned and reached for her hand, which was always available, and they smiled to one another – each knowing the other so well. 'So I am married to a wealthy woman,' he said rereading the letter, and releasing a long low whistle, 'and it all came about because of your legacy.'

'*Our* legacy, my love – yours and mine,' Meggie corrected him. 'If it hadn't been for you, I would have been walking the streets, and God alone knows what would have become of my boy.' Then, to his utter surprise, Meggie burst into tears as all the pent-up emotions of their years of struggle came to the fore, and the enormity of the situation hit her.

'Hey, we'll have none of that, old girl.' Henry put his strong, muscled arms round her slight frame, and she felt safe again. 'If it makes you feel better, we will call it *our* legacy and leave it at that... Nobody need ever know, except us two.'

'Oh Henry, it's not only that. I love you. More than you will ever know. I am so sorry I could never give you the son you longed for.'

'It was God's Will, we had no say in the matter,' he said, smoothing her silky hair, holding her to him, 'I don't blame you. It wasn't your fault. To me, you will always be the nineteen-year-old girl who knocked on my ma's lodging house door looking for a job and walked straight into my heart. I knew I could never let you go.'

'Not even when I arrived with more than a reference for a place of work?'

'You looked so frail, clinging to the babe in your arms, soaked to the skin, with your shawl dripping wet. You had my heart there and then, regardless of your past. I was the luckiest man alive that day.'

'Your mother would never have given me houseroom if she knew I had a child out of wedlock.'

'You made the sacrifice,' Henry said. 'It couldn't have been easy leaving your child in the care of another woman.' He pulled her close to him, knowing times were different back then.

'People were not forgiving in a time when living hand to mouth was a way of life.' Meggie sighed. 'I had no choice.' Henry had secreted her child away under the cover of darkness. No questions asked. 'I had to let the baby go so I could earn enough money to give him the upbringing and education he deserved, I couldn't expect another woman to pay for my flesh and blood.' Meggie's voice cracked. 'I didn't realise I would be denied the chance to raise my own child. But now it's too late to do anything about it.'

'I wish things could have been different...' Henry whispered. 'I wanted to raise the child as my own, but who'd have thought Mother would live such a long and healthy life.' He gave a wry smile. 'A lifelong hypochondriac, she was as strong as a battleship and may still be here yet, had she not been concentrating on getting across the road to the Tavern and knocked down by that tram.'

'Your mother would have disinherited you if she knew you married a woman who bore another man's child. You had no choice either.' She shook her head, her pragmatic voice returning. 'I would never have been able to bear the guilt of you losing the business you and your dear father had worked for.'

'That's what I meant when I said you made the ultimate sacrifice – for me.'

'And that is why I know you will agree with me, when we've saved the business, I can put the rest of the money away.'

'To give the young'un the best life we can,' Henry said, holding her close and looking out of the kitchen window, gazing at the fading sign his father had put up the day he was born fifty-two years ago. *Skinner and Son – Hauliers and Stablemen. 1898.*

He understood why Meggie needed to give her offspring the things denied her.

'I know you had to pay most of your wages over to the woman raising your child every week. It is a parental instinct to look after your young, I believe.'

Well, well, well, Susie thought, *this is getting more shameful by the minute.*

Having heard every word, Susie guessed Skinner was not the father of the child. If Meggie's past became public, it would mark her down as a liar and a fraud. And that would not go down well with her friends in the church. They would snub her in the blink of an eye. And Meggie, who had always prided herself on her good works, while looking down her nose every time she deigned to come into the office, would find the fall a lengthy one. And what was all that talk about an office manager?

'I don't think so,' Susie muttered, 'bloody cheek!'

5

Saturday morning dawned bright and sunny and seeing her ankle was good as new, Evie decided to go and see Mr Skinner about the job Danny mentioned, hoping the position was still available. It would make everything so much simpler if she worked close by, and it would save on the tram fare.

Wanting to look her best, she removed the steel grips from the Catherine-wheel pin curls she had put in the night before. She had grown accustomed to sleeping on clips, securing her pillow in such a way they didn't dig into her head, but last night they seemed to take on a life of their own and she woke up a few times, so it was a relief to take them out and draw the wide-tooth comb through her shoulder-length hair.

Evie's hair fell in pleasing waves round her oval face and she secured it with a pretty ribbon. Her pale complexion making her sprinkle of freckles and aquamarine eyes stand out, she needed a bit of colour in her cheeks. Remembering the tube of lipstick her mother once wore, she rooted through the sideboard drawer until she found it. Even though it had lain untouched for the last three years, it was still useable. Feeling no compunction in applying a slick of red to her generous lips, she then dabbed a spot on each cheek.

She pressed her lips together, wiping the corners with the pad of her little finger before rubbing the red spot on her cheeks, the way she had seen Mam doing it, wanting to look her best when she went to see Mr Skinner, not like a corpse who had just been dug up.

The beaming sunshine enhanced the smell of horses and hay and timber when Evie entered Skinner's haulage yard. And her taste buds tingled when the unmistakeable smell of hot treacle wafted from a small shed where the horses' feed was made up at the end of the stables, making her stomach growl.

The office was tucked away in the corner of the cobbled yard which was busy with several cart lads and van boys mucking out the stables or dropping bales of straw from the loft to the stalls below for the horses' bedding. The entire place was a hive of activity, and Evie knew this job was in complete contrast to her usual office overlooking the River Mersey, where boats and ships of every shape and size sailed each day.

When Evie tapped on the half-glazed green door, signposted with the word Office in black lettering, there was no answer, so she gave another timid knock and turned the handle of the door. It was locked.

* * *

Meggie put the breakfast dishes in the sink and, scooping toast crumbs from the tablecloth, she glanced out of the window. 'Isn't that the Kilgaren girl?' she asked, not waiting for an answer. 'The poor thing looks like the cat who's lost her kitten.'

Opening the back door, Meggie shook the crumbs from the breakfast tray into the yard for the birds.

'He'll be with you now, love,' Meggie called across the yard, and

Evie lifted her hand in a friendly wave. 'Go on, now,' Meggie said to her husband as she bustled about the kitchen. 'Don't keep the girl waiting. Like as not, she'll be jittery.'

'I doubt it,' Henry said, draining his cup and placing it in the sink along with the rest of the morning crockery, 'she doesn't look the type to get the jitters – she's not like that daft mare, Susie...' He lowered his voice, 'You never know, this one might be the answer to our prayers.'

'What prayers?' Meggie asked, her brows puckering. 'And why will she be the answer to them?'

Henry shook his head and beamed a loving smile that told Meggie all was right with the world. The business accounts, though, were another matter and he would keep them to himself to save upsetting her. He had a notion, though, Evie Kilgaren was the girl to fix them. She had been through more than most, and didn't trouble herself with other people's business. Unlike Susie.

Meggie accepted his kiss, as she did every morning, knowing he had been her strength from the hour she met him, and even though she had made a noble sacrifice, Henry had done his best to make her happy. Having no children, he made her his entire world and Meggie's love for him would last until the end of her days.

Reaching for the latch on the door, she noticed a twinkle light his dark eyes when he said, 'Trust me, I will never let you down again.'

'You've never let me down...' Meggie said, returning his reassuring smile.

He and Meggie told each other everything. They were two halves of the same being, which meant that keeping this one enormous secret from her was the biggest burden he had ever known.

'I'll see you later, Love,' he said, believing Evie Kilgaren was the answer he so needed.

* * *

'So, you're Jack's big sister?' Mr Skinner said in that pragmatic way he had about him and Evie nodded. 'He talks of you – proud as punch he is of you and what you've achieved over the last few years.'

'I'm enormously proud of him, too,' Evie said, knowing that, at the crossroads of right and wrong, Jack had made the right decision and, like herself, wanted to hold his head high.

'Susie was supposed to be in today, but she's off sick – again. Typical, that is.' He took a bunch of keys from the pocket of his baggy, brown corduroy trousers and, finding the right one, opened the office door. 'You want a special invitation?' Skinner called from inside the office and Evie all but crept into the dim interior. Her eyes adjusting to the gloom when Mr Skinner pushed back his flat cap and flicked an electric switch by the door. The dim forty-watt bulb hanging in all its naked glory from the ceiling made the myriad lights in Mr Walton's office back at the D'Angelo Shipping look like the famous Blackpool illuminations.

The room was not so bleak that she couldn't see the wooden desk piled high with papers, folders, files and other office detritus. And, if she was not mistaken, there was an overpowering smell of fish.

'How can anybody work in this mess?' she blurted, hoping Mr Skinner hadn't heard her astonished outburst when he headed towards the far window.

'Sit yourself down wherever you please,' he said, removing a blackout blind, a remnant of the war years, allowing a shaft of piercing sunlight through the sash windows, illuminating the dancing dust particles.

Evie tried to summon the enthusiasm to force a smile as he sauntered over to the chaotic desk, but then she caught sight of a stack of dust-covered files and documents lining the cabbage-coloured walls, and noticed a half-eaten pilchard sandwich that appeared to be welded to a copy of *Picture Post* magazine: her enthusiasm plummeted.

Mr Skinner scowled, rolled up the misused magazine and manky sardine butty, throwing the whole lot in to the wastepaper bin, but doing so did nothing to ease the smell of rotten fish.

She didn't have ideas above her station, by any stretch of the imagination, but even on her poorest day, Evie made sure her surroundings were clean. This place was worse than the borough tip.

Smoothing her skirt, she sat on the only available chair, staring at the distempered walls, adorned with dog-eared posters advertising horse feed, out-of-date calendars and a sign that was still advising people to 'Be like dad and keep mum!' – five years after the war had ended.

'I think there's been some mistake,' Evie said, taking in a dull grey coating of dust covering every surface except the black, business telephone. 'I don't clean offices any more.'

Evie had studied for years, passed every examination with distinction, and yet Mr Skinner thought she was here to clean the office. Not that she was above rolling up her sleeves and getting stuck in. Her lips pinched together and the sting of tears at the back of her eyes gave her cause to blink rapidly. She thought Danny was being kind when he said there was a job going. She thought...

'I am a bookkeeper!' Her nostrils flared as the words shot out of her mouth like bullets from a tommy gun and Evie took a deep breath before standing up to leave. 'I studied at night school you see...' She heard the wobble in her own voice. 'I've got qualifications... lots of them.' She swallowed hard.

Mr Skinner held up his hand, looking bewildered. 'Hey up!

Who said I was after a cleaner?' His grey eyebrows pleated above inquisitive eyes.

'Danny didn't mention what the job entailed... This place...' She took in the entire room with one sweep of her eyes. 'It's...' she hesitated to say the word filthy, '...in need of a spring clean.'

'Aye,' Henry said, looking round as if seeing it for the first time, 'I dare say, but it's had none of that since my Meggie stopped working in here. The girl told me she doesn't skivvy.' Evie assumed *the girl* was Susie Blackthorn.

'Though, if she had any nous about her, she'd tidy up now and again.' Evie's words tumbled over themselves to leave her lips. 'You won't catch me spending eight hours a day in this tip!'

'Aye, well, that's by the by,' Mr Skinner continued, unabashed. 'I'm looking for a first-class bookkeeper. Danny said he knew just the girl... Angus vouched for you an' all, said you've been doing a sterling job with the Tavern's accounts and I'll level with you,' he lowered his voice, 'the accounts are in a right state, it's too much for Susie, she can't cope on her own and,' he tapped the side of his head, 'I don't think she's got enough upstairs to do much more than type a letter or answer the telephone.'

'She's a glorified receptionist,' Evie said, knowing it took much more grey matter to run a successful business than filing and typing.

'I said I'll level with you and I will,' Mr Skinner said, perching on the edge of an overflowing desk. 'I've let the business slide, I've had a lot on me plate and trusted the wrong people, made some bad decisions.' Although, he stopped short of telling Evie that he was being squeezed for money. At first, the sum was manageable, but for the last few years it rose to a remarkable level. If he carried on making payments much longer, he would go bankrupt. 'I need to know where the business stands financially.' Henry lowered his eyes to the floor. 'Truth be told, I'm asking for your help.'

How could she refuse, Evie thought, Mr Skinner had been good to her and her family when they needed it most. He had put food on their table, and given Jack a steady job when things could have gone so wrong for him. And now his business was in trouble and she would like to help in any way she could.

'You can count on me, Mr Skinner,' Evie said, and felt a rare sense of pride, knowing Angus had vouched for her, but pride didn't put bread on the table. 'I'll let you know if the job suits when you tell me what the pay is. I won't take a cut in me wages.'

'Does eight pounds a week suit?' Henry asked without hesitation.

'Aye, it'll do. And I think you'll find I'm worth every penny.' Eight pounds a week! That was two pounds more than she was paid now. And where she got the courage from, to say such a thing, was beyond her, but, she assumed, Mr Skinner was a straight-talking man and seemed satisfied. 'But I'm telling you one thing, I'm not working in this chaos. It'd drive me scatty!' She spotted a brown overall hanging behind the door and she put it on over her best clothes, and taking her scarf from her bag, she tied it turban-style, covering her corn-coloured curls.

To think, she was nervous at the thought of working here, but this chaotic muddle soon put paid to those feelings. Then, in her no-nonsense way, she rolled up the overlong sleeves.

'I'd be obliged if you'd fetch me a cloth, a bucket of hot water – and a wheelbarrow.'

'A wheelbarrow?' Mr Skinner cocked a quizzical eyebrow. He liked this girl; she had that same air about her as his Meggie did when she was a young lass. 'What in hell's bells d'you want a wheelbarrow for?'

'To chuck this lot in.' Evie nodded to the out-of-date wall hangings and the stack of knee-high documents leaning against the wall that looked as if they'd not been touched for decades. She went over to the wall and wrote 'Clean me' in the thick layer of dust, making Mr Skinner throw his head back and howl with laughter.

'I doubt you'll get Susie scrubbing out. She spends most of her time filing fingernails instead of invoices.'

'Susie's first job on Monday morning will be to sort out this little lot,' Evie gave a definite nod to the reams of cardboard folders, 'manicured fingernails or no bloody fingernails,' she said, ripping the curling, yellowed posters from the walls. 'I'll let you in on a secret, Mr Skinner,' she said as she began ripping them to pieces, 'we might not have much, but what we do have is clean.'

'Aye,' Henry said in a voice filled with admiration, 'Danny said the King can eat off your floor.'

'Did he now?' the unexpected remark took the wind right out of her sail.

'Listen, lass,' Henry said on a sigh, 'you can do as you please in your own office. You're in charge.' His weathered face stretched in a grin, 'You might even get that Susie to do a bit of work. We can live in hope… I'll go and fetch that water.'

Hands on hips, Evie looked round the ten feet by ten feet room. She would have this place gleaming by the time she finished. And as for Susie, she would have liked to see her face on Monday morning, but she would be working her notice at D'Angelo Shipping.

Fetching cold water from the copper tap in the back room, Evie flicked water over the floor to stop the dust from choking her before grabbing the sweeping brush. With a good dollop of elbow grease, she would have the office just the way she wanted it.

My office. My very own office.

* * *

When Mrs Skinner came into the office carrying a tray laden with tea and a plate of delicious, home-made fruit cake, she seemed flustered. But looking round her jaw dropped, and her eyes widened.

'Hey, lass, you've done wonders with the place.' The office was sparkling. The windows were dazzling, and her face was visible in the Mansion-polished mahogany desk situated on the rust-coloured floor. The colour was impossible to define before Evie got down on her hands and knees to scrub and polish it to a spotless sheen. Meggie's appreciative eyes were never still as she took everything in, 'I didn't know that desk could look so beautiful.'

'Thank you.' Evie found Meggie's praise heartening, she had never been complimented on her cleaning before and it gave her a warm glow. 'I'll soon have this office shipshape.'

'I'm sure you will, lass.' Meggie knew Henry had made the right decision investing some of the money they got from the sale of the land to employ Evie. 'You'll be worth your weight in gold.'

'I wouldn't go that far,' Evie smiled, 'but I'll do my best.'

'We know that.' Meggie offered Evie a cup of tea, knowing the girl could be the godsend Henry was hoping for. 'How's your ankle?'

'Good as new,' Evie said, 'but, I'll have to let Mr Walton know I'm leaving and work my notice.'

'Of course,' Meggie said. 'I won't mention anything to Susie about you coming to work here, either. If she thinks somebody else will do the work, she will try every trick in the book to get out of it, so beware.'

'I know her of old,' Evie said, determined not to let Susie slack, wanting to run the office in the same way as Mr Walton at the D'Angelo Shipping office.

* * *

Susie Blackthorn thought she had come into the wrong office when she unlocked the door on Monday morning. Looking through gleaming windows, she noticed Danny driving into the yard. She waved but was most put out when he didn't wave back, knowing you could see everything through this glass, suspecting Meggie had been busy.

She wondered if Danny would be quite so cocky when he found out his precious Aunt Meggie was not as saintly as everybody thought she was and toyed with the idea of telling Ada what she knew.

Ada wouldn't want anything to cloud her daughter's home-coming on the first of May, now only a week away, and Susie couldn't wait to get a glimpse of Grace's new fiancé.

Imagine the terrible disgrace if the fiancé was met with the family shame, Susie thought. Maybe it would be better if she warned Danny, in case the scandal slipped out after she had a few drinks in the Tram Tavern.

The Skinners had no kids of their own – or so everybody thought – and it was understood by Ada that her Danny would inherit the yard if anything should happen to Auld Skinner. But what if Meggie's offspring should suddenly appear and claim it when Meggie keeled over. After all, the business would go to the rightful heir, or heiress for that matter. Surely Danny ought to be warned there was another contender – Meggie's illegitimate child.

He would be so eternally grateful that she had saved his family from the humiliation and shame of such scandal, that the scales would fall from Danny's eyes and he would realise he *had* loved her for all these years. And he would wonder how he could ever build a business without her support and dedication, and most of all, how he could possibly live another day without her.

Susie couldn't wait for Grace, her best friend since school, to come home. She would be thrilled to have her as a sister-in-law.

Maybe they could have a double wedding - but then she would have to share her big day. *Maybe not.*

All she had to do was get Danny to take her out as a proper couple, not just as friends. If Danny weren't such a good catch, she doubted she would still be friends with Grace, or work in this awful place.

Susie, never to be put down, considered that she had a far superior voice to Grace, and believed she would have made it big if only her mam and dad had allowed her to leave home and meet other men besides Danny.

She watched him bring the wagon to a stop across the yard, knowing most of the girls round here had their eye on Danny, especially since he came out of the army and his mother let it be known he was going to have his own business one day.

Susie sighed gazing out of the window, imagining Danny keeping her in style, with a new house as big as the Skinners, and fancy clothes like the ones in the magazines she read. Danny would take her to eat in the best restaurants, and they would go to the theatre. She would introduce him to a bit of culture, watch a show, not spend Saturday night in the Tram Tavern, the way most men did round here.

Obviously, she would not spend eight hours a day in this awful shed of an office either, even though it didn't look so bad now it had been cleaned up. She would employ some other dogsbody to do the donkey work, and Danny would be knocked bandy by how well she played hostess when she held private dinner parties – because everybody knew that successful businessmen did their wheeler-dealing at private dinner parties. She'd read about it.

Susie had pursued Danny with every womanly charm she could think of, read all the magazine stories about how to make yourself beautiful for your man. Although Danny had shown no inclination to see her as a serious girlfriend, let alone put a ring on her finger and walk her up the aisle – a vision in virginal white.

Though that might be why he wasn't interested, she reasoned. She might have to change her mind on the virginal bit if Danny didn't get his skates on.

He had taken her to the pictures a few times, a dance now and again, and they had a good time, but nothing ever came of it. What was wrong with her? Three years of showing undivided devotion to a man who barely noticed her was becoming more annoying by the day.

Danny may well want to build his own business, but she wasn't getting any younger. Maybe she should try another tack. Meggie had got Auld Skinner up the aisle in such unholy haste and now she understood why.

Mrs Skinner, doing charitable deeds and chewing the alter rails every Sunday, was a scarlet woman of the worst kind. Not only did she have a child out of wedlock, she gave it away so she could marry a man who had money. *Despicable, that's what it was.*

Meggie would be devastated if the news got out. And it would. These things always did. What would Danny think of his precious aunt then?

But what if he told Meggie what she had heard? Then Auld man Skinner would sack her for eavesdropping and telling tales. He had already threatened, if she didn't buck her ideas up, she would be out of a job. Although, who else would be daft enough to work here for the pittance Henry Skinner paid? And, Susie thought, her mind working furiously to her own ends, the information was to her advantage. In possession of a golden nugget, she was not afraid to use it if need be.

She jumped visibly when Danny opened the door, but he didn't enter the office.

'Did you want me, Susie?' he asked matter-of-factly, gazing round the spotlessly clean office. 'I'm in a bit of a hurry.'

So he had seen her waving, she thought irritably. 'I just wanted to see if you fancied going to the pictures tonight?' Susie decided now was not the right time to tell him about his aunt Meggie.

'Not tonight,' Danny answered, 'I've got to have a look at the engine of this wagon.' He had already hatched a plan to get Susie off his back once and for all, but he needed his sister Grace home to offer a comforting shoulder for Susie to weep on, until then he just had to be the Houdini of excuses.

'But you only put a new fan belt on the other week,' Susie was obviously miffed.

'I know,' he said, 'but now the hydraulics are starting to chug about a bit and the old girl's getting jumpy.'

'She's not the only one,' Susie said, dragging the cover off her typewriter, knowing she would have to spend another night listening to the wireless with her mother while Danny would rather play with jumpy dryholicks, or whatever they were called. than take her to the pictures.

Hell's bells, she thought, knowing some people said the quickest way to a man's heart is through his stomach. But she had never been much of a cook, and knew it started much lower down that that. *Well, we'll soon see about that. After all, he's just a man – and all men have needs.*

6

Grace heard the gentle click of the cabin door and inhaled the mellow citrus cologne that soothed her. She had felt nothing so exquisite in all her life as she did when she and Bruce made love on the homeward voyage.

Bruce had been a perfect gentleman. He didn't jump on her and try to take advantage as some men might have. Men like Clifford, who not only had a girl in every port, but one in every cabin.

'It's a wonder Clifford Brack hasn't made a pass at you yet?' one showgirl had said early in her relationship with Clifford, applying make-up in the mirror next to Grace. 'He's a slippery fish, and he's up to all kinds of nefarious activities...'

But none of that interested Grace any more, she had Bruce, the most wonderful, caring man in the whole world, who had truly swept her off her feet. Her every day was a gift, knowing he was going to be in it, spending every possible moment together.

When they were in New York, Bruce took her to Bloomingdale's and bought her a beautiful silk scarf in the most vibrant peacock blue because it matched her eyes, he said. It was the most precious thing she owned. Not because of its luxurious expense, but because

Bruce wanted nothing in return, he was not giving her a gift just to get her into bed - that came later. Their exquisite lovemaking was as natural as breathing, both craving the intimacy of one another.

She bought him a tiepin in the same hue and felt it somehow bound them together in the most intimate friendship she had known. They thought the same way, they laughed at the same things. He called her his soulmate and she called him her wounded sailor, because of his war wound, and Grace could not imagine a world without Bruce in it.

And now she was on her way back home to Liverpool, and Bruce was with her too. He had meetings in head office. He had restored her trust in a way she did not think possible after Clifford's betrayal. Although the less she thought of him the better, and they studiously ignored each other whenever they met, a situation that suited Grace. She would much rather endure Clifford's silence, than his bitter vitriol.

'Am I missing something here?' Bruce asked Clifford pointedly when, once again he did not acknowledge her presence.

Grace had told Bruce everything about Clifford, from the start of their friendship, not because she wanted to get the entertainment director in hot water with the boss, but because she wanted to purge herself of the ugly worthlessness, Clifford had inflicted upon her, and because Bruce was the easiest man she had ever talked to. She felt she could tell him anything.

'I do beg your pardon, Miss Harris, forgive me, I was lost in thought.' Clifford was being over-gracious, and Grace could detect the merest hint of disdain. Clifford was paying lip service to Bruce, and his smile did nothing to warm the chill in his eyes.

'Please, don't mention it,' she replied with equal cool. Grace wanted nothing to do with Clifford, knowing she only had one more week to endure his sneaky criticisms before the ship docked in the port of Liverpool.

'He can be very brash,' Bruce sounded apologetic when Clifford turned and walked away, 'but I won't have him dismiss you like one of his minions.'

'Let's think no more of it,' Grace said, but the catch in her voice told Bruce that she was more upset than she was letting on.

'What's wrong?' Bruce asked, reaching for her hand, gently holding it, when silently Grace pleaded for him not to be kind. She swallowed the tight knot in her throat, but it wouldn't budge. 'He really got to you, didn't he?' Bruce said tenderly and Grace shook her head, unable to speak. 'Come on, I'll walk you to your cabin, you look beat.'

'I'm fine,' Grace lied, knowing Clifford's icy glare had upset her more than she ever thought possible. 'But I would like to go to my cabin where it's quieter.' When nearing the end of a long voyage like this, she always felt the pull of home and could not wait to see her family.

'You merit real diamonds,' Bruce said, and he reached into his inside pocket. 'I wanted to give you this when we got back to Liverpool, but you look like you could do with cheering up now.'

Grace had never expected to be given anything so beautiful and, later that night, the elegant bracelet was all Grace wore when they made love.

She should have slowed things down. But she couldn't, she was in love with the most wonderful man she had ever met, and she would miss him so much when they parted in her home port. The parting was going to be bittersweet, looking forward to seeing her family, yet knowing she would not see Bruce again.

* * *

When Evie collected her cards, she was pleased and surprised when Mr Walton said he would be sorry to see her go. The staff contributed to a small brown leather-bound book of poetry, which he presented her with.

'It is from all the office staff,' he said in his usual stiff, although not unfriendly, manner, and Evie felt her throat tighten. Nobody had ever given her a present, at least not one as beautiful as this. All the staff had signed it and Mr Walton had written a brief message thanking her for her dedicated service.

'I'll treasure it,' Evie murmured, unable to get the words out, steeled herself against bursting into tears and was only able to briefly thank her wonderful colleagues before her throat contracted. She gripped her book of poetry so hard. Everybody hugged her and even Mr Walton, not given to outbursts of senti-ment, told her to come and see them any time she pleased.

Working in the heart of Liverpool was everything she had studied and sacrificed for. And working for the D'Angelo Line one of the biggest shipping companies in the world had filled her with enormous pride. Her colleagues, efficient and self-assured, treated her as an equal and Evie adopted the longed-for mantle of respectability in the office, and in Reckoner's Row.

When she left River Chambers, she was walking on air. Hoping she had made the right decision. But Evie hadn't worked hard to reunite her family only to desert them every day by working miles away. And with the wages she would earn at Skinner's she could even afford to put a bit of money aside for Lucy's future.

She had no choice but to work. If she didn't work, they couldn't afford the luxury of rental money for the wireless, or little treats like a night at the pictures, or even some rarer comforts that rationing allowed, like a bag of toffees or an even scarcer bar of chocolate. And Lucy had a sweet tooth.

Skipping down the wide marble steps of River Chambers, Evie sighed, glad her last day was over. Although she loved working in the hive of commerce overlooking the pewter-coloured waters of the River Mersey, one thing made her even more determined to be closer to home. Their father had been sectioned in a secure hospital indefinitely. But how long was indefinite?

Her breath caught in her throat when Evie remembered how persuasive her father could be. Lucy still thought of him as her Good Shepherd. But Evie knew there was nothing good about him. He was manipulative and sly. Was she being irrational thinking the authorities would let him out early for good behaviour? She could not help but think his actions were premeditated, no matter how much he pleaded his innocence, telling the jury his wife was alive when he left her.

Evie's heart raced, and her mouth dried just thinking about it. She carried her responsibility to her family firmly on her shoulders, to keep them out of his way whatever the cost.

In the Liver Bird's shadow, a little shudder rippled through her slim body, and in the waning sunshine, she could not shake off the underlying fear that her sister may one day come face-to-face with the truth.

The trial had taken place three years ago in St George's Hall, opposite Lime Street train station, only a brisk five-minute walk away. It had been the talk of Liverpool. Evie had prevented Lucy knowing the whole truth by sending her on holiday to Ireland until the trial was over. And even though the news was splashed over the front page of every daily newspaper, Lucy was none the wiser.

Evie reached the arched marble exit. Pulling her paisley head-scarf from her brown leather box bag, she folded it into a triangle, covered her honey-coloured curls and tied it under her chin, before lowering her head against the eddying wind blowing off the River Mersey up Castle Street. Hurrying along the grimy pavement of the bustling port, where soot still gathered in pockmarked bullet holes years after the Luftwaffe tried to annihilate Liverpool docks. She would miss the bustle of the city streets.

'Evie!' Her name sounded distant, and she looked round, about to make a run across the cobbled road towards the bus stop opposite the docker's umbrella. 'Evie, over here.'

Over the noise of rumbling traffic, she noticed the chugging flat-backed wagon only yards away, spewing out diesel fumes into the gusty spring air, and her heart flipped unintentionally when she saw Danny leaning out of his cab. His chirpy grin chased away all reflective thoughts of her father and Evie vowed that she would start a new phase in her life.

Danny put his arm out of the window to let her know he was coming over to her side. Holding up his hand like a policeman on point duty, he stopped oncoming traffic, filling Evie with a fizz of pride, and came to a halt at the kerb opposite her. She felt elated and embarrassed at the same time.

'Come on, girl, get in! I'll give you a lift home,' Danny said in that easy-going way he had about him, leaning over the passenger seat to open the passenger door he tipped his cap. 'Where to, madam? I am at your service.'

'Thanks, ever so,' she said, a little breathless after climbing into the cab. She had liked Danny from the moment she'd set eyes on him. What you saw was what you got. And she liked what she saw.

'So, are you looking forward to joining our happy workforce?' Danny asked. 'I thought we'd been robbed when I went in and saw all the clutter had disappeared.'

'I can put up with most things,' Evie answered, 'but not dirt and clutter. It stems from my days skivvying, I suppose.'

'You were never a skivvy,' Danny said. 'You provided a service and there's nothing wrong with that.'

Evie knew his mother, Ada, had worked as a cleaner in the Tavern for most of her married life. 'I'm not saying cleaning is less of a worthwhile job than any other,' Evie said quickly, 'I just meant that I—'

'I didn't think you were,' Danny cut in, 'we'd be in a right state without our Mrs Mops and the office has never looked so good.'

'Our Jack and Lucy will be relieved they won't have to come home to an unlit fire and no tea on the go,' Evie said, looking out of the window to see the dockside streets whizzing by.

'He's a real trouper, your Jack, he gets stuck in,' Danny said with a nod, 'and he's one of the best workers in Skinner's yard – apart from me, that is.' He laughed, but Evie could well believe that Danny and Jack would make a formidable pair in any task they undertook.

At seventeen, her brother was nearly six feet tall and was as strong as an air-raid shelter. He was also immensely popular with the girls around Reckoner's Row and, after listening to Danny telling of his wartime escapades, decided he was going to sign up for the army when he was called up for National Service.

'You're so modest,' Evie smiled, 'but you've got to admit, peeling potatoes is not a job for a man who's worked hard all day.'

'It'll stand him in good stead when he's called up,' Danny said, reminding Evie that young men, from the age of eighteen were being subscripted into the forces for National Service and could be sent anywhere in the world. 'I think everybody should do a bit of spud bashing, especially if the woman of the house is working too.'

'Well, you are one in a million, Danny,' Evie said. 'Not many men would be so thoughtful.'

'You're not wrong,' Danny replied, knowing his own mother had worked all her life, yet his father never lifted a finger to help her. The thought tightened his grip on the steering wheel. It was probably best he didn't think about Da right now. 'Aunt Meggie told me you were starting in the office on Monday,' Danny said, catching a quick glimpse of Evie's shapely legs. He wasn't one for ogling women, but sometimes Evie's trim calf could brighten this bloke's day a treat. 'Susie will be thrilled to bits.' He kept his eyes on the busy road, but Evie could see he had a twinkle in them.

'I'm sure she won't,' Evie replied, 'especially when she finds out I'm the office manager in charge of accounts.'

Danny nodded as they pulled up outside Number Two Reckoner's Row.

'I'd love to be a fly on the wall when she does find out.' Danny smiled and then, as Evie pushed the handle of the passenger door, he touched her arm. 'Hang on a minute, I've got something for you.' Reaching down the side of his seat, Danny held out a package wrapped in newspaper and tied with string. 'I meant to give this to you before, but I didn't see you.' What he should have said was *I was trying to pluck up the courage.*

Evie took the package as if it were about to explode in her hands. She was not accustomed to accepting presents from men. In fact, she couldn't remember a time when she had been offered one gift, and today she had been given two.

Danny looked ahead, apparently fascinated by a pigeon bobbing about on the bridge steps. He didn't offer a reason for giving her a present.

'What is it?' Evie asked, watching the creeping colour rise up to his throat. 'It isn't my birthday or anything.'

'Open it later, when you get in the house,' Danny said with a casual flick of his hand. He didn't fancy having the gift, which he had managed to buy with the help of Meggie, thrown back in his face.

7

'What kind of a girl does he take me for?' Evie felt her face grow hot when she opened the parcel.

Lucy, fastening young Fergus in his pushchair by his blue leather reigns looked up, was full of curiosity.

'Nylons!' Lucy cried. How she wished she were old enough to wear nylons.

They heard a call from the front door and Connie's voice sailed up the long passageway.

'Cooee, it's only me,' Connie was a welcome visitor and called in every day, or even a few times a day, depending on how much she wanted some respite from her meddling mother, Mim.

'Come in!' both girls replied in unison, and when Connie entered the kitchen, Lucy couldn't wait to tell their neighbour about Evie's present.

'Danny's repaying the ones that got ruined when she fell in the road,' Lucy said, 'but I'll have them if she doesn't want them.' Lucy, more sparky than her older sister admitted, 'I'm not too proud to accept nylons from a good-looking fella.'

'You are your mother's daughter,' Connie said. Although she

could see Evie's lips set in a straight line, and winked at Lucy, knowing that neither of the girls would take offence at her remark because they knew how fond she had been of Rene. Their mother had worked alongside her at the Tram Tavern and was a close confidante when she was alive.

'I think I've got the legs for nylons,' Lucy said, striking a pose she had seen in a magazine advert.

'You will not have them!' Evie stood wide-eyed, hands on hips, outraged at the very thought. 'Thirteen years of age. What would people think if I let you run around in nylons. We'd be the talk of the wash house.'

'Hark at you having time to go to the wash house.' Lucy laughed and Connie, pragmatic as ever, was in her element, resting her bump against the kitchen sink. She loved the Kilgaren family like her own. These two sparked off each other like Aztec warriors and amused her no end. Having no sister of her own, their rapid repartee was a breath of fresh air. 'Our Evie in the wash house? Perish the thought!' Lucy howled with ready laughter. 'And since when did you give a rat's gasp what other people think? Never. That's when.'

'If I catch you wearing them, there will be words, lady,' Evie warned, and Connie could not help herself but laugh.

'She wants the nylons for herself,' Lucy whispered to Connie.

'And why shouldn't she? Danny knows if anybody deserves a treat she does.'

'I am here, you know,' Evie said, 'and I can hear you both.' Her smile broke out and Evie could not feign irritation much longer.

'So you take those nylons, ma'am, and you go flaunt your shapely pins!' Lucy waved her hands with the swagger of a snake oil salesman and in minutes the kitchen was full of female laughter and Evie's pale freckled complexion took on a rosy glow which Lucy was glad to see. In fact, Evie lit up every time anybody mentioned Danny's name. And, if he came to speak with their Jack, she beamed like the Liverpool lighthouse.

'I can't believe Danny would give me something like this,' she said, still holding the packet of stockings.

'Maybe he felt responsible for ruining your last pair?' Connie reminded Evie of the sprained ankle incident, as it was now called. 'After all, it's only a pair of stockings, it's not a proposal of marriage.' She laughed when she saw Evie's jaw drop and her eyes widened in obvious alarm.

'I've got it on good authority from Mersey-mouth Ada, who told my mother, Mersey-mouth Mim, that Danny has no intentions of walking down the aisle. Marriage is not for him,' Connie said. Then, she lowered her voice and said in a conspiratorial tone, 'well, he only has to look at Ada and Bert to see that wedded bliss is a myth in that family.'

Evie felt a zing of electricity shoot through her body and the kitchen was silent for a moment. 'Well, all I'm saying is you're too young to wear nylons, Lucy... And what are you two laughing at?'

'Nothing,' Lucy and Connie answered in unison, 'nothing at all.' They both knew how much Evie liked Danny, even though she had never said as much. The attraction between them was obvious to everybody – except the two people it mattered to most.

In their humble opinion, Evie was more than a match for Danny, who fought in the war and had the medals to prove it, but did he have the backbone to take up with Evie Kilgaren? Time would tell.

'I'll save the nylons for my new job,' Evie conceded.

'Tell me how your last day at D'Angelo's went.' Connie, as interested as any loyal friend, followed Evie into the front kitchen and sat down at the table near the sash window, while Lucy followed with a fresh pot of tea. Anybody who visited was offered a nice cup of tea.

'They gave me this lovely book of poems,' Evie said, glad to change the subject, 'and starting at Skinner's on Monday means I'll be here to get you up for school, my girl,' she told Lucy, knowing her sister was inclined to turn over and go back to sleep when the weather was not as warm as it was lately.

* * *

'Oh it's you.' Susie looked up from filing her red-varnished nails with the rough edge of a matchbox, and even though it was only nine-thirty on Monday morning didn't look happy at being interrupted when Evie entered the office after collecting business files from Mr Skinner. 'If you're looking for your Jack, he's out on a delivery.' Susie sounded bored, sitting behind the enormous mahogany desk that Evie had cleaned a week ago and which was now covered in a thin film of dust.

'I haven't come to see Jack,' Evie answered, seeing the other girl too engrossed in a *Tit-Bits* magazine to raise her head. Obviously, she had no intentions of doing any work as she licked the tip of her finger and flicked another page.

'Skinner's down the stables.' Susie remained glued to the magazine. 'Take a seat. I'll get one of the stable lads to get him in a minute.' Evie sat down on a straight-backed chair near the green wall and studied the girl opposite, wondering how long it would take Susie to show any interest in starting work. It was gone nine thirty and she hadn't even taken the cover off her typewriter. So no time soon, Evie thought when Susie showed little interest in answering the ringing black Bakelite telephone.

Mr Walton would have wiped the floor with Susie for showing such unprofessional behaviour. On the third ring, she deigned to answer it.

'Skinner's.' Susie's jaded tone was an obvious sign this business needed shaking up.

First impressions are everything in business. Evie could hear Mr Walton's voice as if he were standing in the room. But they would fall on deaf ears with Susie as when Danny came into the office her eyes lit up and she cut off the caller, leaving the receiver off the hook so whomever was on the line could no longer get through.

Flicking her bleached-blonde hair, Susie stood up, pulling down her low-cut, tight-fitting sweater to show off her curves and perched on the edge of the desk, ignoring Evie.

'Hiya, Evie!' Danny grinned. 'You made it then.'

'Made it?' Susie shot her usual superior expression. 'Am I missing something?'

'I think you might be.' Evie's voice was steady, her eyes unflinching when she looked at Susie. She had waited a long time for this. 'I'm here for the job.'

'We don't need a skivvy, thanks very much,' Susie said in that haughty way Evie remembered so well, sweeping her hand in a semicircle to take in the whole office, 'as you can see, the place is spotless.'

Evie put down the old newspaper she had been half-reading, not much interested in contraband jewels smuggled through Liverpool docks, wondering what Susie would say when she found out her work-shy days were over.

'The office is spotless because Evie cleaned it.' Danny held Susie's stony glare. 'Although it looks like it could do with a regular dusting to keep it looking the way she left it.'

Susie's dark-pencilled eyebrows puckered, and she looked from Danny to Evie and the atmosphere between the two of them grew tense.

Unflinching, Evie looked back at Susie and wondered if she had made the biggest mistake of her life. However, she didn't have the luxury of being choosy now. She promised Jack and Lucy she would work closer to home and she had no intentions of breaking that promise.

'Well, I must admit we need a cleaner, and even though I say so myself, I haven't met a better cleaner than Evie,' Susie said, while Danny shook his head in disgust and left the office without another word. 'You can start by putting the kettle on,' Susie told her. 'The staffroom could do with a once-over, too.'

Evie cocked an eyebrow. Did this daft mare believe she would come here in her best skirt and blouse to scrub the staffroom? However, she didn't have time to speak her mind as, a moment later, Danny and Jack came in and were heaving a heavy-looking desk through the office.

'Do you mind telling me what you're doing?' Susie asked, pointing to the desk and it drew Evie's attention to her long talons, wondering how she typed.

'We're planting daffodils,' Danny said straight-faced as they positioned the desk near the window.

'What do I need another desk for?' Susie's beady eyes watched every action. The way Danny smiled at Evie, like they were the best of friends. Nodding as if asking her approval about where the new desk would be situated. If there was any nodding to do, she thought, she should be the one doing it, not the skivvy.

'This one is mine?' Evie stroked the mahogany desk. *Her very own desk.*

'Yours?' Susie's neck took on a mottled red appearance, a sure sign she was looking to battle as she picked up the slim packet of five Senior Service cigarettes. The hostile atmosphere broke only when Susie struck a match with such force it broke in two, causing the lit end to fly across her desk and fizzle out. 'You're telling me you are a clerk now, is that it?'

'I didn't say that.' Evie's spirits soared.

Susie thought the Kilgarens were as unpleasant as horse muck on the soles of her high-heeled shoes. And even though she only lived next-door-but-one, she gave a good impression of someone who thought she was better than everybody in Reckoner's Row – except the Harrises and that was because she had her eye on Danny.

'So, let me get this right, you've gone from office cleaner to office clerk?'

'I'm not an office clerk,' Evie said, savouring every word as she skewered Susie with an unflinching glare. She had longed to say those words for such a long time and now that she had she felt ten feet tall. Recalling the compliments she had received from her colleagues at D'Angelo's had given her confidence, and she refused to let Susie intimidate her. That ship sailed long ago.

Danny and Jack shot each other a look. 'Right, well, we'll leave you to it, shall we?'

Evie noticed that they couldn't get out fast enough, thankful that today she could hold her head high and be proud of what she had achieved. And looking at Susie's desk, littered with magazines, bits of paper and cup stains, she noted that the girl had not changed her ways since working at Beamer's. Although one thing had changed, Evie thought, Susie no longer had the power to intimidate her. In fact, she had no power at all.

The air fizzed with unspoken animosity when Evie replaced the receiver on the hook and an immediate piercing ring of the telephone broke the stifling silence.

'Skinner's!' Susie barked the introduction down the receiver. 'No, Mr Skinner is not here, you must ring back later.' Susie slammed it down with such force, Evie winced.

'That might have been important,' she said, but Susie remained tight-lipped, rolling her eyes, her posture stiff. 'That is not the way to introduce the company to a prospective customer?' Was it any wonder the business was failing.

'Why should you care?' Susie asked as Henry Skinner bowled into the office, followed by Jack, who was now carrying a black heavy-looking typewriter.

'Good morning, ladies,' Skinner said as Jack put the typewriter on Evie's desk, 'Susie, I believe you already know our new office manager.'

There was a moment's silence, and nobody spoke as Susie digested his words.

'Office manager?' Her disbelief rose to a high-pitched squeak. 'Office. Manager! I can't believe I'm hearing this right. I've worked here for nigh on three years. Nobody told me anything about managing the office.'

'I was...' Evie began but was silenced by Mister Skinner's large work-worn hand.

'I'm sure Evie would be modest about her skills, but let me tell you something,' Henry explained in his usual forthright manner. He came across as abrupt, but Evie could tell he was a good, kind man. 'She is a first-class auditor. I have it on the best authority...'

'She knows the law and everything,' Jack interrupted, giving the desk a wipe with the cuff of his jacket.

'Jack!' Evie whispered, feeling her face grow hot, not used to blowing her own trumpet, aware that a minute later she could be flat on her arse in the gutter.

'Susie, you haven't got the qualifications that this job needs,' Henry said without a hint of his usual cheeriness. 'Evie will instruct you from now on, and if you don't pull your socks up, you may well look for another job, so think on.'

Susie's black-lashed eyes widened, and her jaw dropped, taking a moment to recover her voice. 'I don't want to speak out of turn, Mr Skinner,' she was finding it hard to control her emotions, 'but if you think I'm taking orders from a jumped-up skivvy, you can think again.'

'That is your choice,' Henry said with a shrug of his burly shoulders, 'but them's the rules. If you don't like the situation, you know where the door is.'

'You're sacking me!?' Susie watched Jack slope out of the office.

'No, I'm not sacking you, I didn't say that. There have been some irregularities with the finances and Evie is here to fix them. Evie, you need only report to me,' he said turning back to Evie, 'and if Susie doesn't like it...'

Without saying another word, Susie scooped up her magazine, her bag and dragged her coat from the back of the door. 'You haven't heard the last of this!' she said, her eyes blazing. 'I can work anywhere.' Marching out of the office, she slammed the door behind her.

'Looks like she's in a right twist,' Evie said, and Henry gave a low chuckle.

'I expect she'll be back tomorrow, have no fear on that score,' he said.

'I can manage,' Evie smiled. 'I've got plenty to keep me occupied.' The telephone rang, and she picked up the receiver.

'Good morning, Skinner and Son Cartage Company...'

'I'll get those other files you asked for.' Henry felt the office was now in the best hands. When he returned to drop an enormous cardboard box on Susie's desk, he said, 'They don't make for exciting reading, and I'd appreciate it if you said nothing to my Meggie. She'll only fret.'

'They might not look interesting to you,' Evie assured him, 'but they'll keep me happy for a long while, Mr Skinner.'

'Just Skinner will do, we don't stand on ceremony here.'

Evie knew she could never call this man by his surname, any

more than she could have called her boss in the D'Angelo Shipping offices *Walton,* it sounded so disrespectful and high-handed.

'Let's hope you can spring-clean my accounts the way you cleaned this office,' he said, and the obvious look of appreciation told Evie he was more than pleased with the new cleaner version of the business.

'Being saddled with that flighty mare,' Evie glanced over to Susie's desk that looked like the corporation tip, strewn with neglected files, 'was doing you no good at all. If you give her a minute, she'll take a month. I know, I've worked with her before.' She had no idea why anybody would choose to keep the girl in a job.

'Talking of saddles,' Mister Skinner grinned, 'I'll be next door in the tack room sorting out the horse brasses for the Netherford Parade.'

Evie had never been to the Netherford Parade. She managed the Mayday parade, when workers all round the world went on a day's unofficial strike, recognising the work done by manual labourers and was celebrated by decorated floats following a marching band.

The floats – flat-backed wagons pulled by horses – were also a good advertisement for businesses, trying to outdo each other with the best decorations. From local breweries and coal merchants to small shops with decorated messenger bikes, every business marketed their wares and the streets were lined with flag-waving people from Liverpool to Litherland. A five-mile stretch of potential customers.

Evie recalled Lucy, in a pushchair, waving her flag in her little chubby fist, being pushed along by her or Jack or Mam, who would treat them to an ice cream from the Italian ice-cream man with his cart on wooden wheels. And she remembered seeing Mr Skinner's float drawn by two huge Clydesdales carrying the May Queen on a golden throne and surrounded by her entourage. Evie felt all nostalgic at the memory of that wonderful day.

'Right then,' Mr Skinner said, heading out of the office and snapping Evie out of her reverie, 'you know where I am if you need anything. The flighty one will be back tomorrow, no fear.'

'No fear at all.' Evie knew he had left some important decisions to Susie for far too long and, by the look of things, she had taken full advantage.

Evie looked round the office with a sense of pride. The entire place smelled of polish and possibility. Things were looking up, at least whilst Susie was out of the office – oh, and she must remember to dock her wages. Start as she meant to go on.

8

'Hello, Evie!' Just as Mr Skinner had predicted, Susie Blackthorn's navy-blue peep-toe shoes clip-clipped across the polished linoleum floor, albeit three hours late, the following morning, and Evie looked up from her rows of figures. Susie was glamorous, in a slender calf-length pencil skirt that hugged her trim figure. A pale blue hip-length swagger coat with deep turned-back cuffs topped off her matching navy-blue peplum jacket. Removing the swing coat, Susie hung it on the hook behind the door as if the events of the day before had never happened.

'Hello, Susie,' Evie said, looking at her wristwatch. She would let the matter go, but only for today. 'I like your suit.'

'Oh, this old thing.' Susie's smile looked forced and did nothing to conceal her look of displeasure as she took her seat behind her desk. 'It's just something I had in the back of the wardrobe. I only wear it for work.'

Pull the other one, it's a call to Sunday mass, Evie thought, returning a matching smile.

'I was sure you wouldn't be coming back when I saw the time

getting on,' Evie said, knowing her lifelong nemesis would try it on just to see what she could get away with.

'I had a doctor's appointment.' Her scarlet smile stretched a little. 'Skinner never asks questions about women's ailments.'

'It is *Mr* Skinner to you,' Evie said, knowing Susie's days of slacking were over. From today, she would do as she was told.

'You might not feel so loyal when you find out they're not as squeaky clean as they seem,' Susie said, 'but I know things. Things that *Skinner* and Meggie wouldn't want made public.'

'Just do your job.' She knew Susie was a troublemaker and loved nothing better than to put other people down to make herself look important, but Evie had no intentions of letting Susie get the upper hand this time. 'I don't listen to gossip and nor should you.'

'You'll kick yourself for not listening when this comes out, and so will Ada.'

'Not interested, Susie.' Evie knew first-hand that rumours could turn even the best of intentions into something ugly and malicious, bringing nothing but misery. Her thoughts sprang to her own father, who had destroyed the woman he adored in a fit of unfounded rage.

'Grace is coming home, and she's only got herself engaged.'

Evie nodded her head, trying to concentrate on her work.

'It's all right for some.' Susie was in the mood for talking instead of working. 'Grace will be a famous recording star one day, according to Ada, but mothers always think their kids will be the next gigantic thing, don't they?' Susie gave a hollow laugh at her own remark and got up to put the kettle on in the back staffroom. 'Grace think she's Vera Lynn.'

'I thought she was your friend,' Evie said, trying not to engage and failing.

'She is my friend,' Susie said in a tone that told Evie she had misunderstood. 'I was just saying she's full of herself sometimes, that's all.'

'Well, she doesn't need enemies while she's got you as a friend, that's for sure,' Evie replied when Susie brought only one cup of tea into the office and sat down behind her typewriter, not even bothering to remove the cover.

'I was only saying...' Susie flapped her hands. 'You've taken my words the wrong way, Evie.'

'Far from it.' Now she came to think about it, Evie realised Susie and Ada got on so well because they were both as bad as each other.

'I'm like one of the family,' Susie said. 'I would say nothing out of turn.'

'Ada wouldn't let you.' Evie kept her tone civil, suspecting an endless day, and she was in no mood to listen any more. 'I'm going for my dinner and have to feed the cat.'

'I didn't know you had a cat,' Susie said, looking out of the window at the yard lads.

'We haven't,' Evie whispered as she covered her typewriter and noticed Danny busy working in the yard. Susie had yet to get Danny to step out with her, Evie knew. The entire street knew she had been trying to net Danny for years. Some even laughed behind her back. It was pitiful, Evie thought, but she had to give Susie top marks for determination. 'Right,' she said, 'I'm off home for my dinner, you can go when I get back.' *Start as you mean to go on* was her new mantra, and Evie said it to herself a few times every day.

9

Grace let the hot water cascade down her face and body, feeling a bit off colour this morning and putting it down to the hard work and late nights with Bruce. Grace had given herself willingly, knowing without a doubt that she loved him, not as a sugar-daddy, but as a person in his own right. And he loved her right back.

'I couldn't let you leave,' Bruce had said as they lay curled in each other's arms after they left New York, 'not without letting you how much I love you and how much I would miss you.'

A gentle knock on her cabin door roused Grace from her thoughts and, wrapping a huge bath sheet round her slim, damp body, she stepped out of the shower and padded over to the dressing table.

The ship had docked in Cork and the Irish weather was calm and sunny – a far cry from the last time the ship visited. Maybe a short walk round Cobh harbour would quell her fragile stomach, Grace thought, wrapping a soft towel turban-style round her mane of wet hair.

'Come in,' she called, having taken the 'do not disturb' sign off the door when she had thought about ordering breakfast, and then doubted she could eat anything.

'Hello, darling, I come bearing gifts. I do hope you're hungry?' Bruce ushered a first-class steward into Grace's suite, and she spun round, feeling exposed without her face on. But she refused to feel self-conscious under his pondering gaze.

'That would be nice,' she said, wondering if she could manage to keep food down. But as Bruce had gone to so much effort, she could not refuse. Bruce was the most wonderful man she had ever met, so kind, so sensitive. He was just wonderful.

It would be heart-breaking when they had to go their separate ways when the ship docked in Liverpool on Tuesday. Two more precious nights together and then it would all be over. Now she knew how women felt when their men went off to war, not knowing if they would ever see each other again.

Bruce pulled out a chair for Grace to sit in before taking the seat opposite, while the white-jacketed steward hovered on the periphery.

'What would you like?' Bruce asked, positioning a pristine napkin on his knee.

'Just fruit juice and coffee for me, I'm not really hungry.' Grace was grateful Bruce didn't labour the point and said he would have the same. With his tender heart and loving respect, he showed her, more than any man she had ever known, how a woman should be treated.

She had not been so naïve as to hope his feelings for her were true love when they first met, suspecting they would last no longer than the outbound trip. His lovemaking, though, was a balm to the raw wounds inflicted upon her by an uncaring, selfish man who used her in a way that nobody who was ever loved should be treated.

'What do you say to taking in a little sightseeing?' Bruce asked. 'It might make you feel better.'

'Do I look ill?' Grace felt a moment of panic and Bruce immediately allayed her alarm with a gentle kiss.

'No, my darling,' he said, 'you look absolutely beautiful.'

* * *

Grace felt much better after a sightseeing trip round the south coast of County Cork. In two days she would be back in Reckoner's Row in the fold of her family, being bombarded on all sides with questions. Ma would get the sherry out, while Da might even shift himself from his chair – if he were not in the Tavern, that is.

'I've got something to tell you,' Bruce said, breaking into her thoughts as they strolled round the sunny harbour and called into a small, intimate cafe. They sat at a table covered with a green gingham cloth near the window. His handsome face unusually bleak. 'I dismissed Clifford Brack from the company,' Bruce said when the waitress, dressed in a black dress covered by a white frilled apron, served tea, and left them to it.

'You have?' Grace was unsurprised at the immediate relief she felt, knowing she would never have to see his glowering face again.

'When you told me what he had done to you, I wanted him off the ship immediately, but that would have thrown up all kinds of problems, which I won't go into right now.' Bruce suspected Clifford of smuggling diamonds into Liverpool, but he needed proof. When customs men searched his cabin this morning, they had found enough stolen gems to keep Clifford in luxury for the rest of his days. But Bruce had no intentions of upsetting Grace with the ugly truth. 'Sufficient to say, he will not be allowed back on board and he will never work on a D'Angelo ship ever again.'

'You did that for me?' Grace said, her hands trembling when she put down her cup on the matching porcelain saucer. Nobody had ever done as much for her as Bruce.

'Why wouldn't I?' Bruce asked as if it was the most natural thing in the world to fire the Entertainments Director because he had upset one of the singers. 'Grace, you really must start believing in yourself. That man should have been flung overboard for what he did to you and, if I had my way, I would have been the one to do it.' Bruce got up and Grace rose from her seat, and right there in front of the other customers, she kissed him.

'I love you Grace Harris,' Bruce said, and she felt dizzy with delight. She may only have this wonderful man for two more nights, but they were going to be ones they would both remember for a long time.

* * *

'Will your family be waiting when we dock?' Bruce asked out on deck, as Grace looked across the River Mersey towards her hometown, her feelings mixed. While the sight of The Liver Birds welcomed her home, her heart was shattered into a million pieces.

'I prefer to join them at home.' *Please don't ask me any more questions about them.*

'I'm in Liverpool for a few nights,' Bruce said, 'I would love to have dinner with you? I could even meet your folks if you let me.'

Grace blanched. She hadn't thought of that, reluctant for Bruce to see the dockside street she came from.

'You could,' Grace stalled, knowing this would probably be their final goodbye. She would miss him so much. Her heart was already broken at the thought.

'Give me your telephone number,' Bruce said while scribbling the number of his hotel on the back of a photograph. A picture of the couple laughing on a Caribbean beach. 'Or I could come pick you up?'

'No, no, I will ring you tomorrow.' She took the number of the Adelphi Hotel, where he was staying, and as they did not own a telephone, nor did anybody else in Reckoner's Row, except Connie and Angus in the Tram Tavern, she wrote down two numbers. 'Here's my number, too.' She knew the number of the telephone box on the corner off by heart and, somebody passing would willingly run and get the person being called. 'If you don't get an answer, you can call this number,' Grace said, writing down the number of the Tram Tavern.

'This trip has been the best yet,' Bruce said, and Grace knew this was the one she would remember forever. She had fallen for Bruce from that first moment, when he was sitting alone, reading *The Great Gatsby*.

'You're the pal I didn't know I needed,' she said, her voice almost a whisper.

'We are more than pals... Much more,' Bruce assured her, and as Grace sank into the depths of his dark glossy eyes, she could see the fire burning deep inside. And she wanted to throw her arms round him. Capture and keep him forever. Never let him go.

'Let's not make declarations we won't keep.' Grace wished she could fight this love she felt so deeply. It would be easier. But she had fallen hook, line and sinker for Bruce. 'I have been asked to go to London,' she told him. 'I've been offered a contract to record a new television show.' Television was becoming popular since the war, but many people could not afford a television set, much less own one, so she was taking a gamble.

'Did Brack organise the contract?' Bruce asked, and Grace nodded. Her eyes registering the belief that Clifford had spun her a web of lies.

'You know I can't keep secrets from you, don't you?' Bruce said, putting the scrap of paper she gave him in his inside pocket, and caught the eye of the purser who came and took her luggage.

'Yes, I know that,' she nodded; Bruce told her everything.

'Well, I was going to tell you something over dinner, but I'm not so sure you will turn up.'

'Why would you think that?' Grace sounded as hurt as she felt. 'Of course I'll turn up.'

'In that case,' Bruce said playfully, his finger trailing the outline of her face, 'I will save it until then.'

'Save what?' Grace was insatiably curious, and he knew it. Her heartbeat quickened. 'Tell me.'

However, Bruce shook his head and, slipping his arms round her waist, pulled her gently towards him and nothing else mattered.

10

'Hiya, Ma,' Danny took off his cap and jacket and gave Ada a quick peck on her upturned cheek.

Ada didn't respond to his greeting as she took five dinner plates down from the shelf and elbowed the ginger tomcat off the wooden draining board. Danny could see his mother was getting herself into a tizzy.

'Does Susie have to come tonight, Ma?' Danny said, reaching for the carbolic soap on the window ledge above the sink.

'Ambushed me outside the Tram Tavern this dinnertime, she did, just as your father was sloping in the other door.' Ada chattered on while Danny washed his hands, 'I can't be doing with her wittering on. Our Grace might bring her new chap here to meet me.'

'He might like to meet the rest of us too,' Danny answered with his usual chirpy tone, also wanting to hear about his sister's escapades at sea.

'You can catch up later, take Susie out somewhere,' Ada said, impatiently. She was looking forward to meeting Grace's *fi-ancee,* so she could pass on every detail to her good friend Mim Sharp.

'I could give him the once-over and see if he's most suitable for our salubrious little family.' Danny was being flippant but knew his mother had not interpreted his comment in such a way when she nodded.

'Aye, I suppose there is that, because we'll get no sense out of your father when he's had a skinful in the Tavern.'

Danny shook his head. He had been all round the world with the army and his mother never showed much interest – until he was handing over money.

'I hope your father doesn't come in sozzled and make a show of me in front of Grace's chap.' Ma believed he depended on her alone and his father let her, knowing full well that's what she needed to feel. Or, maybe that was just his da, who had been waited on hand and foot since the day they wed. Because Ma let him get away with it.

'I can see you've been busy,' he said, knowing she had scrubbed and polished until the house gleamed in readiness for her daughter's homecoming.

'It's only what we're used to,' Ada said, and Danny cocked an easy-going eyebrow, his ma could be so stiff and proper, even though she reckoned she hardly had two pennies to rub together. Although, he had to admit, when money was needed on the quick, she always knew where to lay her hand on some. 'You were brought up a gentleman,' Ada continued, 'and that's an end to the matter.'

Danny knew it would not be an end to the matter. She was nowhere near finished. He knew her superior attitude had been adopted when she worked in upper-class households as a housekeeper, before she married Da, and she had kept it ever since.

He felt a bit sorry for her, if the truth was told, knowing she had not had life easy, working part-time in the Tavern and bringing up two small children while his father was rarely able get a start on the docks. Mortified when she had Bobby after thinking her child-bearing days were over. Especially when his da was more out of work than in it through choice.

'Did you ever travel, Ma?' Danny asked, knowing his mother had never ventured further than she had to.

'Not since coming over from Ireland,' Ada sighed. 'My penance for a hasty marriage was a quick trip up the aisle. I moved in here with two children – both born in the space of ten months – Bobby came much later – it was no joke I can tell you.'

'I'm sure it wasn't.' Danny felt responsible for his mother's irritation and tried to lighten her sombre mood. 'Although, your prayers were answered when you got this house.'

'I had to go through the heartache of living with a bitter, twisted, miserly old aunt to get it though.' Ada's back stiffened and Danny changed tack, knowing his mother could not abide being reminded of her good fortune.

'You did have a lot to put up with, one way or another,' he said, watching her relax as he patted her shoulder, but not for long.

'Aye, and it cost me a bloody fortune to keep it nice for you lot.'

Danny suppressed a knowing smile. His mother would not let a compliment brighten her day when she could wallow in her own umbrage.

'All my life I've thought about others before meself,' Ada muttered. 'I've been a good wife to a thankless husband and a devoted mother, never a word of complaint has passed my lips.'

Danny raised a dark eyebrow, he begged to differ, but reasoned that silence was the best policy on this occasion. 'You've done your best, Ma. Everybody knows that.' Danny felt it wise to humour her rather than have a strained atmosphere when their Grace came home. It wasn't good for the digestion, an atmosphere.

'I've bought some lovely braising steak, so I hope they're hungry,' Ada said looking at the clock. 'She won't be long now. I can feel it in me bones.'

Those suffering bones, Danny thought as he took cups and saucers off the shelf and put them on a large wooden tray.

'It does smell delicious, Ma,' he said, nodding to the oven. 'I'm sure our Grace and her chap will be starving after all that travelling.'

'I'm sure they will,' Ada said with a nod of satisfaction, 'and Susie has invited herself to tea.'

Danny felt his stomach dip when he looked at the clock. It was six o'clock, his Da would be in from the Tavern soon for his tea and Danny didn't think he could spend another moment listening to Susie's tribulations. 'Does she have to come again tonight?' Danny said as he straightened an upended cup. He wanted to listen to the latest Dick Barton show on the wireless at quarter to seven. Susie and his mother would jangle all the way through it, waiting for Grace to come home, and his da would storm off to the Tavern again in a huff because he couldn't hear the wireless properly. Although, Danny knew he didn't need an excuse to take himself off to the alehouse. 'I'm sure some bloke is going to make Susie a lovely bride one day.' *But rest easy, it won't be me.*

'I think she's been lonely since our Grace went away to sea,' Ada said, busying herself round the back kitchen. 'It was good of you to take her to the pictures now and again.'

'I didn't intend our friendship to be anything other than that, though,' Danny answered.

'I've got this feeling in me bones again,' Ada said, ignoring Danny's remark. 'It's trying to tell me something?' His ma always talked in a mysterious way when she spoke about this feeling commonly known to everybody as her *gift.*

Danny raised his eyes to the ceiling, more rational than his mother, he knew *the gift,* which she swore she inherited from Romany ancestors, could be very hit-and-miss.

'Maybe you should see the doctor, you might be coming down with something.'

'Agitation,' Ada said impatiently, 'that's what I'm coming down with. Keeping busy is my only relief from worry.' She shivered when an icy quiver ran through her generously upholstered body. Why did nobody believe her?

'At least we've got Grace's homecoming to look forward to,' Danny said, trying to swerve another conversation about his mother's perceptive powers.

'I know what you're doing,' Ada said. 'I know you don't believe, but look what happened three years ago when I dreamt of water every night for weeks.' Ada waved a fork in his direction. 'Nobody took a blind bit of notice then, did they? And look what happened.'

'What did happen?' Danny looked perplexed.

'That trollop Rene Kilgaren went and got herself drowned.' Ada gave a single nod of her head to stress her words. 'Did a giddy soul believe me when I said I knew something bad was going to happen...? Not on your nelly.'

Danny did not remind his mother that everybody surmised Rene would come to a sticky end, knocking around with Leo Darnel was a dangerous thing to do, even if he weren't the one who did her a mischief. Although, it was Evie he felt sorry for, that girl had not had it easy. But she'd made the best of a bad job and now look at her... He lingered on thoughts of how Evie had pulled herself out of the gutter to make a decent life for herself and her family.

'I don't know what you've got against the Kilgarens, Ma?' Danny's voice betrayed a hint of uncharacteristic annoyance.

'She got over her mother's death very sharpish, I notice.' Ada surmised Danny had a soft spot for Evie, and she didn't want him supporting the whole bloody lot of them, especially when he was going to have his own business. She'd be on him like a fly on a midden.

'She couldn't wallow when she was so busy looking after her family, holding down a job and studying for a career.' Danny felt his blood rising, he felt strongly about anybody, his own mother included, who would bad-mouth Evie. 'I think she did very well, Ma. I imagine she didn't have much time for weeping and wailing.'

'I lost my mother when I was twelve years of age, and I'm still heartbroken.'

'I know you are, Ma.' Danny sounded sympathetic, knowing his ma's mother died thirty-eight years ago and a thought popped uninvited into his head. How long could this woman hold on to such suffering?

'Evie always has a cheerful smile, right enough,' Ada said. 'But I can't fathom what she has to smile about. Imagine what it must be like to carry the knowledge that your father murdered your mother, and only escaped the rope by the skin of his teeth because he was deemed insane.'

'That's enough, Ma.' Danny's low, steel-tipped words betrayed the strength of his feelings and he picked up yesterday evening's newspaper and began to read.

'Hey, Ma, have a look at this, you're gonna cry your leg off,' fourteen-year old Bobby Harris said when he entered the back door, closely followed by Max, Skinner's dog who followed him everywhere.

'I've scrubbed this house from top to bottom for our Grace coming home with her *fi-ancee,* so you can throw that mangy mutt out in the yard,' Ada said, giving the dog a fearsome glare, causing Max to slink under the kitchen table.

'He's not mangy,' Bobby protested, giving the dog's head a pat. He loved Max to bits and allowing the mongrel to follow him around was the only way he would ever be able to look after one. Ma didn't like dogs. 'He's just a bit tatty-looking.'

'Tatty or not, he's not staying in here, send him back to Henry, where he belongs.'

'Never mind that, Ma,' Bobby said, pushing the latest evening paper in to her hand. 'Have a look at page four.'

Ada took the paper and, opening it on the first page, her eye caught the headline:

Smuggled Contraband Intercepted On Way To Liverpool Docks.

'Not that one,' Bobby said, trying to turn the page over, but his mother was engrossed in the thieving down the docks. 'There's nothing new in that,' Bobby said impatiently, 'but you'll be thrilled when you see what's on page four. Turn over.'

Ada tutted, sighed, and turned the page over to see a photograph of her Grace singing on board *The Marine Spirit*. Her very own daughter in the newspaper.

'It says here, she's the star of the show,' Ada gasped, and Bobby nodded.

'That's what I tried to tell you before you got mesmerised by the smugglers.'

'The state of you with your *mesmerised*.' Ada gave a little smile, she liked to hear her offspring use words that were out of the ordinary for Reckoner's Row, and she hadn't heard anybody use that word. 'Doesn't our Grace look magnificent,' Ada said, gazing at the black and white picture, 'I can't wait to see her engagement ring.'

11

'Your family will be thrilled you are coming home,' Bruce said.

'Only to see what presents I've brought them.' Grace laughed. 'You know what families are like.'

'Not really.' His voice was low, husky and that endearing smile made his dark eyes twinkle, melting her heart. 'When you're ready, give me a call.'

'I will,' Evie said, preparing herself for reality. Theirs had been a magical holiday romance, where passengers and crew treated her like onboard royalty. She slept in a cabin the size of which would make her mother gasp. Grace couldn't wait to tell the family of the famous people she had met or dined with and pass on the mementos and keepsakes. The books of ship's matches used by Humphrey Bogart and Lauren Bacall, a fabulous couple, were a reminder, and Grace knew the memories would stay with her until the end of her days.

Bruce asked her again to dine with him while he was in Liverpool, and she thought that, perhaps, it was better they said goodbye now, each going their separate ways. After all, his life was in America, hardly a bus ride away. However, leaving him was not as easy as it sounded. Bruce had shown her nothing but loving kindness, they had spent the best of times together, but she wasn't so naïve to believe their relationship would continue off the ship, away from the balmy beaches, glittering chandeliers and the magic of the moonlight. They were worlds apart.

As the sun began to dip on the horizon, raising Grace's spirits, Bruce escorted her off the ship at Prince's Dock. The sight of the Liver Building made her heart soar, but she would be sorry to say goodbye to the man who had made her life so enjoyable and she would miss him.

Ushered through without so much as a glance from uniformed customs officers, Grace was eager to get back to Reckoner's Row to see her family, yet heartbroken knowing she would not see him again if she didn't have dinner with him tomorrow night. An early-evening chill eddied off the river, causing Grace to shiver and Bruce to put his arms round her shoulders.

'So, is it dinner tomorrow? I'll pick you up.' His head tilting to one side in that endearing way he had when he asked her something, nodding to the luxurious black Bentley waiting on the dock.

She shook her head and noticed his shoulders droop.

'Let me take you home at least.'

'You have a meeting at River Chambers, remember? You won't make it back in time.' Grace rolled her vibrant blue eyes when he smacked his forehead with the palm of his hand.

'That's what you do to me,' he said. 'I'd completely forgotten about that meeting.' He looked at his gold watch. 'I need to see you again. I'll call you.'

'Of course,' Grace said. Standing on tiptoe, she leaned forward to kiss his cheek when he put his arms round her waist and pulled her towards him.

'I will count down the minutes until I see you again,' he said, looking deep into her eyes and Grace laughed.

'You are such a smoothie,' she said, nudging him with her elbow. If she didn't laugh, she would cry. 'I'm sure you say that to all the girls.'

'No,' he answered, 'only you.'

When she refused his offer of a lift once more, he raised a confident hand and snapped his fingers, hailing a hackney cab for her. After the driver secured her luggage into the open-access luggage platform at the front, Bruce leaned into the back of the cab, making sure she was comfortable, and their lips met for the last time.

'I don't want to spend the night without you beside me,' Bruce said, his eyes searching, and Grace felt her face grow hot, hoping the cab driver could not hear what they were saying to each other.

'Neither do I?' Grace whispered, feeling cherished under his close scrutiny. Not seeing him was going to be heart wrenching.

'I will count each moment until I am with you, holding you, loving you.' He said edging out of the cab and closing the door. Grace pulled down the window as the engine of the cab rumbled, and Bruce kissed the inside of her wrist as he had done many times. 'Take care my love, I will see you soon.'

When he walked over to his car, Grace felt a fizz in her veins. Their time together had been more special than anything she had ever known. But, nevertheless, she would be fooling herself if she thought there could ever be anything between them except a holiday romance.

* * *

'I'm that hungry, me belly thinks me throat's been cut,' Bobby said looking like something the cat dragged in, 'so our Grace had better not be late.'

'You and Susie would make a lovely couple if only you'd give the girl a chance,' Ada said to Danny while ignoring Bobby.

Danny pretended he hadn't heard. He was not interested in marriage and especially not to Susie. He had things to do before matrimonial complications took his mind off the really important issue of owning a successful business.

'Here, let me get the meat out of the oven.' Danny took the tea towel from his mother's shoulder and opened the oven door to a delicious aroma of steak in a rich dark beef gravy, which greeted him when he reached in and lifted the large galvanised dish out of the oven. Almost ceremoniously, he placed the dish in the centre of the kitchen table, where Ada nodded in satisfaction hoping Grace wasn't going to be late, this meat was just about ready she thought as she popped it back into the oven to keep it hot.

'I think we'll have the gravy boat out,' she said, 'seeing as we've got company.'

Taking it from the shelf, Danny wiped it with the cloth.

'I doubt there's another family in Reckoner's Row who will sit down to a meal as good as this on *Bally-Ann day*,' Ada said.

'Why do they call it *Bally-Ann day*, Mam?' Bobby asked as he eyed the delicious food he was impatient to get stuck in to.

'It's the name given to a poor day, son,' Ada said, always happy to feed her son's hungry mind as well as his belly. 'The day before payday, when the food cupboard is sparse, and people are forced to scrape a meal together from what little they've got.' She did not inform him that *bally-Ann* was also a code word for *bugger all*.

'Do we have a *bally-Ann* day, Mam?' Bobby asked and Ada's face lit up.

'Not while I've breath in my body, son.' She was proud of the fact she had provided well for her offspring. They didn't go without, if she could possibly help it. 'I've passed many a copper to some poor fellow who pulled his tripes out on the dock, working extremely long hours for a decent pay.'

'Pulled his tripes out?' Bobby had heard the local expression many times, but didn't understand exactly what it meant.

'Aye,' Ada replied, 'he has to work his guts out if he wants a decent wage. If he's lucky enough to get a day's work in the first place, that is.' Dockers would be herded into 'the pen' like sheep every morning and afternoon. 'The lucky ones would feel a tap on the shoulder and be hired for a few hours work.' Ada explained as she bustled about the back-kitchen. 'No tap meant no work.'

Ada remembered that sinking feeling when she heard her husband coming back from the docks each morning after being rejected for work yet again because of his war wound. Or that's what he told her. Some, lucky enough to be hired, took it as a perk of the job to slip the odd tin of this or that into his pocket and sell it for a few bob to feed his brood.

'The Kilgaren kids saw more clean plates than hot dinners after the spiv got his marching orders,' Ada said, and Danny shook his head. Her ongoing hostility towards Evie and her family filled him with shame.

Ada was proud of the full plates which would be transported to the table in the parlour when Grace arrived home. If she hadn't done an expensive deal with the butcher this morning, she doubted she would have managed to buy steak as good. But the price was worth paying with her Grace coming back. Not that Ada would let on she bought black-market meat from under-the-counter. Everybody she knew bought rationed food through the back door if they had the readies. '*The divil looks after his own,*' she muttered.

'What was that, Ma?' Bobby asked and Ada turned quickly.

'Nothing. I was thinking out loud. Now go and wash your hands.'

On his mother's orders, swishing his hands in the bowl of hot dish water in the sink Bobby rolled a block of green soap between both hands, so he could blow bubbles through his finger and thumb. He couldn't wait until their Grace came home. His ma wouldn't be so interested in him, then.

'When's our Grace home then?' he asked, drying his hands on a clean tea towel before collecting the cutlery from the dresser drawer while Danny went to let Susie in the front door.

'Any minute,' Ada said, 'so I want you on your best behaviour, especially if she brings her young man home.'

'I'm always getting told off, lately.' Bobby said heading to the front room to set the table.

'And we'll have none of your old buck.' Ada chastised her young son as she picked up two plates of bread and butter and took them into the front room to see Susie already sitting at the table chin-wagging to Bert, who could talk the leg off a table after a session in the Tram Tavern.

'Hello, Susie, I didn't hear you come in,' Ada said in a tone that barely skimmed hospitable. Susie didn't answer, obviously engrossed in Bert's pie-eyed flannel, she would never offer to lend a hand. 'I'll go and get the rest of the plates out then, shall I?' Ada spoke to the back of Susie's bottle-blonde head, knowing her Grace, *brought up proper, if you please*, would have jumped at the chance to help her in the kitchen.

'We'll eat as soon as our Grace gets home.' Ada said, sure her daughter would be looking forward to a good home-cooked meal.

* * *

Grace Harris's hackney cab rumbled round the corner into Reckoner's Row, and the site that met her turned her stomach. Although it didn't take much to make her nauseous lately. Grace rummaged through the American dollars in her purse, searching for a ten-bob note and decided if she still had this stomach bug tomorrow she would go and see the doctor. Although, she was probably just nervous at being home again and she was tired. She'd worked and played hard and now she was back to this, her family home overlooking the Leeds–Liverpool canal in a war-torn street, with a pub at one end and a small derelict wasteland at the other.

It was hard to describe the vast difference of the two worlds she lived in. One was so opulent, magnificent, peopled by millionaires and film stars – the other was a dockside backstreet where people lived hand-to-mouth most days. She would die of shame if Bruce ever found out she lived here. She hoped he might telephone but wasn't sure now that she was back in the real world. Most likely, he would be off on some other far-flung adventure after his meeting in River Chambers.

Taking a deep breath, the smell of smoking chimneys hit the back of her throat. To think, when she was thousands of miles away, overseas, she longed to be back in this little street. But her rose-tinted thoughts of quaint dwellings opposite meandering waters watching boats sail by were soon dashed by the dusk reality.

The pretty houses were a row of red-brick terraces, and the romantic water was a grey canal. There were no pretty sailing boats, only dredgers and tugs moving stuff to and from the docks. Sailing to exotic places was a natural choice for a girl who wanted more from life than a sink, a cooker and a life of drudgery.

Grace had been to some of the world's most fabulous places: America, Canada, the Caribbean, the Mediterranean. She had been all over the world. She had drunk champagne with Cary Grant, cocktails with Katharine Hepburn. Shared a joke with Clark Gable. Frank Sinatra had sung for her. Kings and princes had conversed. She played roulette with European diplomats and enjoyed spontaneous, late-night concerts with Hollywood stars.

She was discreet and that made her popular with people of importance. She knew their secrets, and she kept them closely guarded. But her biggest secret was the one she held closest of all, and the reason she was not going to be on the next trip.

Grimacing, she gave the cabbie a pound note when she couldn't find a ten-shilling note and told him to keep the change. Tipping back the peak of his cap, he jumped out of the driver's seat and deposited her heavy suitcases at the bottom of the steps leading to her front door.

'Hello, Evie!' Grace said, stepping out of the black cab and dodging a cracked paving flag and seeing the girl from the top of the street. She liked Evie, who was far more mature than she would ever be.

'Hello, Grace,' Evie answered, entranced by the elegant red peep-toe wedge sandals, and feeling instantly dowdy in the presence of such glamour, 'long time no see.'

In a world where drab was the norm, Grace Harris looked like she had stepped out of a Hollywood film, wearing a cream-coloured swing coat that skimmed a figure-hugging dress with a sweetheart neckline matching her red leather handbag and velvet beret. Not that she was paying much attention of course, Evie thought.

Her own appearance had been acceptable when she looked in the mirror over the fireplace earlier, but next to Grace she looked like she had dressed at a jumble sale. She remembered seeing a picture of Princess Margaret in a newspaper wearing an outfit almost identical to the one Grace was wearing now. Grace looked fabulous, and for once Evie wondered what it must be like to afford clothes that matched your shoes, bag and hat? 'I bet you're glad to be home?'

'I wouldn't be too sure about that,' Grace replied, rolling her vivid blue eyes and placing her matching red vanity case in the crook of her arm as she headed to the open front door, where Susie and the Harris family spilled out and down the steps to greet her.

'Coo-ee, Gracie!' Susie's strident tone split the twilight air and a flock of pigeons took flight from their rooftop roost as she increased her pace to get to her friend first. 'Oh let me look at you!' Susie exclaimed, pushing past Evie without a blink of her sooty lashes before throwing her arms round Grace's shoulders.

After admiring everything from her clothes to her suntan, Susie possessively linked arms and corralled Grace towards the front door. 'Let's get inside and you can tell me all about your trip – and your engagement. I don't want you to leave anything out. You have to tell me everything. I can't wait to hear the details…'

Evie smiled as she watched Grace being manhandled by her boisterous family. Noting the word 'Mom', which sounded strange spoken in a Liverpool backstreet. Nobody called their mother, Mom, in these parts. Mam, Ma or even Mim in the case of Connie's mother – but not Mom. That was American, that was.

'Nice to see you again, Evie,' Grace called over her shoulder when she could get a word in edgeways, her suitcases still resting on the pavement.

Susie had seen Grace talking to Evie Kilgaren who she thought was a cut above these days and her nostrils flared. The *office manager*. She should hang her head in shame with a past like hers. But now was not the time for such thoughts. Her best friend was home. And they were going to have a fine old time.

'You don't want to be talking to her.' Susie's voice carried on the quiet evening air. 'What's in the cat must surely be in the kitten and you'll never guess… Auld man Skinner's only gone and employed her as office manager over me – can you believe it?'

A moment later, Danny came out of the house, his chiselled face freshly shaven, if that small white blob of shaving cream on his neck was anything to go by. Dressed in a pair of dark canvas trousers and a white singlet covering his combat-trained physique, he picked up the suitcases like they were empty, and Evie smiled, remembering the cab driver staggering to put the cases on the pavement.

'We'll get no sense out of Susie now that Grace is home, and Ma's just as bad,' Danny said, his cheerful voice a breath of fresh air after Susie's catty remark, his eyes crinkled at the corner when he gave her a lopsided grin.

Evie didn't trust herself to speak, and staring blankly she chewed the inside of her cheek, unaccustomed to the strong physique of tall, dark half-naked men. 'Well, best be off, glad to see Grace is home, she looks very well.'

'Aye, a bit of sunshine can do that for you,' Danny said, watching Evie make her way up the street with her head held high and a natural swagger in her stride. She could do that now, he thought. Evie had earned the right to walk any damn way she pleased and there was nobody to touch her. He liked that. He liked that a lot...

* * *

'Pass me the butter dish,' Ada didn't look up as she pounded the potatoes to a pulp.

'That's a fortnight's ration of best butter you lobbed in there,' Danny said, noticing his ma was agitated and wondering if the reason was Susie, demanding Grace's attention, when Ada thought she should be the one to ask all the questions.

'Our Grace hardly had time to get through the door, Susie hasn't given her a minute – and we still don't know what's happened to the fi-ancee.'

'Are you sure you've got enough...' Danny didn't get a chance to finish his sentence, silenced by Ada's icy glare as she dished out the food that filled the plates.

'I've got more than enough,' she said, knowing there were many women who could not afford cheap margarine to fluff up their potatoes, let alone best butter. 'Nothing is too good for my girl. I know people who know people who can supply me with more butter if I want it. I've got the money.' Ada realised she had said too much when she saw Danny raise an inquisitive eyebrow, and backtracked. 'What I mean is, I'm not having Susie go tell her mother she wasn't properly looked after. Only the best for this family, especially now our Grace is home.'

Danny bent to give Ada a gentle peck on the cheek and she shooed him away with the flick of her hand, although the gesture soothed her. 'You soppy ha'porth.' However, he knew she was in her element, fussing and putting on a show, like they had a steak banquet in the parlour every night.

'She hasn't mentioned her intended yet,' Ada noted. 'Maybe when we can get a word in edgeways, we will find out why.'

'Don't fret, Ma,' Danny said, 'it's not good for the digestion.'

'This'll show Susie what good food my family are used to,' Ada replied, carrying a tray of plates into the parlour while Danny helped by carrying another tray to save time.

'Oh, Mom you have done a fabulous job with all of this,' Grace said, giving Ada a breath-taking hug, marvelling at the dining table, pulled out to full capacity and pristine in her mother's best white tablecloth. She pointedly ignored the D'Angelo Line logo edged in silk, knowing that on her last visit to the ship her mother had taken quite a while going past the laundry on her way to the staff lavatory.

'Come and get it before it gets cold,' Ada said urging them all to tuck in before turning her attention to her own meal.

Grace watched her mother cut into her steak, gather a hill of creamed potatoes and piled a mountain of mixed vegetables on to her fork. She could not drag her eyes away, suspecting her mother's mouth would not open wide enough to shovel that lot in, but it did, and Grace wasn't hungry any more.

'Did you bring back any pictures, Grace?' Bobby asked as he too shovelled food into his mouth making her feel bilious.

12

'You'll never guess who I saw getting out of a taxi half an hour ago?'

'Princess Elizabeth?' Connie answered, wiping her hands on her smock-covered bump, her baby was due around the same time as the princess, so she followed everything she did with heightened interest. Even the customers were running a book on who would have their baby first. 'She might have a hankering to slum around in the backstreets – or maybe Elizabeth Taylor, wanting a pleasant change from Hollywood... Am I getting warmer?'

'No, you're as cold as 1947.' Evie laughed, following Connie upstairs. Nineteen forty-seven was the coldest year on record and, thank goodness, there hadn't been one like it since. It was also the year Evie started doing the pub accounts as payment of gratitude to Connie and Angus's support in those bleak days, three years ago, when her world collapsed beneath her.

With their unfailing support, she pieced together the jigsaw of her life and gave Jack and Lucy the loving security they deserved.

Seated at the table in Connie's furnished sitting room above the Tavern, Evie added the figures while Connie went to make a cup of tea.

'Well?' Connie asked, coming in from the kitchen. 'Spit it out before it chokes you, who did you see?' Connie grabbed hold of Fergus, who was sitting under the table and trying to pull the table-cloth over his head.

'Grace Harris!' Evie said. 'She looked like a film star.'

'We'll never hear the last of it when Ada comes in to see Mim,' Connie said, fastening the blue leather Jumping Jack shoes, which Fergus had kicked off. 'It'll be "our Grace" this and "our Grace" that. There'll be no stopping her and Mim trying to outdo each other in bragging rights.' Connie and Evie laughed, knowing the two older women, who had been friends for donkey's years, had never agreed on anything.

'She's the spit of Maureen O'Hara in that film with Tyrone Power. *The Black Swan*, that was it.' Evie's voice was soft and whispery as she put away the ledger in the sideboard, having finished the weekly accounts. 'You should have seen her, Con. Talk about style. She looks like she'd just stepped off the big screen at The Cameo picture house.'

In the years after the war, the women of Reckoner's Row were starved of a bit of glamour and going to the pictures was their only chance to leave their worries at the door and immerse themselves in a world of make-believe for a few hours.

'Grace had sunshine running through her hair, and her dress matched her handbag, her hat and her shoes... and her coat was the same as one I saw Princess Margaret wearing on the newsreel at the pictures.'

'So you said.' Connie smiled when Evie repeated her description. 'It doesn't sound like you took much notice,' Connie added, tilting her head to one side, never begrudging Evie her daydreaming pleasure. For someone who was so determined that she would make a better life for herself and her family – and Connie had no worries that Evie could make it happen – she was just like the rest of the female population in wanting elegance and personal grooming. Everybody wanted to look their best no matter how little they had. 'Did she speak to you?'

'She did.' Evie sat upright, her eyebrows raised, 'I didn't think for a minute she would, being a friend of Susie Blackthorn, I just thought they were two halves of the same, but she was nice.'

'Here's me thinking I looked nice when I found a bit of red ribbon for my hair, and Grace gets out of a taxi looking like a Hollywood starlet,' she told Connie, failing to hide feelings of dowdiness in a straight black skirt and cardigan over a plain white blouse. 'I've never seen clothes like them.' She stood up, giving a demonstration, 'The red dress fitted into her tiny waist like this,' she squeezed her slim waist, 'and it had a sweetheart neckline showing her tan to perfection.' Anything pretty lifted her spirits a treat. 'On her feet she wore wedged sandals with no back in them, can you believe that?' Evie sighed; her eyes dreamy as an unguarded flash of amusement flickered in Connie's eyes told her she was being daft. She had coveted nobody's belongings before, but there was a first time for everything. 'I'd give my right arm for a pair of red wedges... But they wouldn't look that good on me. The colour of my legs veer towards milk bottles, not Caribbean sunshine.'

'You're as good as any of them out there.' Connie gave her friend an optimistic smile. 'You need to stop thinking everybody's better or wiser or happier than you, young Evie.'

'Hark at you and your *young Evie*.' She laughed, trying to avoid the subject she had heard a thousand times before, 'I am twenty-one'

'And look what you've achieved.' Connie was not side-tracked. 'You've raised two kids, single-handed, while doing a full-time job, and you've turned that house next door into a cosy welcoming home, a place to be proud of.'

'Aye,' Evie laughed in that practical way she had about her, 'and one of these days my halo will fall down and strangle me.'

'More important, didn't I see you talking to Danny, and him only half dressed?' Connie had that knowing look in her eyes, her words tumbling like loose pebbles bent on disturbing still waters, and causing Evie's eyes to widen and for her to shift in her seat. She knew Connie would like nothing more than to see her courting.

Evie hoped nobody would notice Danny leaning on their railings engaging her in a bit of innocent neighbourly conversation, but the slow smile told Evie that Cupid Connie was unconvinced.

'That's the third time this week I've seen you both so deep in conversation that neither of you noticed anybody calling you.'

Connie was trying to coax something from her that didn't exist, Evie thought, and she would not fall into the trap of discussing the conversations she had with Danny Harris.

'He's a free agent,' Evie sounded more irritable than she intended, 'he can talk to any girl he wants to.' Connie was her friend, and she didn't know where she would be without her, but she didn't have to tell her everything that was going on in her mind, or her heart. Her face grew fevered and Evie looked anywhere but at Connie. 'He's just a friend, a neighbour. Nothing more.' Evie shrugged hopefully looking casual. 'He even asked me to go to the pictures and I said no.'

'Why did you say no, you daft mare?' Connie rolled her dark eyes.

'I've got a house to run, and a family to look after, and I've got to manage an office...' *Who are you trying to kid, Evie Kilgaren?*

* * *

'So, where is he then? This new fella of yours,' Ada asked, ignoring Susie, who muscled in on family time. Bert and Danny had already hinted at going to the Tavern to get away from Susie's incessant questions and there was no chance of hearing Dick Barton with all the excitement.

'Are we going to meet your chap before the big day?' Susie asked.

'You mean you don't know?' Grace felt her stomach sink as she watched the sun slip behind a darkened cloud. 'The wedding is off, I wrote you.'

'Off!' Susie's eyes sprung open wide. 'Well, you kept that quiet.'

'It would never have worked,' Grace said, 'we were incompatible.'

Ada looked like someone had just hit her with a wet fish. This news had knocked her for six, Grace could tell by the stunned silence. Her mother hadn't been outside Liverpool since she stepped off the Irish boat, and was not as sophisticated as she liked to think she was.

'What a shame.' Susie's smug tone was palpable.

'No wedding,' Ada said, 'I bought a hat...'

'Oh that's a terrible shame, maybe you can get a refund.' Susie didn't feel the need for tact knowing moments earlier, Ada looked like the cat who had pride of place on the milk float, now she looked like a miserable old moggy thrown out for the night, although she felt thoroughly chastised when Ada gave her a glare that would stun an elephant.

'I wondered where your engagement ring was?' Susie said, knowing there would not be the huge white wedding Ada had been bragging about for months. She looked stunned by the news while Susie wanted all the juicy details.

'We didn't get the letter!' Ada said.

'I've still got the ring,' Grace said, trying to allay her mother's obvious disappointment, 'it's a pink diamond, you know.'

Ada brightened somewhat until Grace took the ring from its

box and Susie lunged, slipping it onto her own finger and pursing her lips, as she gazed at the dazzling sparkle.

'I dreamed of being the mother of the bride,' Ada cried, while Grace put her arms round her mother to console her, knowing her ma wasn't one for sentimentality, but she did like to have a good brag.

'I wondered why you weren't showing it off,' Susie said, pushing her hand under the fringe of the standard lamp in the corner of the room and wiggling her fingers.

'I'm not one for crowing,' Ada said, consoled for now, 'but isn't that the most fantastic ring you ever saw?' She didn't wait for an answer. 'American, I suppose? You won't get one of them round here.' Ada nodded to the ring, knowing the mere mention of the country brought images of Hollywood stars and rich, handsome men, and Susie's eyes widened.

'American!' Susie's dark-pencilled eyebrows shot up to her peroxide lightened hair. 'Trust you to go one better than anybody else in Reckoner's Row. That stone is enormous.' She had seen nothing like it in her life. 'Your chap must have been a millionaire!' she said, twisting her hand one way then the other, examining the ring in forensic detail, while ignoring the disgruntled tut from Ada, who pushed a cup of tea across the table. 'Is it real?' Susie asked, patting platinum curls into place when Danny came into the room. 'I've never seen such an odd-coloured stone before. It's one of those costume jewellery types. I've got an uncle in the trade. He knows everything there is to know about these things.' Susie helped herself to a spoonful of gloopy condensed milk that lightened the weak brew, and sweetened it too, a compromise with sugar still rationed. She watched the milk pour from the spoon into her tea.

But the sight of it made Grace's stomach heave, and she hurried out of the room to the back door. She had to get out of here fast.

Ada's eyebrows knitted when she watched her daughter hurry

down the back yard to the lavatory and worried she might be sickening for something.

'Probably all that travelling,' Susie said.

'Or plain tired.' Ada shook her head. 'She's been travelling for months – she must be used to it by now.'

'What I wouldn't give to have a ring like that,' Susie said, as Danny slid a little further down his chair. Holding up her hand to the bright spring light that had crept over the roof and was now coming through starched net curtains, the myriad colours bouncing off the pink stone entranced Susie, like a child.

'It's amazing how much it looks like a genuine diamond,' Susie said. 'I just thought a stone that size would be beyond the wages of an ordinary working man.'

'And what would you know about "genuine" diamonds?' Ada said with a hint of contempt while Susie remembered how protective she was of her family. The Harrises could do no wrong in Ada's eyes. You were for them or you were an outsider. There was no happy medium. Only the best for her lot. The proud matriarch of the family got so high up Susie's nose it made her eyes water. 'My Grace has the world at her fingertips,' Ada folded her arms and pushed up her proud bosom, 'the talent, the ring. She's got it all.'

'Pity about the wedding though.' Susie's expression was one of pure innocence. But Ada knew better. An only child, her parents wouldn't dream of letting her sail round the world. Not even to mix with the rich and famous. 'Poor Gracie.'

In the drab, post-war streets of broken and dilapidated houses, girls like Susie clung to anything that had a whiff of glamour. A new lipstick. A pair of nylons. A love story on the pictures. Anything to banish the grey world outside.

While Grace, the colour of burnished gold, her mousey hair now shining with caramel and cream flashes, highlighted by the sun, looked every inch a star. Susie who prided herself on making her own clothes, and colouring her hair with peroxide from the chemist, felt dull in comparison. She could only dream of making the clothes Grace wore. Where would she get the material, for a start?

'Her clothes must have cost a fortune.' Susie sighed.

'My Grace could wear a potato sack and look good.'

Susie rolled her eyes. Ada thought her kids so sweet it was a wonder she hadn't eaten them. 'I can't get over the way her voice has changed,' Susie said, alluding to how strange it was that Grace no longer spoke like the rest of the people of Liverpool. 'She speaks posh.'

'She speaks properly,' Ada corrected her, and Susie felt the hairs rise on the back of her neck.

'I was thinking more about the American words,' Susie answered, '*that's swell* instead of nice. Or *Mom* instead of Mam or Ma.' *She was just so false!*

'She's been having her voice trained,' Ada said, 'isn't that marvellous?'

'Marvellous,' Susie replied, deadpan, taking off the ring when Grace came back into the room. It wasn't fair, Danny, the most eligible man for miles, was not in the least bit interested. They had gone to the pictures a few times, but Danny never ventured as far as a peck on the cheek let alone a full-on kiss. Three years! There must be something wrong with him. Then, dismissing the thought she knew Ada would not be able to keep something like a war wound private.

Straightening her spine Susie thought about going home when Ada said, 'I didn't show you the necklace Grace brought me, she gave it to me in the kitchen.' She reached into her pinny pocket for the navy-blue leather box before taking out the necklace that matched the engagement ring in the same dusky pink colour.

Going to the mirror over the fireplace, Ada put it against her and examined her reflection.

'My life wouldn't be worth living if I didn't bring her something back.' Grace laughed, knowing there was many an accurate word spoken in jest.

'This will go with my maroon blouse,' Ada said. 'What do you think, Susie?'

'It's lovely, Mrs Harris.' Susie gave a pale imitation of a smile, wishing Grace had given the necklace to her. She could have made Danny's eyes pop wearing a necklace like that.

'I'll wear it when we go to the Tavern for your birthday,' Ada said.

'Don't go to any trouble on my behalf,' Grace said. The last thing she wanted was to spend the night in the local alehouse being ogled and cajoled to sing another song.

'Aren't you feeling well, Grace?' Susie asked, noting her friend's putty-coloured pallor. 'You love a good sing-song round the old Joanna in the Tavern.'

'Maybe it's something you ate. I'll get you a powder, you'll be as right as rain.' There was something wrong with their Grace, Ada could feel it in her bones. Her daughter was not her usual bubbly self as she had been when she came home last time. 'It's not good for a girl to be away from home for so long.'

'But, Mam...' Grace slipped back into the Liverpool vernacular. She knew that it was traditional to have a few drinks in the local, but the Tram Tavern was the last place she wanted to be.

'No buts, my girl,' Ada said, 'you're going and that's an end to it.'

* * *

Susie was complaining about Henry again as was her wont and Ada was fed up with her muscling in.

'...I said to him, I said, if you think I'm taking orders off a skivvy you can think again!' Susie, on her third cup of tea, had tucked into the feast Ada had prepared for Grace's homecoming without a word of thanks, and Ada decided the girl might not be a suitable choice for Danny after all.

'And what did he say to that?' Grace asked.

Having read all the articles on etiquette, Ada knew, even if your guest was boring the Bejaysus out of you, a hostess must be gracious at all times. Although she felt peeved Susie was taking centre stage at her only daughter's homecoming.

'I told Skinner where to stick his job,' Susie said.

'Meggie fell on her feet when she found Henry, that's for sure,' Ada agreed. 'He's got a good business there and is canny with money, rolling in it they are, money coming out of their ears with the haulage business and the boarding house.'

'Boarding house?' Susie asked, intrigued. She didn't know everything, it seemed. But Ada, being Henry's cousin, knew everything about everyone.

'It's not a boarding house since his mother popped her clogs, God rest her weary bones.' Ada made a quick sign of the cross over her bosom. 'Meggie couldn't get shut of the lodgers quick enough when Aunty Cissie passed,' Ada said, stabbing the table with her index finger, and went on in a voice dripping with malice. 'Now you tell me why they need a house of that size just for two of them?' Her lip curled, turning down at the edges. 'It wasn't like they would fill it full of babbies, now was it?'

'Henry is your cousin, why would you talk about him like that?' Grace said to her mother, having forgotten that in this close-knit community minding other people's business was a way of life.

'Never mind about that now,' Ada said, when she saw the determined set of her daughter's mouth, and suspected Grace did not approve of the way the conversation was going. It seemed like their

Grace had grown out of the habit since working on cruise liners, and although Ada liked to see her offspring bettering themselves, she hoped their Grace wasn't getting above herself.

'Skinner begged me to stay.' Susie had to raise her voice over the criss-cross conversation and Ada, elbow perched on the table, her chin cupped in her palm, made circular motions with her other hand, urging her to get on with it. 'I told him straight!' Susie said, scraping her cup along the saucer, setting Ada's teeth on edge, and sipping her tea with all the indignation she could muster. 'I've kept that office going for nigh on three years and what thanks do I get? None.'

'So you won't go back, then?' Ada asked and Susie gave an evasive shrug of her shoulders.

'Evie Kilgaren can't run that office without me, I've got a system, you see. I was an office clerk when she was the charlady at Beamer's.' Susie had other reasons for not staying away from the office. The way Danny looked at Evie when he thought nobody was looking had not escaped her notice. While the cat's away... 'I can't believe Auld Skinner would use a skivvy to run the office over me.' It incensed Susie. 'I'm not saying she doesn't have her place. The files are in the right order and the place has never looked so neat, but I mean...' She did not say what she meant, knowing she could not disrespect Mr Skinner in front of his own family, but it didn't stop her thinking what would happen if she let him know what she had heard. He would soon change his tune when she told him she was aware of his wife's past. The information would wipe that cocky smile off his face, and put Miss Prim and Proper Kilgaren right back where she ought to be, scrubbing floors.

'Right, I'm just going to see Angus in the Tavern,' Danny said knowing his father had already made his escape there. He had heard about as much as he could take of Susie's whining voice.

'Well, I'd better be off too,' Susie said with blatant haste. 'Things to do. I'll let you walk me up the street, Danny.'

'Didn't I hear you say you wanted to stay and look at our Grace's photos?' Ada's telling tone grated on Susie, who didn't want to miss the chance of being seen walking on the arm of handsome Danny Harris.

'We'll have a look tomorrow, see you then, Grace.' She gave Grace a peck on the cheek and scuttled out, realising Danny was already halfway out of the door.

13

'Thank you, Lord, for all we've had – a little bit more, and we'd have all been glad,' Evie said the prayer her mother used to say after meals when they had little to eat, and even though she and Jack were working and could now afford to buy food, rationing was still a dominant problem. You had to get to the shops early and Evie spent most of her dinner hour in one queue or another.

Stacking the empty plates, she tried to ignore the look of hope in Lucy's eyes knowing her younger sister loved something sweet to finish her meal, but that wasn't always possible with the shortages.

'By the time I got to the front of the queue at the baker's, all he had left was a small bun loaf,' Evie explained, hoping their Jack wasn't going to be late tonight, otherwise his stuffed hearts and mashed potato, which she was keeping warm on a pan of boiling water, would dry up.

'I don't mind.' Lucy's words sounded convincing, but her slumped shoulders told the truth.

'I'll get out early tomorrow and be first in the queue.' Evie turned as the kitchen door opened and she saw her seventeen-year-old brother Jack sauntering into the kitchen with a smile on his face.

'You look like the cat who got the cream,' Evie said, thrilled that he had settled down to work and had not been tempted to listen to talk of easy money from her mother's lodger, who called himself a businessman and lived off various nefarious dealings.

Jack took off his cap and, as was his usual trick, threw it like a flat stone on water across the room, expertly landing it on the cellar door hook. Rummaging in his pocket, he took out a brown paper bag, which he placed on the table like it was the crown jewels. His eyes alight, he nodded to Lucy and then to the package.

'I've got a surprise for you,' he said, silently urging his sister to take a look inside. As they opened the bag, he said proudly, 'the Missus made treacle toffee and she gave me these to bring home.'

'God bless, Mrs Skinner.' Lucy's eyes devoured the dark sweet toffee, hoping her tongue would soon do the same thing. 'This is a rare treat.' Sweets were still on ration, and there was no sign of them being taken off any time soon. 'Treacle toffee is my favourite.' Lucy's lilting brogue took on a wondrous tone.

'Then you are in for another treat tomorrow,' Jack said. 'Danny brought back apples when he went to Netherford, and the missus is making toffee apples.' He always called Meggie *the missus,* thinking nothing of it, harking back to the days of the farmer's wife in Ireland. But everybody knew who he meant.

'Smashing!' Lucy's sweet tooth was a burden in these days when rationing was still part of their everyday life even though the war had been over five years.

Soon the room was filled with a contented silence after Jack handed Lucy a cone shaped paper bag before sitting at the table, and Lucy took out a piece of toffee and popped it in her mouth; closing her eyes she relished the delicious taste.

Jack mopped up the gravy, cleaning his plate with a crust of bread before draining his cup of unsweetened tea. When he sat back, satisfied with his lot, he spoke to Evie.

'So, how did your day go with Lady Muck?' he asked as she unravelled one of her mother's old cardigans so she could knit another one for Lucy.

'Still as hopeless as she's always been, she's spent more time clock-watching than working,' Evie answered, clicking furiously as she filled the knitting needle with the first row of stitches. 'I don't know why Mr Skinner keeps her on.' She clearly remembered the days when she completed Susie's clerical work even though she was only the cleaner at Beamer's Electrical Works, and the girl obviously expected it to continue. 'Susie is a lazy article who is biding her time until something or someone better comes along.' But Evie knew all that was going to change.

'She's all hot air, not clever like you, Sis.' Jack was pleased his sister had got the job in an office nearer home, she was more content, less worried, even though she still worked hard.

'You get nowhere resting on your laurels,' Evie said, determined to make something of herself and her family. 'I worked hard to get the qualifications I needed to have a better standard of living for all of us.'

'Nobody can say you're a quitter, that's for sure,' Jack said proudly.

'I'm not, and nor are you, Jack.' She had been earning good money in River Chambers and Mr Skinner not only matched her wage, he bettered it by two pounds a week, but according to the accounts, positivity may be overlooking prosperity, and sooner or later, sacrifices were going to have to be made.

Evie didn't want to be the new broom that swept some of the workforce out of a job. Hopefully, the situation would not come to that, and she would be able to turn the business round as she was brought in to do. The added incentive of working closer to home meant Lucy would not feel as if she had been abandoned yet again.

'If it's Susie Blackthorn you're worried about...' Jack said, following her out to the back kitchen with his plate.

'Not in the slightest,' Evie answered, taking the plate. She washed it in the warm water, then put it on the wooden draining board. 'I can hold my own with the Susie Blackthorns of this world, and I'm not scared of hard graft either.' She could not contemplate going back to the days when she had to decide whether to pay the rent or feed her family.

'You've made a safe, secure home for me and Lucy,' Jack said, aware his older sister had done better than anybody expected her to after their father was jailed for their mother's manslaughter.

'Thanks, Jack, I wouldn't want it any other way.' Evie wasn't responsible for the sins of her father, and vowed she and her family would stay in their own home, not run away through some sense of shame. She had held her head high, urging Jack and Lucy to do the same, and settled into the dockside community with a sense of hope in the future. Connie, the landlady of the Tram Tavern, was always ready to help when she could. If Lucy needed anything, she only had to go next door. In return, Lucy looked after Connie's son Fergus.

For the first time in years, Evie felt that life had taken a turn for the better. If only it could stay that way. But she couldn't complain. Jack was looking out for the family too, and putting up with Susie Blackthorn for a few hours every day was the least of her worries.

'Don't worry about Susie, she's only hanging on by the skin of her teeth.' Evie laughed, recalling the office manager, Miss Hawkins, from Beamer's, who'd said the very same thing the day the factory closed through lack of fuel during the big freeze.

'I can't see why the auld man hasn't already given Susie the push,' Jack said.

'Maybe she knows something that nobody else knows,' Lucy piped up.

'I thought that, too.' Evie said, her brows puckering. Now she could not get the notion out of her head. There was many a true word spoken in jest.

* * *

Picking up her suitcase later, Grace felt the sudden need to put her head down in her own bedroom and rest. She had distributed homecoming gifts, including Brandy and cigarettes, which Bert, her father stowed away in his own bedroom in case anybody should expect him to share, which he never would. There were trinkets and ornaments from the various countries she had visited for her mother, a sleeve of two hundred cigarettes for Danny and plenty of keepsakes and foreign coins for Bobby, who would add them to his collection.

Grace felt as if she had been on a continuous rollercoaster ride since she got back home. She had forgotten the frenetic energy her family could produce just by holding a conversation. They were eager to get as much information about her trip as possible; her homecoming was always going to be a cause for celebration and a singsong. Her mam had told everybody she met about her return to the Row.

Grace felt she had talked to the whole street at one time or another tonight as they came to say 'hiya' and 'welcome home' and have a look at her engagement ring, but thankfully they had all gone now, Susie included, and she was ready for her bed.

'I will turn in if it's all the same to you,' Grace said.

Her thoughts turned to Bruce as she ascended the wine-coloured carpet that ran up the middle of the stairs, secured by the same brass rods she used to clean every Saturday morning when she was younger. She was missing him already and she only saw him a few hours earlier.

At the top of the stairs, she turned left up another stair onto the landing and pushed open her bedroom door. Flicking on the electric light switch, the pale-yellow light did not touch all corners of the alcove but was bright enough to show off the new flowered wallpaper that had not been there when she left this room several months ago.

The room smelled of fresh paint and disinfectant and she knew her mother had gone to a lot of trouble and expense for her return to the family fold. Dropping her suitcase onto the yellow counterpane, she caught her reflection in the oval mirror inlaid into the wardrobe door and her hand automatically rested on her still-flat abdomen. Thank goodness there was no sign of the expectant mother in her hourglass figure yet.

The large room, with its high ceiling was spacious by local standards but nowhere near as opulent as her stateroom cabin on board the *Spirit*. Nor did her feet sink into the rag rug at the side of her bed as it did into the plush carpet on board. But it was home and she was glad to be here. She had a lot to think about, and plans to make.

However, Grace knew the first thing she must do tomorrow was to visit the doctor. There was no point in wasting time worrying if her monthly 'visitors' were late if there was another innocent reason.

Although if, as she suspected, she was in the family way, she had to make some very quick plans. She could not resume her singing career looking like a landed whale, and nor could she continue to live round here. What would people say? Her mother would be mortified. Susie's mother would say 'I told you so.' She would have to go searching for a place to rent. But that would be easier said than done given the housing shortage since the war.

* * *

'Damn!' Bruce D'Angelo said when he replaced the handset of the telephone after a long- distance call regarding his father who had been taken ill and was in Saint Bartholomew's hospital in London having emergency surgery. Bruce had to leave Liverpool immediately. But first, he needed to telephone Grace and explain.

Dialling the number she had given him; his fingers drummed the desk listening to the constant ring which nobody answered. He tried the second number and a woman's voice on the other end sounded somewhat surprised when he asked to speak to Grace.

'Grace who?' the woman asked, and he told her once more. 'Well, I'm new 'round 'ere an' I don't know no Grace 'Arris. Are you sure you got the right number? This is a public telephone box, you know.'

No, he did not know, and Bruce realised he didn't have time to argue, when the office manager Mr Walton told him the next train to London would leave in half an hour. Luckily, Lime Street Station was only five minutes away by car, he knew having been here many times before, so that would give him time to buy his ticket and ring Grace at the station.

When Bruce got to the station, there was a long queue at the ticket office, which crawled slowly to the small ticket office window.

'Do I still have time to catch the London train?' Bruce was rarely annoyed by much, but his patience had grown thin. Everywhere he looked, there were queues for this and queues for that. A guy could spend his whole day queuing in this country!

'Only if you hurry, sir, it's due to go out in three minutes.'

'Damn!' Bruce exclaimed as he ran past the red telephone box, he knew he had no time to telephone Grace and tell her he couldn't make their dinner date.

* * *

Grace knew she'd fallen long before the doctor confirmed *the rabbit died,* and her test had proved positive. Her mind was in turmoil. Bruce hadn't called and she felt a right idiot. Humiliation flowing through her veins she now realised the only man she ever loved had hoodwinked her, and Grace knew she couldn't have this baby if she was to continue her singing career.

How was she supposed to cope with no man to depend on? Vowing not to return to another cruise ship, she heard her name being called.

'Grace, over here!' She recognised Susie's voice immediately and the sinking feeling of dread returned.

Turning, she flashed a practised smile. Susie was the last person she wanted to see right now. She would want to know every tiny detail of her consultation.

'What brings you here?' Susie asked, not waiting for an answer. 'I've come for a sick note, so I get paid for taking time off. Serves Skinner right for taking Evie on as office manager over me. So what's wrong with you, then?'

'An upset stomach, that's all,' Grace said cagily, desperate to tell someone what she was going through, but Susie was not that girl. 'I've got to be off, see you later.'

When she reached Reckoner's Row, Grace went into the telephone box and picked up the receiver. She needed to speak to Bruce. But her courage deserted her as the heavy door edged to a squeaky close, and she noticed a tired-looking mother pushing a coach-built pram that had probably been an enviable sight in its day, but now it looked like it had been in the war and lost.

A little girl in a knitted pixie hood was standing on the dented, rusting mudguard, while a young child, barely able to walk judging by the size, sat on the pram's canopy. Unseen, deep within the black and silver carriage, the piercing cry of a newborn was making its angry presence known.

The mother was a girl Grace remembered from her class at school, yet she looked ten years older. No make-up to brighten her woeful expression, a headscarf tied under her chin could not hide her limp hair snatched back off her face, and her clothes draped from her hungry-looking body.

I can't live like this. Grace replaced the receiver and the devastating notion that Bruce was just like all the other men she had known, hit her like a wrecking ball knocking her confidence for six. She had been a first-class fool. She knew that now. 'What have you done, you stupid, stupid girl.'

Stepping out of the telephone box, she saw Connie lugging a heavy mop bucket and Grace rushed forward to take it off her and empty it down the grid, but Connie wouldn't hear of it. They were a tough lot round here, Grace thought, much tougher than she felt right now.

'I bet you missed all this soot and muck,' Connie said with a glint of amusement in her eyes. 'I imagine there's only so much tropical paradise you can put up with before wanting to get back to the dockside.'

'I couldn't wait.' Grace managed to laugh and hide her feeling of dejection. She had a fleeting thought. Should she confide in Connie? What with her being a nurse during the war. But then she thought better of it. Grace knew she would have to give her predicament a lot more thought before she involved anybody else.

They shared a bit of local chit-chat before Connie ambled off to answer the ringing telephone, and through the open doorway, Grace clearly heard the landlady say '*Not again*' in a burst of exasperation when the 'phone stopped ringing.

Walking down Reckoner's Row, Grace felt her stomach lurch and the bright sunshine did little to raise her spirits. She needed to get as far away from here as she could. When the child was born, she would give it up for adoption. Grace would not want to know if it was a boy or a girl. Determined she wouldn't even look at it. Nothing must awaken the maternal feelings that she knew must be in her somewhere. Nothing must get in the way of her career.

* * *

Entering a large, soot-covered Victorian building that was the housing department, Grace was careful not to brush against the wall and dirty her blonde-coloured swing coat. She took a seat next to a harassed-looking woman with four young children and a newborn baby in a pram and Grace gave a stiff smile, knowing the post-war baby boom was thriving.

'Have you been here long?' Grace asked the woman as the click-click of a typewriter reverberated round the outer waiting room.

'Half the bleeding morning,' the woman said, rolling her eyes to the high cracked ceiling, probably a remnant of the heavy bombing during the war. 'Another day of begging and pleading, but where does it get yer? Nowhere that's where. I've been here every day for the last three weeks and I'm still no further on. I've got a hole in my roof the size of a football pitch, curtesy of the Luftwaffe, and even the bugs wear wellies!'

Grace was sorry she asked, sure the woman was exaggerating until she saw a flat-capped man pretending not to listen, who nodded in agreement.

An hour later, Grace was relieved when the door of the inner office opened by a straight-backed female clerk.

'Next!' she called in a voice that any sergeant major would be proud of.

Grace stood.

'Name?' the stern one said, examining her clipboard.

Grace Harris.'

'Have you got your green card?' asked the clerk, going down a list of names before holding the clipboard to her flat chest like a shield.

'Green card?' Grace was bewildered.

The clerk gave a long-suffering sigh. 'Your doctor would have supplied you with a certificate of confinement, which you will need as proof of your entitlement to put your name down on the housing list.'

Grace wondered how this woman could possibly know she was pregnant just by looking at her. She didn't know the first thing about having babies. That was something other women did.

'Can't I just put my name down and you contact me when a place becomes available?' Grace asked and the clerk's eyes held a mixture of disbelief and pity.

'Never mind.' The clerk let out a long stream of exasperated air as she opened another door. 'Go straight in.'

When Grace presented herself to the inner sanctum of the housing office, a man with a bushy moustache was talking on the telephone.

'Yes, that's right, in triplicate,' said the man down the telephone, 'one for the ministry, one for the housing committee and one for my files... Goodbye.' He replaced the receiver and looked up to see Grace sitting opposite him. 'Mrs...?'

'Harris, Grace Harris.' She kept her gloves on to hide her naked wedding ring finger.

'Right then,' he said, giving her an appreciative smile, which encouraged Grace, 'let's see what we can do for you.' He rummaged through a sheaf of forms and looked confused. 'I can't seem to locate your forms...'

'What forms,' Grace asked, 'I haven't filled in any forms.'

The housing manager's head shot up and he looked at her as if she had just swiped his sardine sandwiches, sitting in a brown paper bag on the desk.

'Madam,' he said sternly, his smile disappearing, 'you must fill in your application forms, HC1, HC2 and HC3. You can't go on the list without filling in the necessary forms.' He sounded incredulous that she had the temerity to enter the building, let alone walk into his office looking for accommodation. He stood up and headed towards the door and, opening it, he said in a voice loud enough for everybody to hear, 'I should not even be seeing you.'

'But now that I'm here can't you just put my name down on your list,' Grace protested. 'I waited over an hour.'

'Some people have been waiting ten years! You need at least four children to get on the list. Good day to you.' And with that he slammed the office door shut.

'Four children just to get on the list?' Grace exclaimed, realising she didn't stand a chance as she strode out of the building.

'Here, wasn't that Grace Harris?' asked Susie Blackthorn's mother to nobody in particular, waiting to complain about her twisted door. 'I wonder why she's looking for a place of her own?'

* * *

'Have you gone part-time, now?' Evie asked a few weeks later when Susie walked into the office, late again. The girl seemed to please herself when she came in, and Evie wondered how she got away with it. Anybody else would have been dismissed long ago.

'I had to go and get a sick note from the doctor,' Susie said, and Evie lifted her head from the long list of figures. She had little time to take a decent dinner hour lately, with Susie taking so much time off, and had brought a potted meat sandwich to eat at her desk as she worked through the accounts.

'Let's see it then.' Evie was not prepared to allow this defiance to carry on. She was sick of Susie trying to pull the wool over her eyes, knowing the girl only worked here so she could moon over Danny Harris every chance she got. Well, those days were over.

Susie's chin jutted out and she rolled her eyes, handing over the medical certificate. 'See, I am sick,' she said smugly, 'yet I drag myself in here and slave away without a complaint. Look at what it says. Look at the length of that word, I can't even say it. I might have something deadly!'

'You certainly have, Susie.' Evie did her best not to laugh when she saw the colour drain from Susie's face. The certificate said Susie was suffering from 'dysmenorrhoea', the same as her last three certificates. 'If I were you, I would prepare myself for hospital.'

'Really?' Susie's eyes widened. She really was ill? 'It's that bad?'

'I've heard about this,' Evie's face was grim, and she slowly shook her head, 'and to have it four times in a month is deadly, I should imagine. My heart goes out to you.'

'You've heard if it?' Susie exclaimed. 'What happened to the patient? Did she live?'

'Oh yes, *she* lived,' Evie said, her soothing tones becoming more determined, 'she took two Beecham's pills and used a hot-water bottle for her period pain *each month* not *four times a month*?'

'Period pain?' Susie said and Evie nodded.

'Don't think you are getting paid for this.' She waved the sick note under Susie's nose. 'You might have been able to fool Mr Skinner, but you don't fool me!' Evie watched Susie's mouth open and close like a goldfish. 'Your wages will be docked for the time you have had off. You'll be lucky to pick up any money this week, given the amount you owe Skinner in overpaid wages.'

Mr Skinner must want his head read to hire Susie. She couldn't run a tap, never mind sort out this tangle of accounts, Evie mused, systematically going through scraps of receipts, which looked as if they hadn't been given any proper attention since Meggie Skinner had stopped working in the office after the war.

According to these figures, the business had been having a difficult time of it money-wise for a long while. Some outstanding bills had been paid but not all and if they weren't paid soon, the future looked grim for *Skinner and Son*.

'When was the last time we sent a reminder for a final payment to the slaughterhouse?' Evie asked, not surprised when Susie didn't answer because she was too busy gazing out of the window. 'Have you sent out a reminder?' Evie pressed when she got no answer.

There was a heavy silence and she scraped back her chair, going over to the filing cabinet. She was well aware that the other girl had heard her. And if her stony silence was anything to go by, Susie was seething at being found out.

Nevertheless, Evie was not here to make friends, she was here to do a job – and not a minute too soon if this business were to survive.

14

'Aren't you coming in?' Ada asked, standing on the doorstep talking to Connie's mother, Mim, one-time landlady of the Tram Tavern.

'Hello Grace, I saw your picture in the paper.' Mim beamed an approving smile as she entered the house and saw Grace. 'So, we have the top singing artist on the D'Angelo line - right here in our very own street.'

'The best singer in the whole fleet.' Ada said proudly. Straightening her back she stood a couple of inches taller. 'She made headlines in The Echo.' Ada told Mim proudly, and Grace smiled when she heard Mim's sardonic, unhesitating reply,

'Well, she would be wouldn't she.' Then, changing the subject she said, 'your mam tells me the wedding is off?'

'I don't think she wants to talk about it,' Ada replied with a heavy sigh and taking on that pinched expression, which told Grace her mother was the one who didn't want to discuss the big white wedding she had planned and boasted about. Grace felt a bit sorry for her mother, knowing she had saved for years to be able to give her a wedding fit for a star. But there wasn't going to be a wedding.

And very soon she would be asking questions that Grace did not want to answer.

Knowing what she must do, Grace decided to go to London. Clifford had not arranged any of the meetings he said he would. In fact, nobody even knew who he was! But she wasn't going to waste time worrying about him. She had enough money to rent a place and she had contacts. The stigma of an illegitimate grandchild would crucify her mother. She had to get away.

Taking the ring Clifford had given her, Grace decided it was time to make it work for her. She would take it to a jeweller to see if it were worth anything, knowing it was probably worthless if he was anything to go by.

In the unusual likelihood that the ring was worth something, Grace knew every penny would be needed for her new start. She also had savings from her last trip but knew she had no chance of getting cabaret work when her pregnancy started to show. Nobody would employ a girl in trouble.

* * *

'If you are not careful, you'll lose that grand position on the ship,' Ada said when Grace told her she wasn't going back, 'you just don't know when you are well off!'

'If only you knew,' Grace murmured, realising that as her mother had nothing to brag about now she wasn't having the big white wedding, Grace was fast becoming an irritant. And God alone knew what her mother would say if she knew about the child she was carrying. Then a thought struck her, and Grace hurried towards Skinner's Yard.

'Hello, Grace,' Susie said, a smile lighting up her scornful eyes that only moments earlier had shot daggers at Evie, 'to what do I owe the pleasure?'

'Hiya, Susie,' Grace said, ignoring Susie's question and heading straight across the office. 'Evie, can I have a word?' she mouthed the word 'alone,' her back turned to Susie.

Evie gave her a knowing look to let her know she understood and said, 'Susie, will you go and get some more stamps from the post office please?' She waited for a moment. 'Now, please.'

'Slave labour, that's what this is,' Susie said when Evie took a ten-shilling note from the petty cash and handed it to her. Without another word, Susie headed towards the door and slammed it behind her.

'What can I do for you, Grace?' Evie said, when Grace sat on the straight-backed chair opposite. Grace said nothing for a moment, smoothing her hands down the folds of a brown leather clutch bag. 'Is there something you wanted to say?'

'I don't know who else to turn to, Evie,' Grace said opening the bag and taking out a white handkerchief, twisting it into a corkscrew of lace. 'It's like this... What I mean is... Well, I...' No matter how hard she tried, Grace could not find the words she was looking for.

'It's all right, you can talk to me,' Evie said in a tone that was not only friendly but also encouraging. She watched as the other girl's shoulders seemed to cave in on themselves and she let out a long, deflating sigh.

'I wanted to ask you something that is a bit... delicate.' Grace said. 'You worked in the office of the D'Angelo Shipping Line?' She watched Evie nod her head. 'Well, I was wondering if you had access to some information?'

'What kind of information?' Evie's brows pleated. What kind of information could she possibly have that would interest Grace Harris?

'Private information,' Grace said. She was desperate. And,

throwing caution to the wind she poured out the whole story of Bruce, her predicament, everything.

She could no longer hold it in; Evie had been through more than most people she knew, and she had never heard her say a bad word about anybody. Grace could not help herself; she was so over-come that tears welled in her eyes.

'I'm sorry, Evie, I shouldn't have burdened you with all of this.' She liked Evie, salt-of-the-earth, trusted by everybody. 'I have no right to take advantage of your good nature.'

'Oh Grace, I am so sorry, we were never allowed to view the private files of shareholders.' Evie said, getting up to make them both a cup of tea. The situation reminded her of a time years ago when Connie did much the same thing for her. 'But there is some-thing I can help you with.' Evie sat back down behind the desk, and opening her battered leather bag she took out the reference she had received from Mr Walton. 'This has got the telephone number of the company head office in London, maybe somebody there could give you more information about Mr D'Angelo.'

'Oh Evie, you are a diamond,' Grace said. 'I rang The Adelphi, but unfortunately there was nobody who could help me.'

'I do hope you manage to speak to him,' Evie said as Grace stood up to leave, before coming round the desk and throwing her arms round Evie.

'I won't forget this, Evie, thank you.' Grace could not get to the telephone box quick enough. And her hands shook as she dialled the number. Her heart hammering in her chest. She had never felt so nervous. Maybe she should put down the 'phone? As she was about to replace the receiver a woman's voice answered.

'May I speak to Mr D'Angelo, please?' Grace could hear the tremor in her voice.

'I'm afraid he is not here right now,' the woman answered. 'Who shall I say called?'

'Never mind, I'll call back another time, it's fine.' When she hung up, tears were streaming down her face. *It's not fine. It is certainly not fine.*

The following day, taking her courage in both hands, she tried to contact Bruce again, and this time she heard his deep mellow voice, so gentle and comforting.

'Hello, Bruce D'Angelo speaking, how may I help you?'

'Oh Bruce... It's me. Grace...'

'Grace, my darling, where are you? Why didn't you call? I tried to ring you and...'

'Bruce, we have to talk.'

He told her he was in London but would be back in Liverpool tonight.

'I'll fix everything,' he said on the telephone when she was too upset to get her words out properly, although she did not tell him about the baby. 'Meet me at Lime Street Station. Seven o' clock, I can't wait to see you my darling.'

When she got home, Grace hurried past the open doorway of the front room where Ada was knitting and headed straight to her room, and as she suspected her mother wanted to know what was wrong.

'I've got a headache,' Grace called from half-way up the stairs, 'I'm just going to have a lie down.' She needed time to think. To work out how she was going to tell Bruce he was going to be a father.

Rinsing a flannel under the cold tap in the only bathroom in Reckoner's Row, Grace folded it into a long strip, lay on the bed and covered her tear-swollen eyes.

A couple of hours later, Grace, dressed in a lightweight duster coat with deep turned back cuffs and a wide shawl collar, her seamed, sheer-black stockings accentuating her shapely legs and black patent leather stiletto heeled shoes, walked with her head

held high towards the tram that would take her to Lime Street
Station.

Nobody would dream for a moment that she was a walking
bundle of nerves as she blew out a series of short breaths trying to
control her racing heart.

Bruce would look after her. She was carrying his child. He
would make everything right. Her emotions swung between despair
and elation while she waited for the bus, and a meeting that could
be her biggest adventure yet.

Dreams of a new life sustained her as seven o'clock came and
went in the echo of Lime Street Station. She paced up and down the
platform. Eight o'clock... Something must have happened. She
worried. *He's had an accident!*

Nine o'clock...! By now she was frantic. Something had
happened... Grace felt a keen desperation she had never experienced before.

* * *

'I'm sorry to keep you waiting, Mr D'Angelo,' said the chief
inspector of the Liverpool police force, 'but we have had a tip-off
about a member of your employ who has been involved in
diamond smuggling.'

Bruce was giving the address of his entertainment's director to
the chief inspector whose name he didn't catch, but no matter, all
he was worried about was Grace. She would think he had stood her
up. 'Look, I have a particularly important meeting this evening, so if
you could just get on with it.'

'Certainly, sir, we have reason to believe that Clifford Brack and
an accomplice made an exceptionally good living bringing smuggled gems into the country and getting shot of them via a Liverpool
diamond merchant...'

'Well, now you have the address you can go and arrest him.' Bruce looked at the clock. It was nine o' clock. Grace would have gone long ago...

* * *

The following day, Evie started work before anybody else. After a couple of hours, she took a break from the paperwork and, making a fresh pot of tea in the staffroom, she heard the telephone ring in the outer office.

'Skinner's Haulage.'

Placing the kettle on the single gas ring, Evie was shocked to hear Henry's voice clearly through the closed staffroom door. 'Now you listen here, I've nearly run this business into the ground to pay your demands, and I'm not giving you another penny, do you hear me?' Evie had never heard him so angry. 'I'm not having any more of your threats. You've had enough money and it's got to stop, that's an end to it. This month is your final payment.'

Evie heard Mr Skinner slam down the telephone receiver onto the cradle. Whoever he was talking to sounded like a nasty piece of work if the one-sided conversation was anything to go by. The telephone call obviously had something to do with money being siphoned from the business. Although, according to the accounts, Mr Skinner had enough money to pay the men's wages, there wasn't much left over to keep it going indefinitely. A shiver ran down her spine, she had left a bright warm office overlooking the River Mersey to come here, to a wooden hut of an office surrounded by the smell of horses, to do a job she might not even get paid for.

Evie swallowed hard, knowing if this business was to survive, then something would have to be done about Susie. There would be no more swanning into the office at ten past nine like she was doing right now. Susie hung up her coat and pulled out a round gold compact and checked her teeth for lipstick marks.

'What time do you call this?' Evie stood up, she had no intention of looking up to Susie when she told the girl that Mr Skinner was going to let her go, if she didn't start pulling her weight. 'We have both had enough of your slapdash ways, Susie, and if you don't knuckle down and do some proper work...'

'Not you, an' all!' Susie's tone was indignant as she lit an untipped cigarette and blew a stream of smoke that filled the office. 'Auld Skinner just said it's nearly good afternoon, I told him I had to go to the post office.'

'Could you not have gone to the post office at dinnertime?' Evie opened the small window behind her to let out the smoke. This girl had got her own way for far too long, and it was her job to turn the business round, bring it back into profit. Susie's wages might be the first thing to go.

'I had to go to the Netherford post office,' Susie said pointedly, realising Evie didn't have a clue what she was talking about. She had taken the bus into Netherford early this morning instead of yesterday afternoon and when she got there, who should be standing outside but a man who was the image of Bert Harris.

He scuttled off when he caught sight of her getting off the bus, but she knew it was him. And after depositing Skinner's money she made sure she was not mistaken when she sidled back into the post office, and witnessed him drawing a bundle of cash from the Skinner account.

Well, well, well, she thought, putting two and two together. Her job was safe as long as she was in possession of this kind of explosive information. And possibly an opportunity for her to make money, though she would need to find out more.

'I found a huge pile of invoices in an old shoe-box, they should be in the file.' Evie said, glad she had come in early. She had never seen such a disorderly filing system. 'Your days of taking liberties are over,' Evie snapped, and going by Susie's glowering expression the message had got through. 'We've got to get all of these invoices sent out, otherwise you won't get paid.'

There was a moment's silence and Evie waited for a tirade that didn't come and was surprised when Susie marched over and slapped a sheet of stamps on Evie's desk. 'Well, how do you suppose we post the invoices without these?'

Going through the accounts, Evie quickly discovered the figures didn't add up. Every month, a large payment was transferred to a post office account. But there was no name, no business address to contact the payee for an invoice. Evie's brow pleated in confusion, knowing Mr Taxman would not be best pleased about ghostly payments disappearing like a spectre in the night and now she knew the reason. But who could be blackmailing Mr Skinner – and why?

At one o'clock, Evie decided to get out of the office for a while. The sun was shining, the birds were singing, and she needed to stretch her legs. Unless she needed to get something from the shops, she usually ate her sandwich at her desk, but the weather was too nice to waste.

'I'm going for my dinner,' she said, pulling a lemon-coloured cardigan over her white blouse and straight black skirt. She had a lot to think about.

'But I was going to take *my* dinner now.'

'You can, when I've taken the hour I am entitled to,' Evie said, ignoring the indignant flare of Susie's nostrils as she opened the office door. A gentle breeze picked up her hair, stirring the golden strands round her cheeks, and the sunshine, stronger and warmer of late, glinted off broken glass like diamonds.

'Penny for them?' Danny said as he pulled up in the truck at the bottom of the Row.

'They're worth much more than that,' Evie said, realising the sight of him suddenly made her day much more enjoyable. Then a thought struck her. 'Has Mr Skinner said anything to you about money trouble, to do with the business I mean?'

'He's been looking a bit worried lately,' Danny answered, 'why, is the business in trouble?'

Evie knew Danny could be trusted with delicate information and thought it only right he should know Mr Skinner was being blackmailed. 'Every month, he gives money to Susie to put in the Netherford post office account,' Evie told him, hoping Danny might be able to get to the bottom of who was making these relentless demands.

'I'll see what I can find out,' Danny replied, jumping out of the truck.

'Thanks, Dan.' Evie carried on towards her own home at the top of the street. Now that she had told Danny she felt a bit better. Poor Mr Skinner.

15

'Don't you miss scrubbing floors and polishing desks?' Susie asked, feeling that Grace had really rubbed her nose in her new lifestyle, and she wanted to take it out on someone.

'Is that your way of trying to *put me in my place*?' Evie answered. At one time, she would have cowered from the kind of offensive remark Susie made, but not any more, she thought, making her way to the staffroom. The shy, invisible girl who went about her work unnoticed had gone, and in her place there was a competent young woman who knew what she wanted and had every intention of getting it, through diligence and pride in a job. Even when she was scrubbing floors, Evie took satisfaction in a job well done, and nothing had changed since.

'I don't know what you mean.' Susie was putting the cover on her typewriter, ready to go out for her midday meal. 'You work too hard.' Evie was inclined to take the remark as a compliment until Susie added, 'You make me look like a shirker.' It was a complaint not a compliment. 'You wouldn't catch me working through my dinner hour for nobody.'

'I didn't ask you to,' Evie answered, 'but I do expect you to finish the invoices and filing before close of business today.'

When Susie came back from lunch five minutes late, Evie was determined she was going to pull her weight. The business was in no fit state to carry skivers.

'I did my best to keep on top of things,' Susie said, 'but I'm no good with numbers. We had another girl, but she was as useful as a wax fireguard. I've never seen anyone who had so many ailments in my life, she was bloody neurotic, blamed it all on the war.'

It takes one to know one, Evie thought.

'The pay in this place is bloody awful, so you don't get the pick of good staff,' Susie added, and Evie wasn't so slow she didn't see the inference was aimed at her.

'Yes, I can see that,' she said pointedly. Game set and match to Miss Kilgaren.

'Let's face it,' Susie continued, 'what girl wants to work in this dump every day?'

'Well, you, by the look of it,' Evie said, 'but beggars can't be choosers, I suppose.' Susie would not last five minutes in any other office.

'Aye,' Susie said, 'the auld man has a soft spot for a sob story.'

Looking up, Evie stared across the room long enough for Susie to realise she understood what she was getting at.

'I didn't mean you got the job on account of your past, and having a family to look after, or that you got it because you only live round the corner and you're a friend of Connie's or anything like that...' Susie only stopped for breath when Evie interrupted.

'I don't s'pose you work in a place like this for the lovely view either.' Evie followed Susie's gaze from the window to where Danny was harnessing horses in a yard full of wagons, carts and bales of hay and straw, which he then loaded onto the hoist, ready to be sent up to the loft. 'Or because you're partial to the smell of horse dung.'

'Crude.' Susie's nostrils flared, and her red mouth turned down in a disapproving grimace.

'You're lucky I said dung.' Evie didn't give a cat's whisker what Susie thought of her. She was here to do a job, and, by the look of the accounts, there was enough to keep her going for an exceptionally long time.

Wrinkling her nose, Susie took the cover off her typewriter when she saw Henry Skinner. Evie shrugged and said nothing as she filled an envelope with a final notice to The Marrowbone Dog Food Company. She had lost track of the amount of unpaid bills there were, and if something wasn't done about it soon, they would all be out of a job. Because the business was on the brink of collapsing. No wonder she had been brought in.

Evie knew she would have to crack the whip to make this business work. And crack it she would.

'This is not a waiting room, it is a place of work,' she said to Susie, 'so if the yard lads think this is somewhere to hide from Mr Skinner they've got another thing coming. And woe betide anyone who outstays their welcome.' Evie discouraged the yard lads from lingering by flinging a pencil in their direction which usually winged past their ears, reminding them that this was not a canteen where they could cadge a cup of tea any more.

'I'll just pop over to ask Auld Skinner about that pay rise he promised,' Susie said, and Evie rolled her eyes to the ceiling. That girl would use any excuse to get out of doing a bit of work. She was taking a rise all right, but it had nothing to do with wages.

'I was thinking about the old days,' Meggie said, and Henry put his arms round her, knowing his lovely wife, who had denied him nothing in all their years together, had once made a starry-eyed mistake that was never far from her thoughts.

'Money is put aside, don't you worry about that,' Henry said, knowing that the money from the sale of land was now safely in the bank.

'I'm not worried, my love,' Meggie said, content in the knowledge her child would be well cared for and that the careworn expression, her husband could never quite shake off, might disappear now their money worries were not as demanding as they once were. 'The future is mapped out from the day we are born, whether we like it or not.' Meggie gave a low chuckle, gently extricating herself from her husband's embrace when the kettle interrupted with a piercing whistle. 'You love this yard, always have done,' she said. 'Your mother would never have kept this place going without you and if she'd found out about the baby we could never have been married.'

'She was a hard woman, I'll grant you, but times were hard back then.' He didn't like to speak ill of anybody, especially his own dead mother. He gave Meggie a smile that still caused a flutter in her stomach, curling his little finger round her little finger like he always did.

His simple gesture gave his Meggie courage, and as always he listened to her pour her heart out when she needed to talk about the short time she had spent with her much-loved baby. When she finished saying the words he had heard a million times before, she looked at her husband and smiled. 'For a man who was shown little affection as a boy, you give so much.'

'That is because you are so easy to adore, my Meg.' His mother had been skinny with her affection. Any show of love was an anathema to her.

His rich, deep voice was laced with melancholy. 'Ma used to say, *let's have none of that mushy stuff.*' He gazed past Meggie's shoulder to the photograph of his mother in her later years. The sepia tones did nothing to soften the sunken features or the hard, beleaguered glare, nor the black clothes she wore for the rest of her life. 'I would have stood up to her if you'd let me. Backed you all the way, told her about...'

'You married me and made sure my child was well cared for,' Meggie said, stretching her back and wrapping her loving arms round his strong shoulders. Drawing him closer to her, she kissed the top of his greying mane. 'And gave me a proper home, the best I had ever known.' All Meggie had known before she married Henry was work, to keep a roof over her head. 'You paid a high price for marrying me and I will never be able to repay you.'

Henry would not worry Meggie by letting her know he was paying an extortionate amount of cold hard cash to keep her secret child's existence hidden. She would be devastated, and he couldn't bear to see that happen. His huge hands furled round her arms, holding her close.

And the look of regret in his compassionate eyes made Meggie's heart lurch with love for him, when she said, 'I may not have raised my child, but I've been luckier than most. You made sure of that.'

Seeming to shrink as she sat down, Meggie's heart was torn in two by the desperate need to have her child by her side. Every week from the day she let him go, Meggie had paid another woman to take care of her own flesh and blood. The agony of not being able to love her child like a proper mother almost drove her to distraction. But she did not have the luxury of a choice.

'You did your best, lass,' Henry said, taking her hand across the table. 'You needed to earn the money to feed and clothe the child, put a roof over both your heads. The situation was not ideal, I know...'

'The stability of a *proper* family, wasn't that as important?' Rising, Meggie drew the warm air deep within her lungs, putting the flat of both hands on the table in that pragmatic way she had about her. 'We are already halfway through the century. Let's look forward, not back. New beginnings.'

Henry sighed and, with that mischievous twinkle in his eyes, he said, 'I love you so much, Meggie Skinner, and be sure of one thing, when my time comes, your child will have security.'

Meggie's eyes glistened with unshed tears and Henry stretched to his full six feet four inches.

'Right, enough of this maudlin talk,' he said briskly, 'come over 'ere an' give us a kiss...' He smiled when Meggie melted into his arms, each lost in that loving world of their own.

* * *

Finishing historical figures up to February 1948 later that afternoon, Evie stood up and stretched her aching back. The door closed as she put the kettle on and waited for it to boil.

'Danny's taking orders out to Netherford tomorrow.' Evie could hear Susie talking on the telephone, and wondered why she had not taken a job as a telephonist, the amount of time she spent talking to other clerks she knew. '...I *always* go with him, but a certain someone turned up and won't let me out of the office.' Susie was plainly peeved. 'She runs this place like a bloody concentration camp, you should see all the extra work I have to do while she's swanning round to the boss's wife every five minutes.'

Evie stopped what she was doing.

'Well, it's not going to carry on much longer,' Susie said, 'I know what's what about this place, and when I have a word with the boss's wife, things are going to change round here. Queen Bee will be buzzing off back to her posh office in town!'

Evie had heard enough, and she opened the staffroom door to see Susie, wide-eyed, like a child caught with her hand in the biscuit tin. She quickly hung up, as if the receiver were hot.

'Hello, Evie, I thought you'd gone out.' There was a tell-tale quiver in Susie's voice.

'So I gathered,' Evie's tone was cool, 'and what will you be having a word with Meggie about?'

'I wasn't talking about this place.' Susie gave a high-pitched false laugh. 'I was telling the customer about a play on the wireless.'

'I thought it sounded familiar,' Evie said with a knowing look. 'Has Danny been in for the Netherford order list?'

'Not yet,' Susie answered. Then she said in a conversational manner that fooled nobody: 'We used to have a spot of lunch in the little country inn along the way. And the farmer gave us extra rations, you know, butter, cheese, a nice bit of beef or a chicken, things like that.'

'Aye, well there's plenty of work for you to be getting on with. Invoices out and money in to pay the wages.' Evie placed her cup and saucer on her desk and put her head down, concentrating on the accounts.

'Don't you think Danny would make some girl a lovely husband?' Susie asked, breaking her already brittle concentration.

'I'm here to work and so are you,' Evie answered impatiently, 'so I suggest you crack on.' Honestly. Did that girl have anything inside her head beside fluffy white clouds?

'Have you ever thought of actually going to New York, New York?' Evie asked when, for the umpteenth time that afternoon, Susie strangled the tune she heard when she went to see *her most favourite film*: 'On the Town', which was sung by *her most favourite American crooner*: Frank Sinatra.

'Wouldn't that be fabulous,' Susie breathed, ignoring Evie's sardonic remark when the office door opened and Mr Skinner came in, filling the room with pipe tobacco smoke.

The aroma reminded Evie of Mr Walton and, just for a moment, she wished she had not left the brightly lit office for Susie Blackthorn's constant chatter about the film stars she had seen on the Gaumont picture house, or singers she loved to listen to.

'So, how are you finding the work, Evie?' Skinner asked in that deep timbre that kept the men in line.

'I'm getting to grips with it, Mr Skinner, but I need to have a word with you about one of the accounts,' Evie said, unable to ask in front of Susie. She didn't want to embarrass Mr Skinner with awkward questions, but if she had been brought in to balance the books, then there were some awkward questions that could not be avoided.

'I know the one you mean,' Henry lowered his voice so only she could hear. 'You have done a sterling job. We'll talk later.' He didn't wait for Evie to answer. Grimacing, he rubbed his barrel chest. 'Susie, go and get something for this heartburn off Meggie, I'll have a sup o' tea, that ought to shift it a bit.'

'Here, let me make it for you,' Evie said, pulling out a chair to let him sit down. His face drained to the colour of wallpaper paste and she felt more than a twinge of concern. 'You look a bit pale, Mr Skinner, do you want me to call the doctor?'

'I'm not going to see that quack,' Henry said, 'he's more interested in the dog.' He scratched the head of his faithful hound and then said, as if the idea had just occurred to him, 'While Susie's out, could you do me the honour of countersigning this?' He took an envelope out of his pocket and, grimacing, he held out an official-looking document, 'I'd very much appreciate it.'

'Certainly, Mr Skinner,' Evie said, taking the document and picking up a pen. However, when she read the document, she saw it was his Will. And the chief beneficiary was not his wife Meggie, but there was no time to ask and it had nothing to do with her anyway, she was just a signatory. What Mr Skinner did with his business was his affair.

'Meggie sent you this and said you have to go over to the house and rest,' Jack said, coming in and handing over a box of bicarbonate of soda to Evie who mixed it with a little warm water from the kettle.

'Did she now?' Henry sounded distracted as Evie signed her name and, looking out of the window, saw Susie talking to Mrs Skinner

'She's giving the missus every detail.'

'She'll have me dead and buried that Susie, frightening the life out of my Meggie.' He rubbed his chest. 'Don't be letting her pull the wool over your eyes, Evie,' Henry warned, 'she's a sly fly-by-night.'

Moments later Susie came through the office door with such force the door hit the back wall.

'I forgot those files had been tidied away,' she told Evie as Jack left the office, 'they usually stop the door hitting the wall.'

Henry stood up and then sat heavily back on the chair.

'I can manage now Evie's here, Mr Skinner,' Susie said, and he raised his hand for her to be quiet.

'I'll just finish drinking this.' He took a sip of the liquid and Susie rolled her eyes while Evie wondered why she was so reluctant to have the boss here in the office.

'You're still looking a bit pasty if you don't mind me saying,' Evie said as he wiped a clammy forehead. 'Susie, go and fetch Meggie, she'll know what to do.'

'I'll be fine.' Henry pushed his handkerchief into the pocket of his corduroy trousers. 'We're made of strong stuff us Skinners.'

Susie took a slim packet of Woodbines from her bag and lit a cigarette, laying it in the groove of a Bakelite ashtray before rolling a sheet of paper into her typewriter while Evie noticed that, for as much as her movements were quick and business-like, Susie hardly did a tap of work all day, using a lot of energy making no progress whatsoever.

'Meggie swears by a spoonful of bicarb in warm water,' Henry said swigging back the remainder of the drink. 'Works wonders for heartburn, better than all that fancy stuff.'

'Are you sure you don't want me to ring the doctor?' Evie asked for the third time, sure he was not at all well.

'I don't need a doctor.' Henry waved away her concern. 'I'll be as right as ninepence when this stuff does it's magic.' He stood and raised his empty cup. 'Just a bit of indigestion, that's all. And there's no point worrying Meggie,' he said, aiming the comment at Susie, 'she'll only fuss.'

'We're only thinking of your best interests, Mr Skinner,' Susie said, but before he could reply, Evie heard him hit the chair with a thud. The legs creaking.

Her heart gave a little jump and scraping back her own chair, Evie hurried to him, his cup hanging from his index finger and his chin resting on his chest. Her scalp tingled when she heard Susie scream so loud it nearly took the roof off.

Hunching over, Evie could see his putty-coloured face at close range, and he made no attempt to answer when Evie implored, 'Mr Skinner, Mr Skinner speak to me.' She patted his cheek and poked his arm, but still there was no response. She looked at Susie, who, with a trail of black tears rolling down her cheeks, shrugged her shoulders.

Mr Skinner didn't seem that old at close quarters, Evie thought absurdly as she tapped his shoulder. There was still no response. When she lifted his chin, his head flopped back.

Susie, her face devoid of all colour except for the red gash of crimson lips and the black pencilled eyebrows, exclaimed, 'Jesus, Mary and Joseph! He's dead! I'll go and fetch Danny and tell him Auld Skinner's going to miss the Netherford parade.'

'I'll ring the ambulance and Connie.' Evie practical as ever, watched Susie skid across the yard to get Danny, and her finger could not dial nine, nine, nine, fast enough. The new emergency system had been in service in all big cities since just after the war, and would bring an ambulance to the yard immediately.

* * *

'What's up with that dozy mare?' Connie said, arriving in the office before the ambulance and seeing Susie slumped in a chair.

When she had returned to the office and had seen Mr Skinner still unconscious, Susie's heavily mascaraed eyes had rolled, and she'd swooned, falling with perfect accuracy into an office chair.

'She couldn't have aimed herself better if she tried,' Evie said, realising that Susie was spark out. Moments later, the ambulance bell alerted everybody to its presence in the yard. Evie and Connie concentrated on Susie when the medics took over Mr Skinner's care. The office was shrinking by the minute.

'Here,' Connie said, giving Evie a small bottle of smelling salts. 'Waft some of those under her nose.'

'With pleasure,' said Evie, opening the bottle and waving it under Susie's nose. When the pungent smell hit Susie's senses a second or two later, she spluttered into life.

'I think I'm going to go again,' Susie wailed, theatrically putting the back of her hand to her forehead.

'You'll be as right as ninepence in no time,' Connie said when she pushed her head between her knees, and Evie rolled her eyes to the ceiling. Poor Mr Skinner, she thought as Meggie was urged into the back of the ambulance.

'Will you come with me, Evie?' Meggie asked, her face ashen with worry.

'Of course,' Evie answered grabbing her cardigan and her bag.

16

The strong smell of disinfectant clung to Evie's clothes as she hurried along the hospital corridor with Meggie, bringing back memories of the last time she was here, when her mother had *been dragged from the canal.* The smell turned her stomach, but this was not the time to dwell. She must support Meggie, who loved her husband and was worried sick about whether he would survive the night.

'I'm sure everything will be all right,' Evie said when they sat on the long wooden bench outside the examination room for what seemed like hours, patting Meggie's hand. 'He's in the best place.' They had all got such a fright, and when Mr Skinner was stretchered into the ambulance, Evie felt privileged when Meggie asked her to accompany her to the hospital.

'Sitting here worrying won't do any good,' a kindly nurse told Meggie a couple of hours later. 'Why don't you go home and get some rest. We have your telephone number and if there is any change we will contact you straight away.'

'Sooner than that,' Meggie replied and when she heard rapid

footsteps, she turned to see Danny's long strides devouring the corridor.

'Go home and have something to eat,' the nurse said, 'it will do you the world of good.'

'Come on, Aunty Meg,' Danny said, putting his arm round her shoulders. To anybody who didn't know her, Meggie Skinner appeared upbeat about her husband's sudden collapse. But Evie knew different. Behind the business-as-usual exterior, Meggie's world had shattered into a million pieces.

'I can't buckle while the vultures are circling,' Meggie told Evie matter-of-factly. 'And I'd be obliged if you and Danny keep the business going, I'm sure I won't be able to manage, but we will keep that under our hats.'

Evie knew Meggie wasn't given to fanciful notions, preferring instead to look a situation in the eye and tackle it. 'With Danny's knowledge of running this place, and your sharp business brain, I'm confident that the business is in good hands.'

'You've got the brains and the know-how to run the business under normal circumstances,' Evie told the older woman, 'and no doubt you could do it as well as any of us, but I understand that you're worried about Mr Skinner. Nobody could blame you for concentrating on your husband.'

'These are trying times,' Meggie said, suddenly looking tired. 'I don't have the strength to keep the business afloat while Henry's so ill.'

Evie reassured her that there was no need to worry about the business, it was in safe hands.

Meggie's hear skipped a beat when she entered ward seven from the main hospital corridor and looked through the big window of the side ward, set aside for patients who were critically ill and needed extra care, and saw Henry's bed was empty.

'Nurse!' Meggie called to the probationer nurse, trim in her immaculate crisp green cotton dress, starched white apron and tailored cap, who was opening the double swing doors leading into the main ward. 'My husband?' Meggie looked towards the side ward, barely able to get her words out as fear gripped her throat.

'Ahh, yes, Mrs Skinner.' The nurse gave a welcoming smile and said efficiently, 'follow me.' Hurrying down the middle of the ward, where twenty-four pristine beds were positioned equally on both sides of the ward, Meggie was aware of the click-click of her small-heeled shoes following the nurse's silent black lace-up rubber soled shoes.

Meggie dare not raise her hopes as a fleeting thought entered her head. Nurses don't usually smile so widely if they are going to give bad news. Surely.

'Meggie! Over here, Love.' Henry's voice was a little weaker than usual but unmistakeable, nevertheless, and Meggie's heart soared, her face wreathed in a beaming smile, when she saw Henry sitting up in his navy-blue striped pyjamas under a pristine white bedspread that covered the cream coloured iron bed,

She hurried to his bed near sister's large windowed office and kissed Henry's cheek. 'Does this mean you are getting better?' Meggie said taking a white coned paper bag of humbugs, which she had used her own sweet coupons to buy, and put them on the polished wooden locker at the side of his bed.

'Aye, Love,' Henry said and although he still looked a bit wan, he was much brighter than he had been since his collapse. 'I was moved here last night after visiting hour, and the sister said if I carry on making good progress, I could be home next week.'

'Oh Henry that is good news, Love,' Meggie said sitting in the green leather fireside-type chair with polished wooden arms and settled herself. After catching up with each other's news, Henry asked his usual questions about how the haulage yard was faring without him.

'You've not to worry yourself about the yard,' Meggie said patting his hand, 'Danny is doing a grand job and so is Evie – in fact, I think you will be surplus to requirements when you get home.' Meggie gave a small chuckle, but the laughter died in her throat when she saw her husband's grim expression. 'I didn't mean they can't manage without you. Obviously, everyone was worried sick when you collapsed and...'

'That's the point, Meg,' Henry said solemnly, 'I've been told I've got to take it easy from now on, the old ticker is not as robust as it once was.'

'That's a good thing, surely?' Meggie said. 'You were working every hour God sent, you did the work of ten men.'

'I had to.' he said, examining his fingernails in concentrated detail. 'You see...' he paused. 'There's something I've got to tell you, Meg.'

She found it wise not to interrupt when Henry was trying to find the right words to tell her something important. A couple of times he opened his mouth to speak and then closed it again without speaking, and when he still said nothing, she could wait no longer.

'Visiting time will be over by the time you finish your goldfish impersonations.' Meggie decided a little levity was called for and she saw her husband smile, but the smile did not reach his mellow eyes. 'It's about time you slowed down, let Danny take the strain – he is doing a sterling job.'

'Funny you should say that, Meg,' Henry wanted to tell her what he was going to do, but first he had to tell her why.

'We've still got the money from the land sale.' Meggie tried to make it easier for him to tell her this thing that was obviously so hard to talk about. 'Business has been good...'

'That's what I need to tell you, Love,' he said, 'there isn't much money in the pot – and I'm not talking about your money...'

'Our money, Love,' Meggie said, and he waved away her words.

'I'm being blackmailed, Meg,' he blurted out the words so rapidly she only just managed to catch them, 'and I have been for some years.'

Henry aged before her eyes and Meggie reached for his large work-worn hands that now looked so unnaturally clean. Whatever had happened she was going to stand by him, because not for one moment could she imagine her Henry doing something so bad he wanted to keep it hidden.

'Come on, Love,' Meggie said in that quiet persuasive tone he could never resist. 'No matter what, I will always be here, we will get through this no matter what.' Isn't that what Henry always told her when she worried, or when the nightmares of the past came back to haunt her. And didn't he always make sure she was protected and cared for. Now it was her turn to stand by him.

After he had given her a chance to let the information settle, Henry told Meggie about the regular blackmail letters and the telephone demands.

'What are you going to do?' Meggie asked. The danger of her past becoming public knowledge had not only brought Henry to the brink of bankruptcy it nearly killed her beloved husband. 'I couldn't blame you if you want me to leave, I have brought you nothing but bad luck.'

'Don't say that, Meg,' Henry said reaching out to grasp her withdrawing hand gently but firmly. 'You are the love of my life. I am nothing without you.'

'Then what are we going to do?' Meggie asked. 'This cannot carry on any longer.'

'Well, that's what I wanted to talk to you about.' Henry brightened, and Meggie was hopeful. If need be she would forsake her long kept secret for the sake of his health.

'What do you say to me selling the business to Danny?'

'I think it is a wonderful idea,' she answered, 'I can think of nobody better to take over from you... There is just one thing' Her eyebrows pleated, and her caring eyes lost their sparkle momentarily. 'Danny may not have enough put by to afford to buy the yard.'

'You leave that up to me, my love.' Henry sighed, giving her one of his little winks.

* * *

Meggie was beyond thrilled when Sister informed her Henry was on the mend, and ready to come home, but only on the strict understanding he was to take things easy and not rush back to work. The news put a new spring in Meggie's step, filling her heart with joyful gratitude.

'I give you my solemn word that I will keep a strict eye on him,' Meggie told Matron, 'and I certainly won't let him do anything strenuous. He'll be lucky if I let him lift a cup to his lips.'

Evie and Danny, who were there with Meggie, smiled at each other knowing she would not let a gentle breeze tickle one hair on her beloved husband's head.

'I know I haven't been working in the firm as long as everybody else,' Evie told Danny as they left the long ward so Meggie could say goodnight to Henry with a promise to bring everything he needed for his discharge the following day, 'but I feel as if I've known the Skinners all my life.' She was thrilled that Meggie had some good news at last and that Henry was coming home.

When she looked at Meggie as she came out into the corridor

where she and Danny waited, she could see the worried frown had melted from her face.

'It'll be good to have him back,' Meggie said as they crossed Stanley Road to walk back to Reckoner's Row, 'the place has been far too quiet without him. Noisy bugger that he is.' They all laughed, relieved that Skinner was growing stronger.

When they reached the house, Meggie invited Evie and Danny in for a bite to eat and, suspecting she didn't want to be alone, they agreed.

'Mr Skinner was so decent to us when we needed help the most,' Evie said, enjoying the ham sandwich and a fresh cup of tea, 'you both were. And I will do anything to help if I can,' Evie would never forget their kindness, and was so grateful for the food parcels that appeared as if by magic on their doorstep when they had nothing in the cupboards to eat. 'Especially after...' Evie still couldn't bring herself to talk about those awful, dark days three years ago.

'I know, queen,' Meggie said, patting Evie's hand, 'you didn't have it easy, that's for sure.'

'I'm not begging sympathy, honestly,' Evie said, giving Meggie's careworn hands a gentle squeeze, 'I just wanted to say, I understand the worry you've been going through.'

'Uncle Henry is so well liked by everyone,' Danny said, 'I'm glad he's coming home tomorrow.'

'Me too,' Meggie said. Her voice was laced with love and they were all so pleased that Henry had recovered enough to be allowed home under the strict supervision of his adoring wife.

'Something tells me Uncle Henry is in for a terrible time.' Danny laughed.

'Well, this isn't getting the wages done,' Evie said, rising from the table, 'I'll get lynched if they are late.'

'Susie hasn't got a clue about timesheets and hourly rates,'

Meggie said, and Evie said nothing. Realising that Susie might have had more idea than Meggie gave her credit for. Who else could know exactly where those mysterious payments were going each month.

Evie left to go back to the office and Danny was locking up the big double doors on the yard when Meggie beckoned to him from the house.

'Is something wrong, Aunty Meg?' Danny asked as he entered the spacious lobby.

'There's something I have to tell you.' She pushed a cup of tea his way. 'When Henry comes out of hospital, he's not going to be able enough to run the yard.'

'I know,' Danny answered, 'he needs to build up his strength again.'

'That's not going to be as easy as it sounds, you know how stubborn he can be.'

'Aye.' Danny nodded, knowing Henry was not known for being idle, he had to be doing something all the time. 'I suppose we could find him a jigsaw somewhere.'

'Seeing as you have done such a good job with the yard,' – Meggie's thoughts were working double shift and Danny's little joke went unnoticed – 'I was wondering if you would do me a kindness and carry on managing the place until Henry is back to his old self.'

'We want him much better than his old self,' Danny said. 'Of course I'll run the yard. That goes without saying, but you know the auld fella, he'll be up and out ten minutes after he gets home from hospital.'

'Over my dead body,' Meggie said, 'I'm not going through all that worry and upset again – not for a very long time.' He smiled when he saw the determination in Meggie's eyes and knew she meant every word. 'The most he will do is polish the horse brasses for the parade.'

* * *

For the next couple of weeks, everybody, including Jack, Lucy and Evie, along with Henry, Meggie and Danny were preparing the horses for the Netherford Parade. The most prestigious among the North West carters.

Everybody had their own tasks to perform in the Skinner's front room and Meggie was in her element, cooking tea as a thank you to everybody for helping out. Susie told them she had a prior engagement and couldn't possibly help.

Evie suspected Susie's fingernails were far too precious to risk ruination with blacking polish on horse brasses. However, Evie could see that not being so close to Danny was eating Susie up.

Each evening after they finished their evening meal and everything had been washed up and cleared away, they would all gather round the big table, where they would bring out all the beautiful coloured silks and ribbons, which had to be stitched and fringed into different shapes to decorate the bridle, collar and breeching.

Lucy had her own tasks to do. Henry and Danny only trusted her to polish the small buckles and straps. Jack was trusted to do the bigger jobs, such as linking the *brights*. The chains, crank and hame all shone like silver when Jack finished cleaning them, although Henry refused to sit doing nothing.

'I might as well kick up my heels now as sit here doing nought,' Henry said handling the brasses with the same care and attention as he would a newborn kitten knowing nobody was allowed to touch them when they were finished.

Then, when he set to doing all the leather work, he was scolded like a schoolboy by Meggie.

'But Meg, I've got to do something. What good is winning the cup going to be to me if I've done nothing to help?' A practised leather polisher, Skinner even made his own special blacking and kept the secret ingredients to himself, always carrying a tin of it in his working jacket, along with a large washed cloth used to cover lamb and beef carcases, which Meggie got from the butcher.

She boiled the cloths to a pristine white and they were nice and soft, perfect for buffing and polishing. Meggie knew he was right. Her Henry would feel like a fraud if he were to win the cup and hold it aloft after doing nothing to help. 'Here,' she said, 'I've saved this one big cloth to cover the cleaned gears and newly made flowers, it will be your job to keep them perfect until show day.'

Evie looked round the table, happy that everybody was in good spirits, laughing and sharing their hopes and dreams of the future. Their plans and expectations. Danny wanted his own business, everybody knew that, although Jack was putting his plans on hold, knowing he could be called up for National Service when he turned eighteen in September.

'I'm looking forward to getting some service in,' Jack said, polishing away.

'You'll love it,' Danny answered, knowing Jack never shirked his duties to his family or his work. He also knew the lad had been through the toughest of times and had still come through smiling. He was the kind of strong, bright young man this country needed.

'I'll put the kettle on. I think we all deserve a nice cup of tea,' Meggie said, clearing away the silk roses she had been making and rising from the table.

'You look tired, Aunty Meg, let me help you,' Evie said, busying herself getting the cups and saucers down from the Welsh dresser and following her to the kitchen. Since Henry went into hospital, Meggie invited Evie and her family to call her *Aunty.*

Everybody who worked for Mr Skinner called Meggie *Aunty* it seemed, except Susie, who appeared to have a sneering disregard for the older woman, although nobody knew why.

'Aye, I am a bit tired,' Meggie admitted, heaving a sigh. 'It's the worry I suppose. But everything has turned out for the best, as far as Henry's health goes, so the burden of worry is much less now.'

She gave Evie one of her bright smiles, but Evie could see there was still something wrong. Aunty Meg was one of those strong dependable women who could withstand any of life's struggles, but when it came to her beloved husband, that was a different matter altogether.

'He'll be brand new in no time,' Evie said, pulling out a straight-backed kitchen chair from the table and easing Meggie into it, 'especially now he's home and being given the best care possible from you.'

'That's kind of you to say so,' Meggie answered, 'it'll take a while for him to get back to his old self.'

'I'm sure the attack gave him quite a scare,' Evie answered, scooping loose tea from the caddy into the pot and Meggie put her hand on Evie's arm and looked quite subdued.

'If I tell you something,' she said in a low voice, 'you won't mention it to a soul, will you?'

Evie shook her head, honoured to be taken into the older woman's confidence. She would never dream of betraying her. Nobody had been as kind to her and her family as Meggie – and Connie of course. And she was proud to look upon both women as an extension of her own beloved family.

'You know there has been a huge amount of money going out of the business every month, of course you do.' Meggie faltered slightly. 'The worry of it brought on Henry's heart attack. He's worried sick that if it carries on he won't be able to pay the men's wages, or the firm that supply the food for the horses.'

'I know,' Evie said, pulling out another chair and sitting down. 'I have tried to tell him that the business is in much better shape than he first thought.' She could only imagine the worry they had both been going through. 'The accounts were in chaos when I started working here. It was hard to know what shape the yard was in. But, after chasing up all the unpaid bills, the bank balance is looking much healthier.'

'I'm so grateful for what you have done for Henry, for both of us.' Meggie had an affinity with this girl, who had no mother, knowing if she had ever been fortunate enough to have a daughter, she would have wanted one just like Evie. 'Although, I fear it won't be long before the yard goes into decline again.'

'What makes you say that?' Evie asked, knowing Susie had not given a moment's thought to chasing up money that was owed to the business, which was a lot – enough to cripple most of them.

Meggie looked round to make sure there was nobody to hear her and, leaning forward, she said in a hushed whisper, 'Henry has been getting these letters.' Meggie took a large bundle of envelopes from the kitchen drawer. 'I only found them when he was in hospital, after he told me what had been going on. He never said a word to me before that.'

'What are they?' Evie asked and Meggie handed her the bundle. Taking out a note from the top one, she was horrified to see that it was a demand for money. A lot of money, which was to be put into a post office account every month.

Evie had to bite her lips together to stop her jaw from dropping in shock. She could not believe the disgusting claims written in a spidery scrawl. This could not be true. The letter stated that if the money was not delivered by the due date, the whole of Liverpool was going to find out exactly what kind of harlot Henry Skinner had taken as a wife. Evie looked up to see the torment in Meggie's eyes and she knew the words were true. But it did not make them acceptable. And Evie felt her anger rise. How dare this feckless filth write such a thing.

'Have you been to the police?' Evie asked and Meggie shook her head.

'Henry wouldn't hear of it,' she said. 'You know as well as me, we settle our own scores round here.'

'Do you have any idea who is sending these vile letters?' Evie asked, dropping the envelopes onto the table, unable to read another word, and Meggie shook her head again.

'Nobody knew I had a child except Henry,' her voice cracked. 'I came here looking for a place when I left the Isle of Man. His mother would not have given me a job or a roof over my head, if she had known I was an unmarried mother.'

'Oh, Meggie.' Evie's voice was full of concern, she knew there were many women who lived a life of struggle and want because they had hidden the result of a man's lust. 'Do you know where your child is?'

'Yes, I do, but I don't know who is sending these.' Meggie's eyes were glassy with unshed tears, although she didn't seem keen to divulge any more and Evie's heart ached for her.

'Thank you for taking me into your confidence.' Evie said, knowing how evil some people's tongues could be. 'I will do everything to help you and Mr Skinner. Your secret is safe with me.'

17

Grace trudged from Scotland Road to Knowsley Road in the early hours and when she got to the three banks near the North Park, she turned and went back the same way she had come. Her mind in turmoil, she had a lot of thinking to do.

Alongside the quiet shops and sleeping terraced houses, the silent streets were lit by electric street lamps. Tranquillity reigned in the pre-dawn, and the only sound was the distant clip-clop of a horse's hooves on cobbles and the clip, clip, clip of her own high heels that were blistering the backs of her feet. But pain was a small price to pay for the biggest mistake of her life.

Grace needed the enveloping silence that the early hours offered, but she could not lie in bed awake, struggling to find a solution to her ever-growing problem. So when everybody had gone to bed and the house was quiet, she got dressed, snuck down the stairs and let herself out of the house at the bottom of Reckoner's Row.

The early morning was clear and calm and for the first time since she'd docked in Liverpool, she felt she was able to think straight. Mam was always fussing as usual, and she didn't have the heart to tell her she was thinking of leaving Reckoner's Row for good. And it would have to be soon. She would not be able to hide her shame much longer, and wearing two corsets was playing havoc with her breathing. Digging her hands deeper into the patch pockets of her duster coat, Grace was grateful the abundance of material disguised the result of her plight yet still looked modern.

As the sun rose on the horizon, she turned right into Boundary Street, then onward into Blackstone Street opposite Bramley Moore Dock, where the *working girls* and *old tails,* as the dockside prostitutes were known locally, bid each other goodnight as they sloped off foreign ships with a handbag full of money and a weary wave. Returning to their hovels or hungry families to rest their aching bodies in readiness to repeat later on the oldest trade known to man in the knowledge that if they should *fall*, there was always someone like Connie Sharp, or Connie McCrae as she was now, to pick them up.

Traipsing the dock road, Grace watched the sun rise higher in a clear blue sky, when the thought occurred to her: the landlady of the Tavern was a saviour to many a stricken girl or worn-out wife with too many mouths to feed and not enough coppers in her purse when they knocked on Connie's door with a belly full of trouble. Connie was the go-to-woman of Reckoner's Row.

A nurse during the war, Connie came home when Italy fell, turning her back on nursing when she applied to the court for a licence to take over the running of the Tavern from her widowed mother, Mim. She was the one other women went to when they could not afford to pay a doctor or midwife. She would step in and do the business. Connie had delivered every baby born at home in the poor dockside community since the war.

And because of her wartime duties, she also knew her way around a dead body. Often called on to lay out a cherished relative.

Births, deaths and everything in between were a normal part of life in Reckoner's Row, and Connie never shirked what she considered to be her duty to the neighbouring people of the dockside.

It was a little after six a.m. when Grace passed Skinner's yard, which was already showing signs of life by the light in the upstairs window of his adjoining house, as large and imposing as her own home in the next street. Crossing the debris, she heard the low moan of a ship's horn on the river and felt the unmistakable pull of the sea.

Turning into Reckoner's Row, the morning sunshine cast sparkling dapples on the pewter-coloured canal to her right, but she could not appreciate what little beauty there was to be had round here as she hurried past her own house.

The delicious aroma of freshly baked bread that wafted from the bakery at the top of the bridge and down the stone steps failed to waken her senses as worrying thoughts bounced round inside her head.

Slipping down the entry, between Evie Kilgaren's and the Tavern, Grace pressed the brass tradesman's bell on the large gate, her heart beating her ribs like a jackhammer while waiting for Connie. Eventually, she opened the gate and peered out into the entry, blooming in a flowered hip length smock and straight black skirt, and Grace felt her heart sink.

'Is everything all right, Grace?' Connie asked, looking worried as she opened the high gate a little wider, ushering her into the Tavern's yard, where a woman from Beamer Terrace was on her knees, scrubbing the back step with sandstone, disinfectant and hot water.

The image and the smell reminded Grace of the days her mam brought her here as a child, gave her a small bucket of warm water laced with Aunt Sally disinfectant and a scrubbing brush, telling her it was never too early to learn how to be clean. Ada wore her trade like a medal of honour, taking pride in her cleanliness.

Well, thought Grace as she sidled apologetically past the char-lady, there's some dirt could never be scrubbed away, no matter how hard you tried.

* * *

'You mustn't think like that,' Connie said. 'Every child is a blessing, no matter how it was conceived. It is not the child's fault.' Grace was sitting at Connie's kitchen table while the other woman busied herself making porridge for breakfast.

'I know that, Connie,' Grace said in a low voice, 'and believe me, I have walked all night trying to make sense of it all. I can't have this baby.'

'But it's too late to do anything about it now,' Connie said, and Grace swallowed hard as she watched her cup of tea grow cold. 'It will be far too dangerous for you at this stage.' Her words, like shards of glass piercing her heart, were more terrifying than telling her mam. 'Will the father not help you?' Connie asked and Grace looked up to see her caring eyes were not at all condemning like some would be, and for the first time, Grace wanted to share her tale with this wonderful, feisty, compassionate woman.

But she knew the story was often told by naïve girls who thought they were The One. The favoured son, heir to a fortune, takes a shine to the maid – the governess – the singer – who think they are different from every other girl who has been spun a lie.

Her mind suddenly conjured up Clifford who promised to marry her, and even gave her the ring she wore. She imagined that every liar and smooth-talking womaniser looked like Clifford. But none of them were like Bruce.

'Bruce was in a different league.'

'I'm sorry,' Connie said, 'but that's...'

'... What they all say,' Grace nodded. She had been on board ships long enough to know that fairy tales rarely came true. Bruce had gone. He had sounded so happy to meet up with her, pleased they would be together. But actions spoke louder than words. And when he did not turn up, his rejection screamed in her face. He doesn't want you. He paid you lip service and you believed him. She felt her insides shrink with shame.

'Bruce is just like the rest of them after all.' Grace dragged the words from the depths of her heart, finding it hard to believe they came from her own lips. 'Isn't he?'

'Only you know that,' Connie answered and trying to get Grace to open up a little she nodded to the huge stone glittering in the sunlight and let out a low, unladylike whistle. 'Is it real?'

'Never in a million years. The man who gave it to me couldn't afford a ring like this if it were real,' Grace answered and then took a deep breath. 'But he isn't the father.'

'Oh. I see.' She wouldn't pry, Connie told herself, but if Grace wanted to tell her, she was all ears. A paradox of a woman, who loved children and family and was the heartbeat of the community, she was already a loving mother to three-year-old Fergus and cherished each new life she brought into the world. However, for some poor girls, she was just as adept at ending it.

'No, the father of this child is...' Saying the words out loud were more difficult than Grace thought they would be. 'It's the old, old story. I'm carrying the child of the man I worked for.' There, she'd said it. Now her predicament was out in the open.

'More vulnerable girls are caught out by the unscrupulous power of some men than you would ever dream,' Connie said, clenching her fist, her eyes darkening. Then, as if talking to herself, she added, 'The poor starry-eyed mare thinks she has found her one true love. She feels like Cinderella and she has found her prince.

She can't believe her luck: this powerful man is giving her everything she ever dreamed of. But luck and love are rarely on her side.'

'It wasn't like that,' Grace cried hot salty tears that streamed down her cheeks, and Connie hurried over and hugged her.

'That's what they say too, love.' Connie held her until her sobs subsided and she dabbed her red swollen eyes with the handkerchief.

Sitting in silence for a few moments, Grace had never cried so much in her whole life. She was exhausted and felt as if she had been wrung dry. She couldn't have this baby. She just couldn't.

'Everything happens for a reason,' Connie said, pushing a cup and saucer in front of Grace, 'but half the bloody time nobody finds out what that reason is.'

'Mam will go spare,' Grace said. 'I can see it now; she'll go off like an ack-ack gun.' And for the first time that day, the two women smiled.

'Today's big scandal is tomorrow's chip paper.' Her words calmed Grace, who knew Connie would never turn away one of those poor women who had more kids than common sense, or a young girl, like the ones she had seen coming off the ships earlier.

The prostitutes who worked hostile hours to put food on the table, or shoes on their kids' feet were a common sight along the dock road when the ships were in port. She knew Connie felt an obligation to keep them safe from the backstreet abortionists who were not as fastidious or as clean. The dichotomy was not lost on Grace.

'I would have felt safe in your hands if I ever decided to... you know.' Grace could not bring herself to voice the enormity of what she had considered asking Connie to do. 'If I can't even say the word, I'm sure as hell not going to have one.'

'That's good to hear,' Connie said, knowing Grace was luckier than most, with a close family – her bar-hopping father excepted – and a loving if somewhat feisty mother, nor was she destitute, 'it's not worth putting your life at risk.'

The welfare state was two years old and even though hospitals presented free medical care at the point of need, they did not offer the kind of treatment required by a pregnant mother, desperate because she could not feed the hungry children she already had, let alone another mouth to add to her troubles.

'I shouldn't have disturbed you, Connie.' Grace said, and Connie could detect a hint of desperation in this girl's voice and worried that Grace would do anything.

'If I can help in any other way Grace, I will.' Connie said without malice. 'Some men promise you the earth because they can provide it.'

'But their words are hollow and meaningless? A shortcut to getting what they want?' Grace never dreamt Bruce would do that to her. 'Bruce wasn't like that, he was kind,' she told Connie, 'and loving. Nothing was too much trouble. What a bloody fool.' Grace stood up and swayed a little. The emotional deluge had left her depleted.

'I'm sorry, love.' Connie put her arm round her once again and hugged her. This poor girl who had the world at her feet was as naive as any other. 'I wouldn't... proceed, even if you were not so far gone.' Connie placed two protective hands on her own abdomen, 'not in my condition.'

'I shouldn't have come, laying my problem at your door. I'm not a bad woman, Connie. I just got myself into a spot of bother.'

'I know that, love, but these things have a way of sorting themselves out, trust me.'

'I hope so,' Grace said. It would be nice to look forward to the day when she would be like Connie. Married. Content. Waiting for the birth of her baby with a loving husband beside her, she said simply, 'This just isn't the right time for me.'

'For some women it is never the right time, but they have no choice.' The two women headed towards the door. 'I fervently hope I'll see the day when women will be independent, like they were during the war. They will have a choice, with nobody telling them what to do or how to behave.'

'Like you?' Grace asked, descending the stairs to the side door and stretching over the step which the charlady had finished cleaning. 'Would you give up the life you have now and go back to being independent?' Grace asked and Connie thought for a moment.

'Would I hell as like,' she laughed as she opened the side gate. 'Take care of yourself.'

'I will,' Grace answered, 'but before I do anything, I'm going to Saint Patrick's to pray me mam won't skull-drag me when I tell her.'

'If she lays one hand on you, come and tell me,' Connie said with the hint of a smile, 'I'll set Mim on her.' With a small wave, taking in the warmth of the morning sun, Connie turned and went back inside.

* * *

Dipping her fingers into the marble font, Grace dabbed her forehead, chest and each shoulder, making the sign of the cross with holy water. She had not been inside a church since she was on board the cruise liner, but now she felt the urgent need of this sacred place, which never closed its doors, giving sanctuary to the lost and needy. And if anybody needed a safe haven right now, Grace thought, it was most certainly her. And she also needed time to contemplate what she was going to do next.

Grace took the scarf Bruce had given her and slipped the exquisite fine-silk square over her head. Immediately, she felt the light touch of his gentle caress on her hair and, turning, she expected to see him behind her, and her heart dipped with disappointment when he wasn't there. Confused, she had come here to ask forgiveness. Yet Bruce was uppermost in her mind.

Her footsteps echoed in the cold, empty church of Saint Patrick and, compelled by the serenity of this holy place, Grace stepped lightly into the nearest pew, not daring to go as far as the alter just yet. Grace knew she must pray for her terrible sins.

The last few weeks had been a nightmare of sleepless nights and indecision. She had even given serious thought to contacting Bruce again, but when it came to write the letter, she could not find the right words. Her pride would not allow her to ask for his help. Begging did not come easy to a headstrong girl who looked and acted like a woman of the world, but who was as lost and afraid as a child alone in a strange and crowded place.

Grace could not bear it if Bruce ignored her again. Or worse. What if he denied he was the father of her child? She couldn't face that. If Bruce wanted nothing to do with her, she would have proof she was a blinkered fool. A rich man's plaything. She lost her heart to Bruce. Grace knew that now. But she was not the kind of girl he considered taking as a wife.

A backstreet girl she might be, but she had standards. She didn't fall into bed with every man she fancied. In fact, he was the only man she had ever slept with and she knew for certain this baby was his.

Clifford could not bear that she was saving herself for their wedding night, and had cast his net into other waters. Yet, when it came to Bruce, the thought of saving herself could not have been further from her mind. And it had nothing to do with his money. He could have been the glass collector for all she cared.

Grace knew she had not only lost her heart, but lost her head too. She allowed herself to believe that Bruce really did love her in the way he said he did. She allowed her enjoyment of his company and his lovemaking to cloud her judgement. What girl wouldn't?

Grace stared straight ahead at the altar with its marble steps and golden alter rails. In her heart of hearts, she believed Bruce did love her. But she didn't want him thinking she was trying to trap him.

You've made your bed, my girl, her mother's voice was as clear as if she were sitting beside her, *now you must lie in it.* Her intentions became clearer. Grace knew what she had to do. And staying in Reckoner's Row was not an option. The scandal would end her singing career, and the shame would follow her round for the rest of her days.

Alone and penniless, she would be forced to bring up a child she could not look after properly and might even grow to resent. If she must have this child, it deserved a better mother than she would be in that situation.

Lowering her head, Grace rested her forehead on clenched hands and begged forgiveness. 'Bless me Lord, for I have sinned...'

After lighting a candle at the feet of the statue of Mary Magdalene, Grace hurried down the side aisle and out of the church.

Dazed through lack of sleep and a little unsteady on her feet, she walked to the market, taking deep breaths of hazy air that smelled of chimney smoke and the khaki coloured canal. Horse and carts vied with cars and wagons for space along the busy main road, and women in headscarves held wicker baskets across their arms like shields as they queued for their day's shopping.

Grace couldn't go back to sea, but nor could she stay here, knowing she would start showing soon and tongues would certainly wag. There was nothing like the fizz of another's misfortune to get the women of Reckoner's Row excited. Her mother would be in church night and day, chewing the altar rails and begging forgiveness for giving birth to such a worthless, wicked daughter, and Susie's mother would nod her turbaned head and say, 'I told you so.'

No, she could not stay round here. She would take off for London first thing tomorrow. She knew people there. They would help her out.

18

Curling blue smoke rose from the long cigarette and Grace watched it with concentrated fascination, ignoring the cylinder of ash hovering over the tin ashtray, she tried to force down the rising nausea as the greasy smell of fried bacon vied with the cigarette smoke.

The market cafeteria was bursting at the seams with shoppers who appeared like hunting packs, searching the stalls for tasty morsels to liven their ration-jaded palettes and Grace parted the net curtain covering the lower half of the window, wiping the condensation from the steamed-up glass.

Where was Susie? She should have been here by now. Grace should have known better. Susie would be late for her own funeral.

Grinding the unsmoked cigarette into the ashtray, Grace pushed it to the other side of the table, sickened by the charred remnants of blackened tobacco, watching shoppers elbow their way through a large throng, while a man in a demob raincoat was selling second-hand shoes from a dilapidated pram. Housewives in headscarves rooted through, examining the merchandise, while others hovered by the next vendor, giving battered utility furniture the once-over, and haggling a price. But there was still no sign of Susie. People who were waiting to sit down gave her the evil eye for hogging a table.

'Can I get you anything else?' the waitress in a flowered pinny asked pointedly, pad and pencil at the ready.

The couple casting the evils found a seat and Grace breathed a sigh of relief.

'Could I have two more coffees please.' Then, feeling obliged, she added, 'I'm waiting for my friend – she's been delayed.'

'It's all the same to me, love,' the waitress answered, distinctly uninterested as she removed the lipstick-stained coffee cup and wiped imaginary crumbs off the table.

'Oh, here she is now...' Grace's voice trailed off when she realised the waitress had already gone and had not heard a word she said.

'Sorry I'm late.' Susie was breathless as if she had been rushing.

'I've ordered us a coffee each,' Grace said above the loud chatter of stallholders and shoppers in the smoke-filled, steamed-up café.

'I'm not too keen on coffee, to be honest,' Susie said, blowing smoke to the ceiling, 'but seeing as you've already ordered, I might as well drink it.' Her presence immediately irritated Grace and she felt no inclination to confide in her friend the way she would have done in the past. Talking to Connie had done her the world of good, and the time she had to think while waiting for Susie to show up had cemented her thoughts for the future.

'Here,' Susie said, leaning forward and lowering her voice, 'I heard something about Meggie Skinner that will make your hair curl.'

'What did you hear?' Grace asked, realising she had outgrown the small-town mentality that thrived on gossip and insinuation.

Looking round, to make sure nobody could overhear, Susie said, 'I'm not sure I should say. Not with you being related and all that.'

'You've started now,' Grace said, tapping her fingernails on the table.

'It's not the kind of thing I should repeat,' Susie replied mysteriously, taking another drag on her cigarette.

'Then why mention it in the first place?' Grace said, knowing Susie should have outgrown this desperate need to be always in the know. 'You're as bad as my mother.' It made Grace realise this was one of the reasons she left Reckoner's Row in the first place. The small-mindedness got on her bloody nerves.

'This is just between me and you,' Susie said, and Grace nodded, 'you mustn't breathe a word.'

Grace nodded again. *Get on with it.*

Susie's world was what happened at the yard, and who said what to whom. She lived a little life and had no ambition but to marry Danny just to get away from her overbearing parents, who would not let her out of their sight. Although God only knew why, she never shut up talking.

'Aunty Meggie had a baby.' The pleat of her brow gave Grace a look of disbelief and now it was Susie's turn to nod. 'I'm telling you, straight up, not a word of a lie.' To enforce her words, she slapped her hand on the table. 'She had a baby before she married your uncle Henry.'

'It's nobody else's concern but theirs,' Grace said, realising she had more in common with the old woman than she thought possible. Nevertheless, she had no intentions of repeating the news. After all, she wouldn't want people gossiping about her. She decided to change the subject before Susie really got her teeth into it. 'Don't you fancy travelling, seeing the world, open your mind to new ideas?' Grace asked.

'If I went on a ship, it would probably sink.' Susie was peeved that her news did not have the explosive impact she had hoped for. 'So come on, tell me, all about how you and Clifford split up.' She was dying to know why Grace wouldn't talk about her chap in front of Ada.

'Clifford?' Grace's brow furrowed in momentary confusion. Clifford seemed so long ago, and she shrugged her shoulders. She couldn't talk about her tangled love life with her one-time friend. who was more interested in other people's business. 'I don't want to talk about him.'

'I've been looking forward to every juicy detail.' Susie recalled the ring. 'He must be rolling in money to afford a dazzler like that one he gave you.'

'It's not worth much, I'm certain,' Grace said, 'but I'd like to know for sure.'

'It looks real enough to me,' Susie answered, and a light went on behind her eyes when she said, 'I could ask my uncle for you? We could go now if you like.'

'That would be good,' Grace answered, knowing they could escape the smell of fried food. 'I've got it here in my bag.'

'Well what are we waiting for?' Susie said and they got up from the table.

Watching the two girls chatting he ground out his cigarette knowing he had done the right thing in not approaching her before the blonde joined her at the table. The place was packed. She may have kicked up a fuss. Picking up his cigarettes and lighter, he stood up and followed the two out of the cafe.

'It's not like Beaverbrook's, or any of those posh jewellers,' Susie said in hushed tones. 'I suppose if you walked past it you wouldn't even notice it was there, not your usual kind of jewellers...'

'Here, you're not talking about anything, you know... Shady?' Grace knew she was in enough trouble as it is.

'Why would I do that?' Susie was affronted. 'I'll have you know these are diamond merchants, they buy straight from source from all over the world.'

'I didn't mean any offence,' Grace said, remembering how quick Susie was to take umbrage.

'None taken.' Susie felt appeased. 'These people value the merchandise, bring it back and sell to other jewellers who make up fancy bracelets and necklaces, you know, like the one you brought back for your mam.'

'He must be loaded,' Grace said as they hurried along Stanley Road to the bus stop, 'dealing in gold and diamonds.'

'He isn't the owner,' Susie replied as the bus showed and they had to run to catch up, 'he's learning the trade.' Jumping on to the open platform at the back of the bus, they heard the ding-ding of the bell and flopped down on the brown leather seat as it lurched forward not taking any notice of the man who got on and went upstairs.

'He won't be interested in a bit of old tat then, will he?' Grace said patting her bag. They looked like a couple of starlets and the bus conductor couldn't take his eyes off them. When the bus came to their stop, they stood up and the conductor gave them both an appreciative smile as he let them get off the bus.

'The shop is closed today; it gives Uncle a day each week to complete the orders that need to go out and update the stock,' said Susie

'You were right when you said the place doesn't look much,' Grace said taking in the chipped wooden door and blacked-out windows.

'Uncle knows everything there is to know about precious stones,' Susie trilled when she rang the bell, 'he'll tell you exactly how much the ring is worth – if anything.'

* * *

The inside was nothing much to write home about either, Grace thought, her gaze spanning the unpolished wooden floorboards that creaked with every movement and the L-shaped counter stretching the length of the dusty shop. From floor to ceiling, there were rows of shelves filled with brown cardboard shoeboxes.

Susie's uncle locked the door behind them, making Grace feel a bit uneasy; this didn't look like the kind of place that housed such treasures Susie had spoken of. She had expected it to look like one of those large diamond merchants she had seen in America, but this looked more like a run-down shoe shop.

'We can't have just any Tom, Dick or Harriet walking in off the street, you know.' Susie's uncle said, and Grace realised she did not even know his name, but she didn't ask, being quite content to know him only as Susie's uncle. 'Too much valuable stock. And I know every single piece.' Those six words sounded like a warning to keep her mitts off. But the last thing Grace wanted was more junk jewellery.

After examining the ring in forensic detail, Susie's uncle made a small noise at the back of his throat. Something between a grunt and a sigh, and Grace thought it sounded quite rude.

'Exquisite,' he said eventually, 'just... exquisite. A fine piece.'

'So it might be worth something, then?' Grace was surprised because Clifford wasn't known for being at all generous.

Then his eyes narrowed, and he spoke in a whisper, 'Where, may I ask, did you get this ring?'

'From my ex-boyfriend. It was an engagement ring.'

'He's very wealthy, this boyfriend?' Susie's uncle asked and Grace began to feel a rush of dread and excitement. She didn't answer. It must be worth a few bob, she thought and knowing Lime Street Station was just a little way down the road she could nip in and purchase her train ticket while she was in town. If she got enough money for it, that is.

'I would say somewhere in the region of twenty thousand pounds...'

'How much?' she and Susie said in unison. Grace in a state of shock, was rooted to the dusty floorboards and could not raise her voice above a gasp. 'How much?'

'I am not an expert, you understand, but, with an educated guess, I would say this ring is worth well in excess of twenty thousand pounds.'

'That's what I thought you said... Bloody hell!'

'Where did your fiancé buy it, might I ask?'

'Where did he buy it?' Grace looked puzzled. She had to think fast. What could she say? If the ring was worth that much, then how much would the necklace be worth. And, most important of all, where *did* Clifford get the money to buy them? 'I think it is a family heirloom,' she said quickly. Something was wrong here. Something was very, very, wrong.

'Do you have the certificate?' Susie's uncle asked, and Grace shook her head, still finding it difficult to string a few words together.

'What does she need a certificate for?' Susie asked and seemed satisfied when he told her it was for insurance purposes.

Grace looked at the ring in a different light. It didn't look quite so gaudy now. In fact, it was quite beautiful. But if it was so valuable, then maybe Clifford still had the certificate. Or had he won it in one of his many card games from one of his wealthy clients? Did he know it was worth so much money? And if he did, she began to wonder, why had he given it to her?

'I wanted to know how much it was worth because I want to buy property in London,' Grace said later when she and Susie were getting off the bus at the top of the bridge leading down to Reckoner's Row. The news put a skip in their step as they descended into the Row and headed down the sun-drenched street.

'You could buy the whole street with that amount of money!' Susie squealed, and as she opened the gate to her own home at number six, she leaned forward, looked round to make sure nobody was within earshot and said to Grace, 'Uncle told me, if you ever want to sell the ring, he'll give you a good price, or rather, his boss will. They are always on the lookout for something out of the ordinary – for the foreigners, you understand.'

'I'll keep it in mind,' Grace said. But her mind was on other things. If Clifford saved every penny he earned from now until doomsday, he would never be able to afford a ring like this.

She looked down at it again. Something wasn't right.

* * *

'Coo-ee, Evie, are you in?' Connie shouted up the lobby.

'Come in, Connie,' Evie called, and a moment later Connie let herself into the kitchen, where a play was airing on the Light Programme. 'Come out here, I'm in the back-kitchen.'

'I just wanted to know if you could give me a hand tonight,' Connie asked. 'Grace Harris is going to London for a big audition tomorrow. Ada told Mim she's going to be a big star on the television.'

'Well, nobody round here will see her because they haven't got a television.'

'That's what I said,' Connie answered, 'but guess what? Ada said they were going to buy a brand-new television just to watch their Grace sing.'

'That'll be a treat for them,' Evie said, rolling her eyes. Trust Ada to be the first to get one.

'Bert will sell the telly to the highest bidder. He's flogged Ada's furniture from under her in the past, especially when he needed the price of a pint.'

'She hasn't had it easy with Bert, that's for sure,' Evie answered.

'The family are giving Grace a bit of a send-off in the best end,' Connie said, 'a buffet and everything, Ada's pushing the boat out this time.'

'She might as well, seeing as there isn't going to be the big wedding she had planned for Grace.' Evie was feeding a wet towel through a mangle in the back kitchen, letting the water pour into the white galvanised bowl underneath.

'Mim was so looking forward to wearing her wedding hat,' Connie said, and the two women burst out laughing, recalling Mim's maroon velvet Cavalier hat that she wore to Connie's wedding. It had been the talk of Reckoner's Row. 'Ada called it a monstrosity and vowed never to be seen dead in anything like it.' Tears of mirth ran down Connie's face, 'Ma's steamed the feathers and everything.' She could hardly get the words out as she and Evie were overcome by another bout of laughter that rang round the kitchen.

'Yes, I'll do a couple of hours,' Evie said, folding the wet towel when they had calmed down a bit, knowing she would do anything to help Connie, who had given her more than just a helping hand three years ago. Connie had been her backbone, her strength, *and* her sanity.

* * *

'Sounds like the bloody rent man,' Ada said when she heard a loud ran-tan on the front door.

'I'll get that for you, Mrs Harris,' Susie said. She had decided to call in on her way back from the post office, but Grace wasn't feeling well and was having a lie-down.

Moments later, she rushed into the back-kitchen, where Ada was making pobs – a concoction of stale bread soaked in hot milk and sprinkled with sugar – to keep Grace's strength up for the night ahead. She didn't want anything to spoil Grace's big night.

'I think you'd better come and see.' Susie's eyes were glittering with excitement and Ada sighed, she could do without callers today.

'Can't you see to it for me, Susie? Tell them I'm busy.' Ada stirred the milky mixture.

'I don't think it's a social call.' Susie could see the visitor was in no mood for niceties, and did not want to miss a minute of any impending drama.

'Tell them I'm indispensable. I'm not buying today.'

Susie rolled her eyes to the ceiling. Nobody suffered the way Ada did. 'You mean indisposed, *Mrs Harris*,' Susie said, 'and you're not.'

Ada stopped what she was doing and wiped her hands on her pinny.

'This one says she's not leaving until she gets some answers.' Susie noticed a spark of interest light up Ada's eyes.

'She?' Ada's head was on a swivel and she seemed infused with a new energy. 'She, you say. Out of my way.' Ada nudged Susie out of the way with her elbow. 'I suppose if a job needs doing, I'd better do it meself.' Heading to the door, Ada looked like a cat stalking a mouse and Susie knew her curiosity was an itch that had to be scratched. Suddenly, it seemed like Ada was back to her old, bombastic self.

A woman stood on the top step. She was dressed in a black coat with an astrakhan collar and matching hat, standing straight-backed, like a dancer. Her poise elegant and proud. Perusing the single row of terraced houses, her offended facial expression told its own story.

'You must be Mrs Harris?' the young woman said in a voice that wasn't local. In fact, Susie, who had joined Ada at the front door, would've laid money on it not being familiar to the North West at all.

'I'm Ada Harris,' Ada said importantly, her back ramrod straight, her hands clenched under a buxom bosom. She looked the younger woman up and down. 'What can I do for you?' She hadn't seen this woman before. She would have remembered. But she had a feeling in her bones that the woman was not here on a friendly social visit.

'You are the mother of Grace, I take it?'

'What if I am?' Ada said, giving nothing away. It was a common response to answer a question with a question when probing strangers came calling. For all Ada knew, this woman might be anybody from a debt collector to the authorities, and what they needed to know was nobody's business.

Susie noted the tall, thin woman whose hair, cut into a sharp bob, peeped below the rim of her cloche hat, while on her feet she wore black Mary-Ellen shoes and lisle stockings, reminding her of the pre-war thirties.

The woman, looking down her slim nose under the rim of her hat, eyed Ada with something akin to suspicion. 'You don't know me,' she told her, 'but you do know my husband.'

'And you are?' Ada developed a sociable smile that dissipated when the woman replied.

'My name is Mrs Brack.'

Ada's brows creased in confusion. She'd heard that name before. Brack. Brack? That was the name of Grace's fiancé, wasn't it? Brack wasn't a common name round here.

'Brack, you say?' Ada queried after a moment's pause.

'My husband...'

Ada, aware of the small gasp, spun round as if suddenly remembering Susie was still there and said with a sniff, 'I'll tell Grace you called, Susie.'

She bundled Susie out of the door, looked both ways to make sure no nosy buggers were poking their sticky beaks into her business and ushered Mrs Brack into the lobby before closing the front door, an unheard-of action on a warm, sunny morning in Reckoner's Row – unless you had something to hide.

'Your husband's name?' Ada demanded, steering Mrs Brack into the front room, which was kept neat and tidy for important circumstances such as these, or when the priest called round.

'Clifford... Clifford Brack,' the black-clad woman said, opening her bag. She showed Ada a small photograph and Ada felt herself shrink when her straight back stooped a little.

'You're mistaken!' Ada's annoyance caused a warm glow on her neck and face. 'This is the man who was going to marry my Grace before...' She couldn't tell this woman why the relationship was over, because Grace had given away no details. None at all.

'He is the father of my sons!'

'Clifford isn't married, he can't be!' Ada skewered the other woman with a venomous glare before dropping the black and white photograph like it was hot. 'What's your game, missus?' Ada forced the words through clenched teeth, aware they didn't sound like her own.

'What's all the shouting?' Grace asked, entering into the parlour to see a stranger sitting on the best sofa dabbing her eyes with a linen handkerchief.

Ada gave her daughter a warning glance as Bobby came into the front room, followed by Skinner's dog, Max. Lucy Kilgaren was standing on the top step leaning against the door frame and Grace pushed Bobby out of the room into the narrow passageway.

'Here's two bob, go and get you and Lucy some fish and chips.'

Bobby's eyes lit up, he didn't need telling twice, and in seconds he and Lucy were running towards the steps that led to the top of the bridge and the chip shop.

Sitting on the sofa in the parlour, Grace was overwhelmed by the cloying sweetness of white lilies that her mother insisted made the house smell nice, but which turned Grace's stomach. They reminded her of funerals. But that wasn't the only reason she felt sick.

'Clifford is married?' she whispered, when her mother introduced her to Mrs Brack. 'I knew there was something not right about him,' Grace said, glad now that she hadn't given the cheating toad his ring back. If she was honest with herself, this was the perfect excuse to quell any guilt she had about breaking off their so-called engagement.

'W... what the hell has been going on?' Ada asked and Grace lowered her head. She would like to know, too.

'There's something I have to tell you,' said Mrs Brack, 'and once I've done that, it is completely up to you what you do about it.'

'Look out of that window and tell me what you see,' Susie said when she rushed into the office and headed over to the window, her face alight with expectation.

'I can't see anything,' Evie said, replacing the black telephone receiver after another call to remind their debtors they needed to pay up.

'Any minute now you'll see her.'

'See who?'

Susie had given some fantastic excuses for being late, but she had never acted like this before. Without a word, her back to Evie, she beckoned her over to the window.

'The wife! His wife has only gone and turned up.' Susie's voice was full of glee and she could not hide her excitement when she said, 'There'll be skin and hair flying later.'

'Whose wife?' Evie asked, looking up from her work.

'His wife if you please,' Susie nodded her head. 'Clifford Brack. Married.'

'Never!' Evie's eyes widened. 'Poor Grace.'

'This is a turn-up for the books,' Susie said, and Evie gave her a withering look of disapproval. Did the girl have no heart. Grace might seem as if she had the world at her feet to the other residents of Reckoner's Row, but Evie knew better given what Grace had told her last week, the poor girl's world was falling apart at a rate of knots.

19

Grace knew she was putting her pride on the line when she picked up the receiver in the telephone box outside the Tram Tavern. Her back towards the bridge, her eyes wandered the length of Reckoner's Row, along the dismal detritus strewn canal, across the cobbled street to the row of three-up three-down terraced houses with cold-running water and the lavatory in a tiny shed at the bottom of the back yard.

She wanted more than this.

Having grown up on this street, Grace realised every smoke-filled dingy minute left her yearning for something better. She could not get out fast enough and when her singing career took her all over the world she thought she had everything she ever wanted.

Travel was her escape from a clingy, small-minded mother whose nose was always stuck in some other poor bugger's business. Her life could be anything she wanted it to be. The punters loved her. She had seen most of the world, met people that her mother could only dream of meeting, and Grace had wallowed in the attention, soaked up the adoration, was swept up in the elation of the encores. Loving every moment... But none of it came close to how she felt when she was with the man she genuinely loved.

The ringing tone ended abruptly, and the clipped tones of efficiency gave her a start. 'I am sorry, Mr D'Angelo is out of the office, may I take a message?'

No matter how many times Grace telephoned, the woman at his London office said he was out of town and she did not know when he would be back.

Replacing the receiver, Grace had difficulty swallowing the hard lump in her throat. Her mind jumping from one confused emotion to another. How stupid she had been to believe every word. Not once, but twice. She lowered her head, resting it against the cold wall above the payphone and her limbs felt heavy in defeat. She had lost Bruce. They had their good time. But, she was in no doubt that her *holiday romance* was well and truly over.

What made her believe that Bruce genuinely loved her? Her vanity had, once again, taken her down the wrong path. She had been blind to her own naivete. The realisation filled her with disgust.

Grace really wasn't in the mood for a shindig. But it wasn't going to go away.

All she wanted to do was go home and pull the covers over her head until the whole damn situation went away. 'Gracey girl, you are going to have to face the music and see it through to the finale.'

'Touching...' She nearly jumped out of her skin. Grace hadn't noticed the missing pane of glass that allowed her desperate words to be heard.

'That ring I gave you...' Clifford said looking round, his words low and eager, 'I'll have it back since we're no longer engaged, and the necklace too.'

'Who says I've still got them?' Grace knew quite well the ring was still in her bag back at the house and the necklace was going to adorn her mother when she played hostess at the party tonight.

'Let me explain,' Clifford stepped towards her and Connie moved back. He needed a shave and there were dark circles under his eyes. Even his clothes, usually so immaculate were crumpled – like he'd slept in them. This wasn't the suave, sophisticated man who could command a room full of millionaires, have anything he wanted with the snap of his fingers. This man looked haunted, bedraggled, desperate.

'You got off the ship in Ireland, and nobody saw or heard from you again.'

'I'm not going into that right now, Grace, tell me where the jewels are!' Clifford's tone was sharp and impatient as he glanced at his watch. She knew something was very wrong.

'You're not helping your cause, Clifford,' Grace replied pulling her cardigan round her slim frame like an added layer of protection. Looking at him now, she wondered what she ever saw in him. No longer the naïve starlet who clung to his promises, she had troubles of her own.

'I have to get home,' Grace said knowing she had to get ready for her 'big' night in the Tavern. Tomorrow she was off to London.

'All I want is the ring and the necklace.' Clifford explained as the loud church bell made him jump.

'I've been offered a hundred pounds for them.' Grace wanted to see his reaction. Would he own up about the ring being worth a small fortune?

'I will give you five hundred pounds,' Clifford said.

'You don't look like you have a penny.' Grace's words were tipped with ice.

'You need not concern yourself about that.' Clifford said edging towards her. Grace knew she only had to call if he threatened her in any way, and she would have help in an instant.

'You won't get away with this.' Grace felt her stomach tighten; her mouth dry. But she had no intentions of showing him she was worried.

'I'll be in the Tavern at seven o' clock.' Clifford leaned forward. 'Be there and bring the jewellery.'

'How come it's taken this long to come and claim them?' Grace asked.

'Ask no questions and be told no lies.'

Grace knew that if what his wife told her was true – Clifford was a bigamist who left her with two young boys, and the reason she came to see Grace was to warn her that he had put her in jeopardy when he gave her the jewels, which were not his to give. Unknowingly she had taken contraband through customs. The blood froze in her veins. Grace knew she could spend many years in prison for bringing diamonds into the country without paying duty on them.

'I will meet you in the bar at seven o' clock,' Grace said, 'you can have what you came for, and good riddance.'

* * *

Angus McCrae, landlord of the Tavern, had a nose for a villain since his days in the police force. He was putting a wooden crate of empty beer bottles on top of a stack when he recognised Grace's voice, and he paused, hardly daring to breath. He had heard every word and having been asked to keep his ear to the ground with regard to contraband being brought through the port, his investigative antennae twitched, and he knew he was in the presence of a crook.

Angus listened as a pair of male footsteps retreated down the alleyway. That meant Grace was still outside the gate.

'Grace,' Angus whispered beckoning her with his index finger, 'can I have a word?'

* * *

'You're late.' Grace's brittle tone sailed through the thick smoky air and even though every door was open to the evening breeze, the air inside the Tavern was still hot, thick, and uncomfortably sticky. Grace sat near the door so she could see Clifford as soon as he walked in. He still needed a shave but at least he looked as if he'd washed and Grace told him she had already ordered, nodding to Connie, who brought over a tray containing a glass of lemonade, a pint of beer and a small whisky chaser. It wasn't what Clifford was used to, but beggars could not be choosers.

'Thanks, Connie,' Grace said thinking Connie looked uncomfortable in the sixth month of pregnancy.

Even lifting the wooden flap of the bar was an effort for Connie who nodded to a couple of customers at the far end. Every night this week their sleep had been interrupted by the telephone ringing in the middle of the night. If it carried on much longer she was going to complain to the Post Office. Clifford looked over his shoulder before downing the whisky in one gulp. The bar was almost empty as it was too early for Grace's guests to arrive but just then Evie came in, lifted her hand in a little wave before taking off her cardigan and slipping behind the bar to relieve Connie who disappeared upstairs for a well-earned break before the party started. Except for a couple of dockers and a sleeping drunk on the next table, there were no other customers.

'Have you got the ring and the necklace?' Clifford asked, 'I'm in a hurry.'

'Have your pint,' Grace nodded to the golden liquid, 'relax. I'm not going to get rare pink diamonds out in the middle of the bar now, am I?'

'Who said they were rare?' Clifford's brows puckered and Grace shrugged.

'I looked it up in a book,' Grace said showing no emotion. 'Bruce dismissed you in Ireland. You didn't have time to collect your contraband, is that it?'

'In a nutshell.' Clifford said as if talking to a child who didn't quite understand. 'I knew you'd do a far better job of getting the sparklers into the country than me.'

'You knew Bruce would escort me off the ship,' she said, and he nodded.

'Being the son of one of the richest men in the world,' Clifford added, 'Bruce wasn't going to get stopped by customs.'

'You went on the run?' Grace asked, understanding the reason for his tatty appearance.

'You're not a dumb as I thought you were.' The ropey veins in Clifford's neck stood out, and he scowled, his lips pinched. Sitting back in his chair, he pulled out an untipped cigarette. 'When the diamond merchant offered you all that money, you should have took it.' His eye looked past her rather than at her, keeping an eye on the door, 'You could have made yourself a nice little nest egg.'

'How did you know I had the jewellery valued?' Grace asked.

'I followed you. I have contacts in every major city,' Clifford said, 'and now I have come to collect. That con man only offered a fraction of what the diamonds were worth.'

Grace could not believe Clifford could call anybody a con man. 'You didn't think twice about putting me in danger.' Her voice sounded calmer than she actually felt.

'I'll send you a little something for your trouble.' Clifford was as cocksure as ever.

'I don't want your tainted money.'

Clifford's posture was stiff and unyielding as he took another long drag of his cigarette. 'Hand them over. You can't keep them.'

'I don't want them.' Her voice sounded determined and Grace

took a deep breath, putting in place the same tactics she used to combat the stage fright she had suffered on a nightly basis.

As he ground out his cigarette, she picked up her handbag, his eyes watching every move. Grace had persuaded her mother to part with the necklace by telling her it was fake and that she would buy her a real diamond necklace when she signed her new contract.

'I never took you to be an international jewel thief,' Grace said with more than a hint of mockery in her voice. 'A louse, a two-timing rat, but a jewel thief? Now that is a first. I've never dated one of them before.' She slid the necklace and ring across the table, her insides jumping, she felt queasy.

'There's a first time for everything.' Clifford, taking another cigarette, lowered his gaze to light it.

When he lifted his eyes again, he was surrounded by uniforms. Police uniforms. And at that moment the sleeping drunk in the corner lifted his head, took off his greasy flat cap and stood beside the officers – it was Angus. It did not take much for him to persuade Grace to help the police with their enquiries. She jumped at the chance.

'Clifford Jeremy Brack, I am arresting you for smuggling in international waters, you do not have to say anything...' The police inspector accompanied by uniformed officers quickly overpowered Clifford and snapped handcuffs on his wrists.

'You tricked me!'

'Not nearly as bad as you tricked me,' Grace replied. Glad to see Clifford get his comeuppance. Did he actually think she was going to protect him after what he had done? She hoped he would rot in gaol. It was no less than he deserved.

* * *

The evening was in full swing and Grace even got up to the piano and sang a couple of duets with the locals. She looked fabulous in pale blue with a waspy white belt accentuating her tiny waist in layer upon layer of calf-length tulle and was glad her years of performing had taught her to not only hide a broken heart but also wear a sparkling smile when she felt like dying. But she couldn't let her mother down. Ada had gone to a lot of trouble and called in many favours to put on a fabulous spread.

'I just need to go and powder my nose,' Grace excused herself and made her way to the Ladies.

'Oops, one too many?' Evie asked when she heard heavy retching behind the door of the ladies' toilet in the Tram Tavern.

'Probably,' Grace said between heaves and Evie's eyebrows rose when she recognised the voice. She had been brought up by seafarers. Her mother had been a stewardess on ocean liners before she married Da. They could certainly hold their drink. And Grace hadn't had any alcohol, as far as she was aware. The family had only been in half an hour and Grace hadn't had anything stronger than a lemonade. And she ought to know, she served Danny with their round. 'Maybe it's something you ate. I'll go and get you a glass of water.'

Grace heard the creak of the door hinges, telling her she was alone once more.

'Please make it stop,' she prayed as another searing pain gripped her and bent her double. When she was able, she clutched the waistband of her drawers, pulled them down and hit the wooden toilet seat with a thump. 'Oh dear God. No!' she gasped. The white gusset was now stained bright red. 'I'm going to die,' she said aloud, unaware of the creaking hinge of the outside door.

'Grace, Grace are you okay?' Evie's voice was full of concern and

Grace pressed her lips between her teeth, careful not to call out, knowing her own voice would sound painfully distorted. But she could not hold on to the involuntary urge to push and let out a groan that, even to her own ears, sounded inhuman. Her mind no longer able to comprehend the passion and love that had created this terrible situation. This pain was her penance for loving a man she could never have.

'Grace?' Evie's unease threaded her voice, sounding far-off to Grace, who could barely think straight. She needed help. But she couldn't stand to open the door. 'Grace...? Grace can you let me in?'

'Evie...' Grace didn't recognise her own voice. 'Get Connie. I need some help, here.'

Evie didn't like to leave Grace when she sounded so frightened. So, grabbing the chair that was set aside by the sink, Evie pushed it up against the lavatory door and climbed on it. Looking over the top of the door, she could see Grace sitting on the toilet, her head buried in the crook of her folded arms against the wall.

'Jesus, Mary and Joseph,' Evie whispered a quick prayer, her voice trailing to nothing. She knew exactly what that red gash of colour meant. She had seen the same thing when her mother lost a baby after Lucy. 'I'll go and get her now!'

Susie craned her neck, looking round the best end of the Tavern. People were packed like sardines and it was hard to see past the first group of revellers. She had been lucky to get a seat near the window, being moved from side to side in time to the strains of 'Roll out The Barrel'. When the singing stopped for a little while, Susie drummed her long fingernails on the table, fanning herself with a beer mat, her rigid shoulders getting tighter as her tension grew. She had been sitting here forever and there was still no sign of

Grace who had disappeared into the lavatory ages ago. Who asks someone out and then ignores them completely to gasbag with her 'audience' in the lavatory!

Danny was talking to Angus, the landlord, and the plink-plonk of piano keys showed everybody was having a whale of a time, except Susie. She felt like a spare part, perched on the end of the red, leather-covered banquette. She was in two minds whether to go home. She couldn't hear a word of conversation over the singing and if she stayed here much longer, she was sure to die of neglect.

'Susie, what are you having?' Danny asked, coming over with a tray full of drinks.

'About time too,' she said under her breath, but instead of firing a quick retort, she smiled. 'I'll have what Grace is having,' she said, noticing Evie Kilgaren beckoning Connie towards the ladies'. After waiting another ten minutes for her drink, she was not in the best of mood when she tasted the lemonade. 'What's this?' she asked Danny.

'You said to get you whatever Grace is having,' Danny said apologetically, and with still no sign of Grace, Susie decided she had waited long enough. Picking up her bag and cardigan, she squeezed through the throng of men and headed to the door. Not one person said goodnight or persuaded her to stay as she hoped they would. When she saw Grace, she was going to give her a piece of her mind.

* * *

'Connie's here now, Grace, hold on!' Evie's voice sounded calm, but inside she felt anything but.

'I don't think I can hold...' Grace whimpered as Connie took a bunch of keys from the pocket of her smock and pushed the key into the lock of the lavatory door.

'Hold on, love, I'm just going to open the door,' Connie said as the door swung open. 'All right, love,' Connie said when she saw Grace who was by now sitting on the linoleum floor in a pool of her own blood, 'we'll have you safe in no time.' She turned quickly to Evie and whispered, 'Go and ring an ambulance! She needs more help than I can give her.'

Evie was gone before she finished talking.

Grace was issuing low groans and Connie lifted her wrist to check her pulse.

'Grace, you have to tell me before anybody gets here,' Connie ordered, 'did you go and see anybody else after you came to see me?' She knew desperation could drive many a girl to take drastic and sometimes fatal action. She could see that Grace did not have the strength to speak and she tried to shake her head, but lifting it slightly it fell back and lolled to one side.

The cramped cubicle was growing cold, but Grace was loath to move because she felt wet. She wanted to go home. Get into bed. Everything would be all right once she was in bed. She tried to stand, but her legs gave way and she banged her head on the wall. Somebody was holding her shoulders and she must have wet herself but didn't have the strength to look as the warmth spread between her legs. It felt good. The pain was gone.

'Hold on, Gracey, love. Open your eyes, darling. Open your eyes.' Someone was patting her cheek.

Stop it!

More warm wetness. Gushing behind her knees.

I didn't go to anybody else, Connie. I didn't.

'Grace, tell me, love, have you taken anything. A tablet? Medicine? Anything?'

Connie, listen. I told you already. Although Grace thought she was speaking loud and clear, no words came from her lips.

'It will help if we know before you get to the hospital.'

Hospital? What for?

'If the ambulance doesn't get here soon...' The deep-set frown on Connie's face told its own tale, and Evie's suspicions that Grace might not make it were cemented when Connie whispered. 'This is bad.'

Oh Bruce... None of this should have happened... What will me mam say? It doesn't matter now... I'm falling... It's going dark... She drifted into oblivion.

'I'll go and get Ada,' Evie said. 'She should know.'

'Don't tell her what's happened, keep her outside. We don't want her to see this.' Connie nodded to the blood, which had spread across the floor.

Evie hurried over to Ada's table as the singing stopped, and the clink of beer glasses fell silent. An unusual hush descended when two uniformed ambulance men cut through the swarm of happy drinkers.

'What's going on, here?' Ada asked, rising from her seat.

'Ada, don't panic, but your Grace is not a bit well, and we had to call an ambulance.'

'What sort of "not well"?' Ada looked indignant. 'And why didn't somebody come and get me before they turned up?' She nodded to one of the ambulance men guarding the door so nobody could enter the ladies'.

'I don't know,' Evie lied for the sake of discretion. 'She had a pain in her stomach. Connie thinks it's for the best.' That was all she was prepared to say on the matter as Ada pushed her way over to the medic.

'That's my Grace in there,' she said, 'so you've got to let me in.'

'Sorry, madam, no can do,' the medic said emphatically, and Evie could see Ada was going to get nowhere here. She'd seen his type before. The uniform's word was law. It must be all that military training during the war, she thought. The power went to their head.

Ada went and sat at the nearest table. Someone brought her a brandy for the shock, and she downed it in one gulp.

'My poor girl,' she wailed when another brandy arrived and was gone as quickly as the first one had. 'She could be at death's door and I am out here, hapless. If you give me a subscription I can take it to the chemist.'

'No, missus, a prescription will do her no good in this case.' The medic stretched a little taller, 'My colleague will be doing everything he possibly can.'

'It's gonna be a tight fit round that corner by the door, Fred,' said the navy-blue uniformed medic, 'you'll have to get a chair.'

'Make sure she is well covered,' Connie said as she padded Grace with towels to stop blood seeping when the ambulance men put Grace on the chair, then, cocooned her in a red, woollen blanket. She followed them to the door of the Tavern, along with every other customer, while, probably with the help of copious brandies, Ada fainted clean away. But Connie left her to sleep it off as the ambulance took Grace to the hospital.

* * *

'Bruce...' The enormous effort for Grace to speak left her sinking into a deep black hole, her voice barely a whisper, 'Bruce...'

She was being moved and there was a strong smell of disinfectant. She wanted to get up, but couldn't. Bound by something rigid. She could hear the sound of running feet. People were talking in urgent voices. Grace could not understand the tangle of orders being fired like shots from a machine gun. She started to shiver. Her body shaking uncontrollably. Somebody grabbed her wrist and held it tightly.

'Sharp scratch!' A deep pain in her thigh and the voices receded.

* * *

'Grace... Grace, honey. I'm here...' His voice sounded far off in the distance. 'I went to meet you at the station.'

Grace felt a tear roll down her cheek, but she could not form the words she wanted so desperately to say. 'The woman wouldn't let me speak to you...' Her thoughts were muddled. She could not focus on why she was here. When Grace opened her eyes she was alone, lying in the darkness. And Bruce was not here.

Grace heard his voice again as bright sunshine pierced her eyelids. There was another. A woman's voice, whispery and incoherent. Her eyes felt glued shut and the strong smell of disinfectant told Grace she was not at home. She was lying down. Her toes rubbing the stiff sheet binding her tightly to the bed. She could not turn.

Slowly and with great effort Grace forced her eyelids open. But the white tiled room was too bright, and she quickly closed them again. She saw Bruce but knew he wasn't there.

Somebody was holding her hand, stroking her fingers. It tickled and she pulled her hand away. 'Shh, shh, shh.' The gentle rhythm of ocean waves lulled her.

'It's going to be okay, Grace.' His voice sounded so clear she could imagine Bruce sitting next to her. 'I'm going to take care of you.' A smile stretched her dry lips.

'You are my dream...,' she whispered, 'one I don't want to wake from.' She stretched her hands and felt her little finger being caught in a gentle tug. A touch she would never forget.

'My Bruce,' she whispered, 'my darling Bruce.' Somewhere in the distance she could hear a bell and she surrendered herself to a dream...

* * *

'Please wait outside, sir, madam.' The nurse's tone was efficient, her words spoken with some determination as she urged Bruce and Ada out of the ward. Ada sat on the wooden bench outside, while Bruce traipsed back and forth along the shiny floor of the long corridor, each thinking the same thing for completely different reasons. Ada needed her daughter to live. She needed answers. Grace must have known she was in the family way. She had been five months gone. And not a mention. It was little wonder she had not been her usual self when she came home. And who was this American chap, who turned up at the hospital and was sitting by her daughter's bed when she arrived. He had tried talking to Ada when she entered the clinically white side-room, but she was not here to chew the fat with strangers. Then that nurse came in and ordered them outside.

'Bloody cheek!' Ada muttered, loudly blowing her nose on a white handkerchief made from an old bed sheet.

Bruce could not keep still. His thoughts were tripping over themselves to get attention. But he could not focus on any one thing except his beloved Grace.

He had been only moments away from being with his father when he took his last breath. Bruce tried to call Grace many times. But nobody answered. He had to see her. Explain. But before he could do that, he needed to go back to the States. His father was buried in Arlington Cemetery with full military honours, for service to the American Navy during World War One and Two.

As sole heir to the D'Angelo fortune, Bruce had spent weeks going through his father's papers with lawyers and shareholders. He was in America for nearly a month, locked into meetings and itineraries that took him from one end of The United States to the other.

'So, did you work with my Gracey?' Ada asked as she stuffed the handkerchief into her pocket. Her head felt as if it were bursting and she would give every penny she possessed for a cup of tea.

'No, I didn't work with her,' Bruce said realising he had not introduced himself to Grace's Mom. 'I am Bruce D'Angelo, I...'

'Oh I'm sorry, I didn't know.' Ada stood up and almost dipped a small curtsey, but her drink-sodden brain would not allow for the dipping of knees. 'You're her boss!' Bruce tried to explain, but Ada was in full flow.

'It was a terrible shock, you know,' she said, not letting Bruce get a word in until she'd had her say. 'One minute she was right as ninepence, the whole Tavern was in raptures with her singing, they couldn't get enough of her.'

'I'm not surprised,' said Bruce, 'she has the voice of an angel. You must be so proud.'

'Proud is not the word,' Ada explained, 'I'm more than proud, I'm inflated.' She lowered her voice. 'Then without any warning, she took bad with her appendages, and the landlady of the Tavern had to call an ambulance – I was overcome, as you can imagine, and nearly needed an ambulance, myself.' Ada was getting into her stride when a young nurse came out and told her she could go in to see her daughter, but only for a short while.

'I'll tell her you called Mister D'Angelo.' She held out her hand. 'Nice to meet you.' Bruce shook Ada's hand and went to find the matron. Wild horses were not going to keep him away from Grace.

Later, Bruce watched Ada walk, straight-backed out of the hospital. As soon as she was out of sight he snook into the side ward where Grace was lying with her eyes closed. He stood in the doorway, watching her take a breath with such force it shook her whole body. Bruce could not keep his distance as the nurse urged him to when he saw the tears run down Grace's beautiful face even though her eyes were still closed. He moved forward and the ward door with its porthole window gave a small squeak as it closed.

'Don't upset yourself, Mam.' Grace said in a groggy voice, 'just let me sleep.'

'Oh my darling Grace,' Bruce was by her side in a couple of strides. 'When you are better, I am going to take you away and make you strong again.'

'Go away, Bruce,' Grace said as a tear ran down her cheeks, 'I know you are not here.'

'I am here, my darling, and I will never leave you again. I can't live without you.'

Grace could not focus, her eyes filling with happy tears when he took her in his arms.

'I am so sorry you had to go through that, honey,' Bruce said. 'But I am going to make it up to you.'

'I think I am still dreaming,' she managed a half-hearted smile but the effort was too much and Grace closed her eyes. Bruce was here. She should be the happiest woman in the world. But how could she be? She had lost the child she was carrying. Bruce's child.

20

Evie had been swamped in the tangle of accounts for weeks. She was proud of the work she had done getting everything in order, but there was still one outstanding payment that could not be attributed to the business account. There was not one single receipt for the money that was still going out regularly every month since 1947.

Was Mr Skinner still paying the blackmailer? After all he had been through, he still had this worry hanging over him.

She looked up at the clock. Nine thirty, and Susie was still not in the office.

Evie caught sight of her assistant through the window. Susie was strolling along Summer Settle like she had all the time in the world. *And why not*, she asked herself, *when she's got a mug like me to do all the work.*

By the time Susie arrived in the office after a cheery good morning to the lads in the yard, and a little natter to Meggie, who was bringing some letters over, Susie was another fifteen minutes late.

'Meggie kept me talking, you know she likes a good natter,'

Susie said, removing her lemon cardigan and putting it on the back of her chair before she put the letters on Evie's desk. 'These are for you to sort out. The new postman delivered them to the house by mistake.'

'Just leave them there, I'll get round to them in a minute,' Evie said, studying the figures, while Susie went straight out to the staffroom to put the kettle on.

'Tea?' Susie popped her head out of the door.

'Never mind tea,' Evie said, reaching for the first envelope, 'you're late enough as it is.' The first was an electric bill. The next one was handwritten, addressed to Mr H. Skinner at the business address, so she thought nothing of slicing open the envelope, but she was not prepared for what she read. It was another demand for payment, and the amount was substantial. The usual time and the usual place, it said, and Evie looked at the plain white envelope. The postmark said Netherford.

She pondered on what to do next, knowing the Netherford farmer's invoice was paid regularly, on time, every month. This was something different.

'I'll be going with Danny today,' Susie said, putting a cup of tea onto her desk. 'I go every month if you remember.'

'I remember,' Evie said, knowing Susie always made an extra effort to look nice when she was going out with Danny, and she was vaguely aware that was Susie's reason for being late this morning. Her thoughts still on the letter, Evie decided a change of plan was in order. 'But not today, you're not.'

'Why not?' Susie's pencilled brows furrowed, and she speared Evie with a direct glare. 'I go every time. I collect the accounts and...' Susie could hardly tell Evie about the time she went to Netherford when she went to the post office and clearly heard Bert Harris's voice. He was not pleased when she stepped in to see once again that he was in the process of collecting money from the

Skinner account and Bert had paid her to keep shtum after telling her why Mr Skinner was paying him. Who would have thought it? Bert Harris would do something so nasty as to blackmail a member of his own family.

'And what?' Evie asked.

'Nothing,' Susie said quickly. 'It doesn't matter.' She savagely hauled her chair across the linoleum and dragged the cover off her typewriter. Thumping each letter with such ferocity, Evie imagined the top of her head would spout steam like a boiling kettle. Susie suddenly stopped typing and her head shot up. 'I always go,' she said stabbing the desk with a crimson fingernail. 'Every month. Rain, hail or sunshine.'

'Well, not today,' Evie said, keeping her voice even. 'Anyway, out of curiosity, can you tell me why you have to go?' Susie was hiding something, she could tell.

'I can't say,' Susie answered quickly, too quickly.

Evie cocked her head to one side, like she always did when she was trying to work something out, and she was silent for a moment. Susie was making a right song and dance about not being able to go to Netherford. Was it because she would miss out on a day's skiving on such a beautiful day like this: when the sun was shining, and the sky was the colour of a baby boy's matinee jacket? Or was there more to it? A thought popped unwillingly into Evie's head. Surely not? But the thought niggled, refusing to go away. Was Susie writing those letters to Mr Skinner?

But she had no time to ponder when the telephone rang. It was Danny, to say that Grace was going to be fine. He nipped round to the hospital first thing.

'Give Grace my good wishes when she's up to receiving visitors,' Evie said before replacing the handset.

'What was that about Grace?' Susie asked, curious as ever.

'Oh, you don't know, do you?' Evie said, wondering how Susie managed to miss the sirens and flashing lights. 'You left early.' Her words were loaded with accusation. How could she have left Grace like that when she was supposed to be her best friend?

'I'd been sitting on my own while Grace was in the lav chin-wagging,' Susie replied, most put-out. 'She'd been gone ages, I felt like a spare part.'

'Did it not occur to you to go and see what was keeping her?' Evie asked, disgusted that this girl who claimed to be such a good friend to Grace and her family would think of storming out of the Tavern with her knickers in a twist.

'I'm not her keeper.' Susie's lip curled upward. 'She's a big girl, she can find her own way back from the lavatory.'

'Did you not consider the possibility that she might not be well?' Evie could feel her blood pressure going through the top of her head. How could anybody be so selfish?

'Grace is never well, she's always got something to moan about, if it's not sunburn then it's a broken nail or—'

'This is much more serious than a broken fingernail, Susie.' Evie glared at the girl who was still gazing out of the window watching the stable lads working. 'Grace was rushed to hospital last night. She needed an emergency operation.'

'What?' Susie's head whipped round, and she was suddenly attentive. Leaning forward on her desk, she was all ears. 'Why, what happened!?'

'I found her on the floor in the ladies', she had collapsed and was writhing in agony.'

'What? When? Oh my God!' Susie jumped up from her chair.

'It's a bit late for you to do anything now,' Evie said. She had promised Danny she would not give away the truth of why Grace had been admitted to hospital as an emergency.

'She had appendicitis. The surgeons operated through the night.' Evie made it sound as sombre as she could, knowing Susie was hanging on to every word. She would never stoop to such levels under normal circumstances, but she knew Susie needed to be taken down a peg or two and understand the world did not revolve around her, as she had always been led to believe by her domineering parents. 'Danny and I stayed all night waiting for results. It was touch-and-go at one stage. They had to give the poor girl a blood transfusion.'

Evie felt a hint of satisfaction in the look of horror on Susie's face when she realised she had got the situation spectacularly wrong.

'You spent the whole night with Danny?' Susie chose her words carefully, Evie could tell, and she nodded.

'I didn't get into bed until the early hours,' Evie said, giving a small yawn, 'although, the way I'm feeling now it was hardly worth the bother.' She could not judge if Susie's face had turned the colour of putty because she had let her friend down, or if it was because Evie had spent the night in a hospital corridor with Danny. Telling Susie that her friend had been rushed into hospital with appendicitis would save Grace's reputation at least.

'Nobody told me,' Susie answered, most put-out. 'I thought Danny would've let me know, seeing as Grace is my best friend.'

'I suppose he had other things on his mind,' Evie answered. 'Grace still isn't out of danger. But don't worry, she has somebody with her.' Evie suppressed another yawn. She was owed a couple of hours for coming in on Sunday, so she was leaving early.

'I have to go and see her,' Susie said, pushing back her chair so hard it fell over and, not even stopping to pick it up, she headed towards the door.

'There's no point,' Evie offered, 'only one person is allowed in her private room and that's Bruce.'

'The millionaire?' Susie said. 'She mentioned him a couple of times, but I never thought they were that close.'

'Really?' Evie said, 'I thought you knew everything there was to know about the Harris's family, but obviously not.'

'I didn't say I knew everything,' Susie was still reeling from the knowledge that Evie had been Danny's shoulder to lean on when it should have been her. If Evie weren't the office manager, she would tell her exactly what she thought.

'Bruce is taking care of Grace. He said he has nurses and doctors on hand and when she is feeling up to it, he will have Grace moved to a private nursing home in the countryside.'

'If I'd known, I would have helped her, you know I would,' Susie said to Evie. 'What will Danny think of me? You can't keep news like this quiet,' Susie said, lighting another cigarette, blowing a long stream of dissatisfaction.

'Ada made sure Grace had everything she ever wanted. Nothing was too good for her only daughter.' The gleam in Susie's eye was malicious. 'And now she's fallen on her feet again with a bloody millionaire! Some people have all the luck.' Her voice had turned to ice, and Evie realised Susie's anger was the result of her own sense of entitlement as Susie sucked in a long shuddering breath of injustice. 'I'll never get out of Reckoner's Row.'

Evie was more than ever convinced Susie had no compassionate bones in her body.

'Shouldn't you be doing something useful, like working for a living?' Evie asked stiffly when Susie's long nails were tap... tap... tapping the desk, aggravating Evie like a stone in her shoe and setting her teeth on edge.

'Are you trying to provoke me?' Evie asked, her patience worn thin. And Susie had the gall to look innocently surprised.

'Who? Me?' She stopped tapping.

'Yes, you,' Evie answered without lifting her head from the row of figures. If the other girl did as much work as she was supposed to do, she would have no time for drumming her nails on desks. Susie continued, ignoring Evie's glare from the other desk. 'I need those files today, Susie,' Evie said, following a long vertical row of figures with her fingertips.

When Susie opened her mouth to speak again, she shot her a glare so sharp, Susie said nothing and got to work, and Evie was relieved when the only sound in the room was the tick of the clock and the clack of the typewriters.

Five minutes later, Evie drew in a lungful of air and rolled her eyes. She wanted these figures signed off before she left the office. It had been a long night at the hospital and her hand shot out, gripping the weighty black receiver as she removed a clip-on earring and answered the ringing telephone.

'Good morning, Skinner and Son... How may I...'

'Hello, Cinderella – I just wanted to say thank you for staying with me last night?'

Evie felt an exhilarated burst of energy and dropped the pen she was holding. Retrieving the pen before it rolled off the desk, the office was suddenly hot and airless, and the silence on the other end of the line told her that Danny Harris was waiting for her to say something. And by the questioning expression on Susie's face, so was she. Evie took a deep breath.

'Oh hello,' she said brightly, reviving her docile response by sitting upright and sounding more business-like, 'what can I do for you?' She averted her gaze, not looking in Susie's direction.

'You were a real pal, waiting up so late.' Danny's voice sounded deep and warm and intimate.

'It was nothing,' Evie tried to keep her tone light, she didn't want Susie to know Danny had walked her home when they were given the good news that Grace was out of theatre and the procedure had gone well. She was sure it was not her imagination, recalling his arm lingering longer than was necessary when he draped his still warm jacket round her shoulders. But her mind wasn't playing tricks when she relived the moment when he leaned in and kissed her cheek.

'Thank you for making the long night bearable.' Danny's voice sounded different, warmer, and Evie tried to keep the conversation light because Susie was watching her like a cat ready to pounce.

'Think nothing of it,' Evie said, rolling the pencil between finger and thumb.

'Susie's in the office, earwigging, isn't she?' Evie could hear the smile in Danny's voice, and she nodded even though he couldn't see her.

'Yes. Yes, that's correct,' she said. 'It is good of you to call and let me know.'

'Oh,' Danny said lightly, 'if you are wondering where the flat-back is, I took it first thing for a dockside delivery, I'll be back soon.'

'Oh... okay, I would have assumed that was the case if I'd known it was gone.' Danny was the only one who used the flat-back truck.

'And just one other thing... I really, really wanted to hear your voice,' Danny said and Evie, pitying her poor ribs being pummelled by her racing heart, turned the small gasp in to a cough, making a stab at a more professional approach and failing.

'Well, that's just wonderful...' she replied. 'I will expect the wagon back this morning.'

He doesn't need your permission. Fool.

'See you later,' Danny said, and Evie heard the pips going on the other end of the line and took a deep breath. Back to business. Daydreaming was for later.

'Susie, I need you to go along to the slaughterhouse and pick up this month's invoices. They are long overdue. You were supposed to chase them up last week.'

'I'm not going to the slaughterhouse,' Susie's eyes were round as side plates, and her defiance was wearing Evie's patience. 'Why do I have to go?'

'You don't,' Evie said. Enough was enough. If this were her business, Susie would have been long gone. So why should she allow her to stay, sucking the life out of Mr Skinner's business. She was fed up to the back teeth with Susie's hostility. Evie was the one running this office, putting the long hours in. Bringing everything up to date had been a long hard slog and she felt she was carrying Susie. Well not any more! Susie was a hindrance with her lazy ways and arrogant put-downs. 'There are plenty of girls out there who could do your job, and now that I think about it, they would be far less trouble.'

'You're sacking me!' Susie's jaw dropped. 'Well, we'll soon see about that Miss High and Mighty. I know things about this place and I'm not afraid to tell all.'

'You do what you have to do, Susie.' Evie was too tired to care. 'But know this, Mr and Mrs Skinner are well respected in this town, whereas you are just a petty troublemaker who needs to grow up and stand on her own two feet. Get your head out of the clouds and stow the veiled threats – nobody is listening.' She opened the office door just as Danny arrived. 'Your cards will be in the post. Goodbye Susie.'

'You haven't heard the last of this,' Susie threatened as she collected her handbag from her desk. 'You'll be sorry.'

'I am sure I won't be,' Evie said as Susie crossed the office floor and glared at Danny.

'And you... You...' Susie was obviously lost for words, looking for someone to blame. But she had nobody to blame but herself, Evie thought as Susie stormed out, slamming the door behind her.

'I thought you were on the dock?' Evie said, confused as Danny stood in front of her with a twinkle in his eyes. He told her he rang from the 'phone box outside the Tram Tavern.

'What was all that about?' Danny asked, perching on the edge of Susie's desk, and when Evie told him, he shook his head, giving her cause to think she had done the wrong thing, but she couldn't be more mistaken.

'It was a long time coming,' Danny said, 'you had more patience than most.'

'They stayed at the hospital until Grace came out of theatre,' Ada told Susie, both dabbing their eyes with a handkerchief. 'She looked really ill. I would have changed places in a heartbeat,' Ada wailed. 'Everything I have done has been for my girl, nothing but the best for my Gracie. My only daughter.' She looked over to her husband, sitting at the table, his head in his hands. If looks could kill, he would have been six feet under. 'To think, my Gracie has travelled round the world and not a scratch, not a sniffle. Then she comes back here and in a crowded room, surrounded by people who processed to love her...'

'I think you mean *profess* to love her, Mam.' Ada's crushing glance told Bobby she was in no mood to be corrected.

'She must have felt so alone.' Ada, mindful about giving too much away, saw Susie's suspicious eyes narrow and she said, 'Poisoned by her own appendages.'

'I should have been with Danny,' Susie said. 'Holding his hand, keeping him company.'

'Mm,' Ada, not so distracted, said in a voice loud enough for all to hear, 'that's all he needs, a simpering drama queen.'

The single-bed ward was quiet when Bruce crept in to see Grace still sleeping off the effect of the anaesthetic. She looked the most beautiful woman he had ever seen. So serene, so pale, so still.

'My darling, I am so sorry I wasn't here when you needed me most,' he whispered, holding her hand in both of his and gently kissing her fingers. He was beside himself with worry. If she did not pull through, he would never forgive himself. All that worry and pressure she had to endure alone. He had not yet told her his father had died, and that he had to go back to the States to tie up business loose ends.

If she didn't pull through... Bruce did not even feel the tears running in rivulets down his suntanned face. He could think only of her recovery.

'I will make sure you are never hurt again, my love. I love you so, so much. Please, don't you leave me too.'

He didn't know how long he had been sitting beside her bed, stroking her face, her hair, her hands. Willing her to wake up. He watched the sun rise and beam in through the window and when it shone on her face, Grace moved her head, her beautiful, gentle eyes slowly opening to see Bruce sitting in the chair beside her bed.

'What happened?' she asked not recalling she had seen him earlier, her voice thick from the anaesthetic. Then everything came flooding back and her tears fell too. Bruce held her in his strong arms and they both vented their grief together.

'I love you so much my darling,' he said, 'I was so scared I would lose you.'

'I love you,' Grace answered, 'I thought I had lost you too.'

'Never, never, never,' Bruce said with such depth of feeling she knew he meant it. 'When you are feeling stronger, I will take you away and we will talk everything through, but for now, you must get your strength back. I am going nowhere.'

* * *

'Grace is not feeling well, and I don't want her disturbed,' Ada

Harris told Susie, who felt she should come and visit her best friend every chance she got. 'The doctor will only allow two visitors at a time, because she needs her rest.'

'What about the fete, Mrs Harris? Will she still be going?' Susie knew her friend's life was touch-and-go for a while and a day out in the countryside was just the ticket she needed to cheer her up. Also, she didn't fancy going on her own, not now that Danny had lost all interest.

'Having your appendages taken out is not a walk on water, you know, Susie.' Ada was fully aware her daughter had lost the child she had been carrying but had put the story about that Grace had to have her appendix taken out. 'Grace needed a blood transfer and everything.' Ada's misuse of her words was more acute when she was worried or upset, although she had no intentions of letting Susie, who had a mouth as big as the Mersey Tunnel, know that her only daughter had been in the family way and lost the baby. Susie would have spread the news quicker than the blink of an eye and filled their neighbours' mouths in no time. Friend or no friend.

Bert, embarrassed by the whole thing, had taken solace in the Tavern and he made every excuse he could think of to get out of the house. Not that he needed much of an excuse.

'Bruce is taking her away for a few weeks' rest and reciprocation to get over the operation.' Ada knew she would never be able to show her face in the Row again if the news got out. Her Grace would be a social piranha, an outcast, Bert had said. Ada had cut him off at the quick, deciding, the time had come to close ranks. 'As far as anybody's concerned, our Grace was rushed into hospital with poisoned appendages.' The truth would soon be lost when news of her new rich man seeped into the public domain.

* * *

'Evie, will you add this invoice to the Skellen farm account,' Danny said when he entered the office, 'I forgot to give it to you when I was here earlier.'

Evie had worked tirelessly to bring the office files up to date, making it known that all bills must be handed in to her before the end of the working day. The system had worked extremely well in bringing to light a few worrying discrepancies concerning the accounts.

21

JUNE

'Mam, my face hurts,' Bobby was trying to have a day off school, Ada could tell. It was the end-of-term tests and he didn't want to do them; she was sure.

'Don't come the old tin soldier with me, Bobby Harris 'Ada said, 'I know your game. You've got a school test.'

'But it's killing me, Mam,' Bobby said, holding his jaw. 'I won't be able to think straight.'

'You can beg 'til the cows come home blue in the face, but you're going in.' She knew when her kids were up to something, and Bobby wasn't pulling the wool over her eyes.

'What's wrong with our Bobby?' Danny asked as he picked up his flask and headed towards the door.

'He's trying to wangle a day off school because he's got tests all week,' Ada said clearing the table, she had an important errand to run and she wanted the place tidy when she got back. 'He must think I was born yesterday, so I sent him to school with his head between his legs.'

'I bet that was awkward,' Danny was going to correct her but thought better of it when he saw the determined look on her face.

'Right-o, don't forget I'm going to Netherford today, so I won't be home for me dinner.'

'I have to go out today too,' Ada said, 'I've left some money on the sideboard for Bobby's dinner, he can go to the chippy today.'

'Where are you going Ma?' Danny asked conversationally, 'anyone I know?'

'That's for me to know,' Ada said, 'and you to mind your own business.'

'Sorry I asked,' Danny said. He'd had this conversation a thousand times and it never ended well. His mother had a little jaunt every month and told nobody where she went.'

'So, poor Susie got the push,' Ada said changing the subject, 'you should take her to the pictures. Cheer her up a bit.'

'I'm not taking anybody to the pictures,' Danny answered. 'I've got to save enough money to get me own yard. And another thing while I think on,' he said, not looking in Ada's direction, 'even if I did think of getting wed, it wouldn't be to Susie.'

Before his mother could answer, he was out of the front door, down the steps and in the wagon.

* * *

'I told you it was sore, didn't I,' Bobby said when he came home in the middle of the morning, accompanied by one of the masters of Saint Patrick's Senior Boys.

'I would suggest an immediate visit to your family doctor, Mrs Harris.'

'Right away, sir,' Ada said and Bobby, feeling rightfully justified in his grievance of his mother, thought all she was short of doing was bobbing a curtsy. His mother was of the opinion that when authority spoke, the little man or woman obeyed, no questions asked. 'If I'd have known he was in such pain, I would have took him straight away, wouldn't I Bobby?' Ada nodded, but Bobby wasn't in the mood to be pacified. 'Thank you so much for bringing him home, sir,' his mam said in that voice she used when she was talking to the priest. 'I will take him straight round to our doctor, we won't need an appointment as he is obviously suffering.'

Bobby was hardly able to open his mouth when he tried to examine the inside in the mirror over the fireplace when his mam came back into the kitchen.

'Come here, and let me have a look!' Ada, impatient, allowed herself a fleeting twinge of guilt when she saw the swelling of Bobby's cheek. She could have done without this today, she wanted to go out to Netherford with Danny to check something Susie mentioned would be of interest. 'I've got a million things to do, and now I've got to take you to the doctor.'

'I couldn't concentrate on me tests this morning,' Bobby laid it on thick, knowing his mam could look a bit more guilty than she did at the moment. 'Even Miss Evans said, if I were her son, she would never have let me go to school in this much pain.'

'All right, Laurence Olivier, don't milk it. I said I'll take you and I will.'

When they arrived at the doctor's surgery on Stanley Road half an hour later, the waiting room was already full, and Bobby knew his mam was not pleased. Her lips looked like they were glued shut.

'We'll be here all flipping day,' Ada said when she did speak. Letting out a loud sigh and taking the only chair available, she looked at the clock again. She was going out to Netherford today, and was going to ask Danny to take her. *But by the time I get out of here, he will be long gone.* 'Straighten yourself up,' she told Bobby, who was leaning against the frame of the open sash window, 'and take your hands out of your pockets.'

A few minutes later the door opened, and everybody looked towards a lady in a tweed skirt and horn-rimmed glasses.

'Jennifer Nichols!' the receptionist called in a voice that was too loud for such a small, cramped room filled with people, and a young girl in pigtails got up from the seat next to Ada and walked round the large, polished table that displayed copies of *Town and Country* and *Hare and Hounds* magazines.

'I bet they belonged to the doctor,' Bobby said to his mother, 'because nobody here's reading them.'

'What d'you expect?' Ada's nostrils flared in disgust. 'They wouldn't know good breeding if it jumped up and bit them on the arse.' She nodded to the vacant chair beside her, but Bobby decided it was more comfortable to stand, his undercarriage felt painful too. 'Thank heavens for this new National Health Service,' Ada said to the woman next to her.

'I know,' replied the woman, whose nose almost touched her chin like a Punch and Judy puppet. 'I had all my teeth out yesterday.' She opened her mouth, showing two rows of pink wet gums and Bobby couldn't look away quick enough. 'It's not all bad, though,' the woman lisped, 'I'm having a new oven put in later.'

'Fancy.' Ada shrugged and looked at the clock, half-past ten. She glared at Bobby who rolled his eyes. His mam never listened. He told her yesterday that he didn't feel right, and she said he was swinging the lead because he wanted to stay off and listen to the football on the wireless. Women didn't understand nothing, he thought miserably, the World Cup only came round once every four years.

'Robert Harris!' the horn-rimmed one called, coming into the waiting room, and Bobby noticed his mam was up out of her seat like she'd been fired from a gun.

'Come on, let's get you into the insulting room and see what's what,' Ada said, heading towards the doctors consulting room, and Bobby, who soaked up words like a sponge, was anything but amused when the doctor took one look at him and said to his mother, 'The boy has mumps.'

'Mumps!' Ada looked at Bobby like he was a ticking bomb about to go off and she backed away to get a better view of his face.

'I told you it hurt.' Bobby was lying on the doctor's couch and feeling a deep sense of satisfaction that, for once, his mam was wrong.

'Right,' Ada said, looking suitably shamefaced. She had raised three kids. Surely she should have recognised mumps when she saw it. But that was the problem. She didn't see it. Because she wasn't looking. She was too busy thinking of other things.

As Bobby was easing himself from the doctor's couch, he felt another sharp pain in his *down-below*, the name his mother gave to anything she found too embarrassing to give a proper name. He winced and the doctor put his hand on his shoulder and gave him a sympathetic look.

'I'm afraid mumps can affect other glands as well.' Then, turning to Ada, he said, 'I suggest you take him straight home, put him to bed for the next two weeks.'

'Two weeks in bed?' Bobby tried to look suitably disappointed but was quietly thrilled. 'What a pity I will miss the end-of-term exams.' And he could listen to the World Service coverage of The FIFA World Cup on the wireless. The competition was being held in Brazil and the first since before the war, and, although he was in a bit of pain, Bobby was sure he could manage to 'persuade' his mam to let him listen to the matches. It was the least she could do for putting him through the ordeal of sending him to school when he was obviously so ill.

* * *

'If you're that sick, you won't be interested in listening to the football,' Ada said bringing him a glass of water as he languished on the sofa, a soft pillow under his head and melting under the eiderdown off his bed. 'Plenty of fluids the doctor said, so drink up.'

'I don't think I can,' Bobby croaked like a bullfrog. 'He looked worried that doctor, like he wasn't sure if I'm at death's door or something, and he said mumps is highly contagious.' His innocent-sounding words bit Ada and she relented.

'I suppose it won't do no harm to listen to the football, if you keep the wireless on low,' she said, knowing she could have infected the whole school by sending Bobby in. 'D'you think I'll get reported to the authorities?' Ada didn't like the authorities. Once they got their sticky beaks into your business they never let up.

'Who knows.' Bobby shrugged, he could see his mother looked worried. 'He did say contagious diseases have to be reported to the health people. You might only get a warning.'

'A warning?' His mam looked at him like he had just grown another head. 'But how was I supposed to know you had mumps, even your own teacher thought it was a bad tooth?' Ada stood by the window, looking down the yard. She watched next door's ginger tom sauntering along the back-yard wall.

When Henry opened the letter with the familiar handwriting that oozed malice as it scrawled across the page, he knew what he had to do. He had discussed everything with Meggie, and she agreed completely.

'I am glad,' she told her husband, 'we should have done it years ago.'

Going to the yard, she called Danny, who came over, his expression full of concern.

'Is everything okay?' Danny's brow furrowed into a frown. 'Is the auld man all right?' He looked relieved when she smiled.

'Aye, lad,' she said, 'never better.' And with that she went and fed the chickens that Danny brought back from Netherford, so they would have more room to run around and grow than the birds would have in their own back yard. They were getting big and plump with all the seed and grain Meggie fed them each day, along with the potato peelings that had been boiled and mashed.

'Come in, lad,' Henry said as Danny went into the spacious sitting room that was identical in shape and size to his own home, but the atmosphere was much more cordial here. Nobody would think his mam and Uncle Henry were first cousins, different as day and night.

Is everything all right?' Danny asked, taking a seat at the other side of the fireplace.

Henry nodded. 'As you know, my Meggie wants me to take things easy, and to tell you the truth, I quite fancy that too. However, there is something that's been worrying me of late.' Henry put his pipe between his teeth. It was unlit and had been since he went into hospital. 'You know the old ticker is not as strong as it once was, and if truth be told, I don't want to put any more pressure on it than I have to. Me and Meg want to grow old together, and we can't do that if I spend all my waking hours out in that yard.'

'What do you propose to do?' Danny felt his heart sink to his boots. He had hoped to carry on working here until he had enough money to set up a place of his own, but that could take years.

'I have a question,' Henry said, 'what do you think about buying the yard from me?'

Danny could see that he was deadly serious and that sinking feeling he had earlier turned in on itself and he felt sick. 'You know I can't afford to buy you out; it really would be the never-never.' Danny could hardly get the words out, picturing his dreams fading to dust. He thought that Henry would keep this yard until he dropped. But now he thought about it logically, Danny realised his uncle had almost worked himself to death, and if he didn't retire now, he and Aunt Meggie would never see the autumn of their years together.

'I haven't told you the price yet,' Henry grimaced, getting no satisfaction from his unlit pipe. Danny knew the yard. In his hands, it would be worth a fortune. Then there was the unused land that went right down to the docks. 'There is just one piece of land I don't own,' Henry said, 'we sold that off a while ago to keep the business afloat.' It was only a small lie, he thought, knowing there was plenty of land for Danny to work with. The money Meggie raised for the plot of land that was sold to the Dock Board was of no concern to anybody except him and his lovely wife.

'It doesn't matter how much it is you're asking; I won't have enough money saved to buy a business this size.'

'One pound,' Henry said, and Danny had to ask him to repeat himself.

'I'm sorry I thought you said—'

'One pound. Not a penny more, not a penny less, take it or leave it.'

'If I thought you meant it, I would bite your bloody hand off.' Danny laughed. 'And you know I would. This is my dream. My own yard.' Then his pale blue eyes lost their sparkle. 'I think it's a bit cruel of you to build up my hopes, only to knock them down again with such a ridiculous price.'

'I am serious,' Henry answered, his determination obvious in the set of his jaw. 'I will have the deeds drawn up by the solicitor, everything legal and above board – and I want every penny, in cash.'

'You're having me on?' Danny thought he must be dreaming. Things like this didn't happen to an ordinary bloke like him. Not in real life.

'I'm not kidding you,' Henry said, giving his unshaven chin a raspy scratch, 'I owe you more than you will ever know, and I can't think of anybody more able than you to run this business.'

'But why only a pound?' Danny asked, waiting for the catch, the bit of information that would pull the rug from under him. Although, thinking on it, that had never been Henry's style. So why would he change now?

'You've put as much, if not more, work into this place over the last few years than I have. This yard is you, and I would never rest easy if anybody else got their greedy mitts on it.' He sucked hard on the unlit pipe and his face crumpled into a scowl before he reached into his pocket and extracted a well-worn tin.

'You're talking about the person who's been threatening you?' Danny outlined the lace pattern of the tablecloth with his forefinger, unable to meet his uncle's gaze when he heard Henry let out a small but audible gasp. Danny hadn't meant to blurt out that he knew Henry was being blackmailed and did not probe the reason why, because he didn't have a clue. If Henry wanted to tell him that was up to him. But Danny would not fish for explanations. That was not his way.

'Not me, lad,' Henry said. 'I'd have stood up to the bugger, challenged 'em, like. But I've been sworn to secrecy. I'm not the one in danger of losing everything I hold dear.' He was quiet for a moment and Danny realised his uncle was going to say no more on the matter.

'One pound, though?' Danny shook his head, 'I can't take it in.' There was being generous and there was downright madness. 'Are you sure your head wasn't affected when you were ill?'

Henry gave a low chuckle, pushing tobacco into the bowl of his pipe while keeping an ear on alert for the sound of his Meggie's footsteps; he had no intentions of lighting the pipe. 'The situation is this, if I sell you the yard, and you pay the asking price, no matter

what that price is, then you are the legal owner. No ifs, ands or buts.
I can't tell you what to do with it.' He put the pipe in his mouth.
'You could turn it into a Saturday night dance hall – I'd have no
say...'

Danny laughed as the proposition sunk in. 'That sounds like a
good idea,' he said and bobbed out of the way when Henry threw a
polishing cloth at his head.

'Joking apart, you can do whatever takes your fancy. Nobody
can ever take the yard from you.' Lighting a taper from the low
burning embers, Henry showed the flame to his pipe, but he still
did not light it. Instead he put out the taper on the fender and lay it
on the high mantle shelf.

'If I popped my clogs, there is the chance that the Will could be
challenged, and believe me, it would be.' He put the pipe on the
table out of temptation's way. 'I know my family better than
anybody. It's not in their nature to be benevolent. They would fight
tooth and claw to get the business from Meggie.'

'But what will you live on?' Danny asked, and Henry shook his
head, holding out his hand and drawing Meggie into the room.

'My Meggie has made sure we will both be well looked after,'
Henry said, knowing they had the money from the sale of the land.
Money that nobody except him and Meggie knew about. Money
that she could never be hounded for. Because it was hers and she
had the papers to prove it.

'But what about the blackmailer?' Danny asked. 'Won't they still
try to extort money from you?'

Henry shook his head. Depending on what Danny said about
taking over the business, he could handle the blackmailer. 'Leave
that to me,' Henry said. 'So, what do you say? Do you want the
yard?'

'You are serious, aren't you?' Danny asked, half laughing, half
incredulous when Henry and Meggie nodded. He stood up, gath-

ered them together in his arms and, hugging them both, buried his head in Henry's shoulder so as not to show the tears running down his face.

When he looked up, Danny was surprised to see Henry and Aunty Meg also had tears running down their faces.

'What a lot of soppy ha'porths we are,' Henry said, taking a huge handkerchief from the pocket of his brown corduroy trousers and blowing his nose with such force, Meggie said she thought he was going to blow his brains out. 'I'll set the wheels in motion first thing tomorrow morning.'

'Well, don't go popping your clogs before then.' Danny laughed, unable to believe his good fortune. 'Can I tell Evie?'

'Aye, lad, but tell her not to let on to anybody else until after the papers are signed.'

22

The sweet scent of hedgerow stippled with creamy blossom perfumed the balmy summer air and Evie could not think of a better day in her life. Danny told her they needed to be going. The wagon trundled down the bumpy lane, leading to a row of four farm cottages. Evie wondered what it must be like to have all this space to live in. Meggie had offered to look after the office to let Evie have a day out in the countryside.

'Do you think you expand upward when you've got more space to grow,' she asked, 'because our Jack and Lucy are like beanpoles, I'm obviously the runt of the litter.'

'I think you're perfect just the way you are,' Danny said, and Evie took a sideways glance and saw the corners of his mouth curl upwards into an unabashed smile, even though he kept his eyes on the narrow dirt road.

Evie did not speak. She couldn't. Trying to get the sense of his words straight in her head, she was more confused than ever. What did he mean by that? she wondered. Looking straight ahead through the dusty windscreen, she tried to force herself to think of other things, anything but what he had just said to her. But the words kept going round inside her head.

What if he was just being his usual friendly self? She would look a right lemon if she took his words to mean something else, something deeper, and respond in a way that the heroine did on the pictures, by flinging her arms round him and declaring her undying love. He would think she was a bit doolally, especially if he had to explain that he was just making conversation.

Evie shifted in the seat. Did the words 'undying love' just saunter into her head and take up residence?

'We could not have picked a better day,' Danny said. 'I love this place, but even more so in the summer.' Netherford was a quiet, gorse-scented hamlet with red-roofed cottages dotted about the lanes. They passed a sixteenth-century inn called The Wheatsheaf, separated from the medieval church by a small graveyard. 'I usually go there for a ploughman's lunch before heading back,' Danny said, and Evie felt a buzz of excitement in her stomach. She had never eaten at an inn before, and didn't even know what a ploughman's lunch was. 'We could have it outside if you like?' he said as they passed a post box and telephone box standing like scarlet sentinels guarding the vast fields.

A little further on, he stopped to let her out of the truck. The post office was not like any Evie had seen before. This one looked like a stone cottage, with its mullioned sash windows and pretty flower garden, and to her right as she walked up the path, she noticed an area cordoned off with wire to allow various coloured chickens to roam free.

She was going to enjoy finding out for sure who was blackmailing Mr Skinner. There had been another demanding letter this week.

'I have come about the Skinner and Son account,' Evie said to the post mistress behind the iron mesh.

'No Susie today then?' the postmistress asked. Evie supposed in a place as small as this, not much went on without the knowledge of the postmistress.

'Not today.' Evie said determined to talk only on a 'need-to-know' basis, like they did during the war, and feeling like a character in a Dick Barton play, which Danny had told her he liked to listen to on the wireless, a zing of excitement shot through her ribs and made Evie's heart thump faster.

'So I take it you are depositing the money this month.' The postmistress said conversationally.

'There is no payment going into the account this month.' Evie told her. Opening a cash box the post mistress took out the official savings book, and wrote something under the date.

'I could take the book back with me if you like?' Evie said and the postmistress looked up, her eyebrows raised.

'Why on earth would *you* do that?' she said. 'The book stays here until it is collected at one o' clock.'

'Of course,' Evie gave an apologetic laugh, she would love to ask the name of the person who would be picking up the book – and usually the money. But if the post mistress didn't trust her with the savings book, Evie doubted she would give any names. 'I've a head like a sieve when I'm ready for my dinner.' Evie hoped her light-hearted laugh sounded genuine as she left the post office, astonished that in a beautiful chocolate box village like this, skulduggery was being carried out on a monthly basis. And whoever was demanding outrageous amounts of money was crippling the business.

* * *

'Are you in a hurry to get back?' Evie asked as they waited for their home-made cheese and warm crusty bread in the garden of the country pub, surrounded by ancient, lopsided headstones and verdant countryside

Danny leaned back on the bench, putting his hands behind his head. Closing his eyes, he offered his face to the brilliant sunshine.

'What do you think?' he asked. 'Uncle Henry gives me as much time as I need when I come out this way.' For the time being he decided against telling Evie he was taking over the business. He still hadn't got used to the idea himself.

Evie would not voice her suspicion that Susie had been stealing Mr Skinner's money. But she couldn't stay silent either. 'I don't really know how to say this...' Evie took a deep breath, and Danny sat and waited for her to find a way. 'I think... Well, I know...'

'What do you know?' he asked quietly, not wanting to rush her. 'If something is troubling you, Evie, I would be only too glad to help if I can.'

'I know you will,' Evie answered, giving him a reassuring nod, and trying to find the best way to voice her concerns. 'It's like this... You know Susie usually comes here every month?'

'Yes,' Danny said patiently, taking the first bite of delicious home-made bread and cheese, while Evie's remained untouched.

'And you know she goes to the post office every trip?'

Danny nodded and there was a moment's silence between them. Evie decided if she didn't speak now, she never would.

'I think Susie's got something to do with Mr Skinner being blackmailed!' Evie's words tripped over themselves in their haste to be out in the open, unable to keep the information secret any longer. 'And, what with you running the yard while Mr Skinner is recovering, and knowing Susie as well as you do, you must think I'm a right cow for suspecting her, but...'

Danny put his finger on her lips, and she stopped talking.

'Slow down, there's no rush.' Danny said in that soothing manner that immediately relaxed her and Evie took a deep breath.

'Susie usually deposits a large amount of money into the post office account.' She swallowed hard, knowing she had his full attention, and it gave Evie the courage to go on. 'Then the blackmailer collects the book and the money at one o' clock...'

'Why one o'clock?' Danny asked. Mulling over the new information.

'That's when the post office closes for the day,' Evie answered allowing herself to enjoy this feeling of solidarity. They both wanted what was best for Meggie and Henry who were like two halves of the same person and absolutely devoted to each other. But this business was taking its toll on Mr Skinner's health and Evie was going to get to the bottom of it once and for all.

'How could Meggie carry on if anything happened to Henry?'

'That's what I thought,' Evie answered watching Danny look out across the miles of crops and green fields. How handsome he was, she thought, taking the opportunity to gaze. He would make someone a wonderful husband.

'We will have to stay until one o' clock then,' Danny said suddenly, and she jumped a little. 'Do you think you could hang around that long?'

'It's only another hour or so, I think I'll manage,' Evie was delighted to spend longer with Danny and her heart pitter-pattered at a rate of knots.

'I couldn't believe what Meggie and Mr Skinner have been going through, all this time,' Evie said, relieved her suspicions were out in the open.

'Do you know why he's being blackmailed?' Danny's voice was low and grave, and Evie shook her head. She was not going to repeat malicious gossip. So, what if Meggie did have a child out of wedlock. It was nobody's business but hers and Mr Skinner. 'I'm not being evasive,' Evie didn't want to speak out of turn, 'but I don't like to surmise.'

'No, of course not,' Danny answered. She was a good sort was Evie. One of the best. And if he ever put his trust in anybody, it would be her. 'Penny for them?' Danny asked, after a few moments of silence, his smile as dazzling at the day.

'They're worth much more than that, you old skinflint.' Evie let out an easy laugh even though her heart was beating nineteen to the dozen.

'Less of the old, if you don't mind.' Danny laughed. 'I'll have you know I am in my prime.' He flexed his bulging biceps and Evie laughed, realising what had changed. She wasn't scared of life any more, nor did she automatically wonder what new hell the day would bring.

'If it didn't swell your head, Danny Harris, I would agree with you.' Then suddenly she stopped laughing. Did she just say that out loud?

'Well, if we're exchanging compliments, Evie Kilgaren, you scrub up very nicely too, if I may say so.'

His words made her feel good about herself, made her feel worthwhile, like she meant something. Not a pumped-up-important-kind-of-something, but worth more than she had ever given herself credit for. It was the same feeling she got when Mister Skinner told her she was in charge of the office.

But Danny's compliment was so much bigger. She had never known a man to give praise without wanting something in return. Danny was nothing like that. And for that she would be eternally grateful. Something akin to the weight of a giant concrete boulder lifted from her shoulders, and in that moment Evie realised that not all men were made from the same mould as her father.

'Why doesn't Henry give you the package to deliver?' Evie asked the mundane question to break the silence between them and not out of some Marple-like curiosity. Danny shrugged.

'I suppose he didn't want me to know,' Danny answered as they ate their tasty lunch. 'He didn't want anybody else involved I suppose.'

'We should know who is doing it by the end of the day,' Evie said, looking out to a cloudless baby-blue sky bursting with golden sunshine. Who wouldn't jump at the chance to get out of a smoky office and into the wide blue yonder with Danny Harris? The thought brought a rush of heat to her face. There was something liberating about having this much space for just the two of them that gave her the courage to rib Danny and, just for today, she felt complete.

In that moment, when she saw the dazzling sunshine bounce off a piece of glass, she thought the sparkle was as precious as a diamond and felt something she had never truly experienced before. If she could put into words this glorious epiphany of happiness, she would describe it as the diamond sparkle of broken glass.

'Stop here a minute,' Evie said, and Danny's dark brows furrowed to see Evie get up from the rustic bench attached to the wooden table, throw her arms open wide, and run through the wheat fields.

Danny laughed like he had never laughed before. Evie was like a child let out of school at playtime, and he loved the joy in her. He sighed, seeing this ancient place through new eyes. Her elation gave him hope that seeped deep inside his heart. Unable to tear his gaze from her, Danny knew this was the most carefree Evie had ever been, and his heart swelled with love for her as she made her way back.

'Did you think I'd gone scatty?' Evie asked, breathless as she sat down opposite him and Danny gazed at her, shaking his head, smiling, longing to take her in his arms...

'What?' Evie laughed unable to suppress this wonderful feeling of joy that was all thanks to Danny.

23

'Let's go and see if anybody's turned up' Danny said, never wanting this time to end.

'Hasn't the day been glorious?' Evie replied mirroring his own thoughts.

'More so because you're here,' Danny said as they headed to the post office. He realised that, from his early years, on the rare occasion the thought of a wife should ever enter his head, she always came in the shape of Evie Kilgaren. The most perfect, self-educated, resilient girl he had ever known.

'I hope we haven't missed the blackmailer,' Evie said, covering her elation with the practical matter in hand, although, thrilled Danny found her company as enjoyable as she found his. The time had flown by, with no let-up in their conversation and they had not noticed the time. Hopefully, they had not missed whoever was stealing Skinner's money.

As they approached the post office Evie put her hand on Danny's arm when she noticed someone they both knew well, and Evie had to hold Danny back.

'What is he doing here?' Danny had fire in his eyes when he saw his father step inside the vestibule of the quaint stone cottage that doubled as the village post office, and as they got nearer, Evie could clearly hear Bert Harris's voice. And he did not sound pleased as they entered the vestibule and could hear voices inside the post office.

'What do you mean, no money? The girl brings it every month. Look again.'

'I'm sorry, Mr Harris, the usual girl did not turn up and there has been no money deposited in that account today.'

'You're lying, there should be plenty.'

Careful not to move a muscle for fear the rickety floorboards would creak, Evie and Danny listened.

'Check it again. It will be there. If not, there will be trouble.' Bert's overconfident retort could be heard clearly, and when Evie saw a look in Danny's stormy eyes that she had not seen before she held her breath.

'Can you tell me who sent the money order?' the postmistress sounded unconvinced. 'There has been a considerable amount of money going through this account.'

'Mr Henry Skinner...' Bert responded, obviously confident his answer would get him what he came for, 'and I have my National Identity Card as proof of who I am.'

'I see you have, Mr... Harris.' There was a pause and Evie presumed the postmistress was checking his identification card.

'My father is blackmailing Henry Skinner,' Danny said, his fists clenched, 'But why? What's my father got on him?'

'Susie dropped off the money when you brought her here each month.' Evie said, 'but she didn't give me the impression she knew what the money was for. She told me she just enjoyed the pub lunch.' Evie had no intention of telling Danny that Susie saw him as a get-out-of-Reckoner's-Row-free ticket. 'The strain almost killed your poor uncle.' And to think Bert Harris had the gall to demand more and *more* money. There was greed and there was downright wicked.

'Don't say anything for the time being,' Danny said, and Evie agreed. The ball was suddenly in his court and he would play the situation whichever way he saw fit.

'But what about Henry?' Evie asked, 'what will he say when he finds out who has been doing this to him.'

'I'll sort it all out,' Danny said in that reassuring way he had about him, 'and there will be a lot to sort.'

'It's not your fault,' Evie said, 'none of us can be blamed for the sins of our father.'

Danny could not look at Evie. He felt too ashamed, 'You go on ahead. I'll see you back at the truck.'

Evie left without another word, knowing Danny needed to do this by himself.

'You make me sick to my stomach.' Danny's mouth turned down at the corners when Bert came out of the post office, momentarily taken by surprise. 'Leeching the lifeblood out of Uncle Henry's business for years...' Danny, blazing angry, could hold his tongue no longer. 'I could kill you for this!'

'I don't know what you're going on about.' Bert Harris obviously thought he could wheedle his way out of the situation with his flippant remark, the way he had for years.

'What has Henry done, that is so bad you almost killed him and sent his business to the brink of ruination. Tell me.' Danny edged closer, his fists clenched, longing to put this seedy cretin of a man flat on his back, unable to believe he had been sired by someone so low.

'You mind yer own, Danny,' Bert answered, 'you don't want to know.'

'That's where you are wrong – I do want to know. I want to know all of it.'

'Then you'd better ask your mother,' Bert said, 'she's the one with all the answers.'

'I have never despised anybody the way I despise you right now.' Danny's words were pushed out through clenched teeth and he edged closer. 'Was it because you wanted a comfortable lifestyle without working for it?'

He watched his father raise his chin while backing off. It would only take the one punch to put Bert on his backside, but Danny worried he might not be able to stop at one, because that comfortable lifestyle his father enjoyed had been provided by cowardly threats and the sweat of his mother's brow.

'You are a disgrace. A jumped-up little nobody.' With every word, Danny's rage grew and he edged forward, scared of what he would do to this poor excuse of a man yet unable to stop himself.

'You've never done a hands-turn to help Ma. When she finds out what you've done, I hope she turns you out onto the street to be judged by your sorry deeds, you despicable runt of a man.'

'Now you listen 'ere,' Bert said, still backing away, 'you've got no idea what I've had to put up with. Ada is a very demanding woman.'

Danny, who prided himself on being level-headed, could take no more, and even though it went against everything he believed in, he gave into a base instinct and thumped Bert so hard he went flying across the road.

'Danny, no!' Evie's voice cut through the fog of anger and reached that place where reason and good sense dwelt. Turning, Danny heard Evie's voice and stopped in his tracks. Beating the man to a pulp would certainly make Danny feel better, having watched him take advantage of his ma's good nature for years, but the satisfaction would not last. Every time he set eyes on him Danny would lock horns. Life would become even more unbearable for his ma, who had encouraged him to join the army at the earliest possible chance to get away from his poison.

* * *

'I am sorry you had to be involved in any of that,' Danny said to Evie as they went back in to the post office. He had asked the post mistress if she would be good enough not to discuss Bert's outburst with anybody.

'He has been under a lot of strain lately.' He told her.

'He ought to see a doctor,' said the post mistress and Danny nodded his head in agreement.

'I can assure you he will be getting treatment very soon.'

'Danny, are you OK?' Evie whispered, and he gave her a reassuring smile.

'Let me do that for you,' Danny told the post-mistress who had come out to collect the boxes of fresh fruit and vegetables that were on display outside the shop, 'as a way of saying sorry.' While Evie unconsciously took in the antics of a large brown cockerel strutting around his harem of chickens. They were all clucking and pecking the ground at the bottom of a sloping plank of wood leading to the chicken coop. At the bottom of the wooden slope was a sign that read, 'Chicks for sale,' and a big fat hen made her way to the coop and urged a line of fluffy yellow chicks into the wire mesh pen.

Heading towards the truck a short while later, Danny was carrying a hessian sack, which he handed to her before he jumped into the truck. Evie felt the heat rush to her cheeks that had nothing to do with the warm weather. Flustered, she made an exaggerated show of settling the sack on her knee.

'Gosh it's hot in here, shall I open this window?' She felt the space in the cab was much smaller than it had been on the journey out here. She had never seen Danny so angry, as he had just been, before and she could see he was trying to control his feelings by the way his knuckles turned white as he gripped the steering wheel.

Then, taking in a huge deep breath, Danny let out a long stream of air that seemed to calm him, and Evie surmised that his army training had taught him the discipline he needed right now. Especially when they saw Bert walking along the dusty lane holding a blood-stained handkerchief to his face, and Danny drove straight past the man to whom he had nothing in common.

'Comfy?' Danny asked and she nodded, unable to speak. He had every right to be angry with his father, and she could understand why he raised his fist to him. If she had been a man she would have done the very same thing. Bert Harris was a drunk and a gambler who dragged Ada down every chance he got. She could see that now. He must have given her a dog's life.

'At least we had the weather on our side,' Evie said. Accustomed to the rough-and-ready attitude of the dockside, she tried to lighten the heavy atmosphere, wanting to tell Danny she thought he had done the right thing, but unable to find the words.

'Every cloud, hey, Evie.' Danny's voice was laced with sadness when he gave her a playful nudge with his elbow. 'At least Uncle Henry won't be fleeced for money ever again.'

'Oh Danny,' Evie said, 'I understand exactly what you're going through. My old man was a wrong'un an' all.'

'Thanks for not judging,' Danny said, as they drove out of Netherford and home.

'Never,' Evie answered.

'Oi! What you got there?' Connie demanded the following day when Bobby Harris tried to sneak under the bar with a hessian sack slung across his shoulder. Bobby had been a pot lad since he was ten years old and even though he was nearly fourteen, he still came into the Tavern to help out, although Connie felt he came in not only for pocket money wages but also to get out from under his

mother's feet. 'I hear your Grace has been swept away on a Mediterranean cruise?' Connie said, as she rinsed glasses and put them on
the shelf above the counter.

'To help her get over having her what's-it's out, Mam said...'
Bobby's voice came from under the wooden counter flap. '...her
appendages.'

'Appendix,' Connie corrected him, realising that Ada wanted the
emergency kept under wraps, especially since Bert had done a
moonlight flit yesterday.

Bobby's eyes rolled heavenwards. 'I knew Ma said it wrong, but I
didn't know the proper word either, though I knew you would,
Connie.' The afternoon closing time had not come soon enough for
Connie, who was feeling dead beat in this heat.

Mim had taken herself off to the hairdressers earlier in the
afternoon and hadn't come back yet, so she put Fergus in his
pushchair and kept him down here in the bar until Lucy came after
school.

Luckily, the heat had knocked him out and the child's afternoon
nap lasted a bit longer when she put him over by the window where
it was nice and sunny. She didn't like him being in the smoky bar,
but could do little about it. Angus had gone to the coach station to
order the charabanc for the street outing.

'Come out here where I can see you,' Connie demanded, hands
on hips, ignoring Bobby's cocky cheerfulness. 'You're like the artful
dodger lately.' If someone didn't pay him a bit more attention,
Bobby might be in danger of going astray, she thought. There had
been so much going on, with Grace being in hospital, Danny
working all hours and Bert off to who knows where. Bobby, much to
his delight, had been allowed to do as he pleased.

He was a good lad really, Connie knew, but he had a sense of
adventure that may lead him up a blind alley if he wasn't careful.
Although Bobby, like his brother, had a strong work ethic. Danny

had been a good example to the lad, unlike their glass-back father Bert, who was always on the cadge after losing money to illegal bookies.

'What's wrong with your face? And don't say nothing.'

'Nothing,' said Bobby automatically and Connie raised a cynical eyebrow.

'What's in that sack?' He might be as tall as she was, but Connie could still put him in his place. 'Come on, spit it out before it chokes you.' She glared at the sack, which was moving, and he placed it on top of the bar. the Tavern was closed for the afternoon and they were the only people here except for sleeping Fergus.

'Chicks.' Bobby's innocent expression did not fool her for a minute, he looked so proud he might have hatched them himself.

'Chicks?' Connie wondered if she was really in the mood for this. She was hot, uncomfortable, and she longed to soak her swollen feet in a nice bowl of soapy water.

'You know, baby chickens!'

'I know what chicks are, soft lad. I didn't come over on the last boat.'

'I'll show you.' His voice was almost breathless with excitement.

She watched him undo the loose string round the neck of the sack and she stepped forward, craning her neck to get a view inside the bag.

'I'm sure you will.' Connie peered inside to see six cheeping baby birds that would one day grow big enough to make someone a nice Sunday dinner. 'Where did you get those from? And I want none of your stories!' Ada would have these sold if they were any bigger, for sure.

'Our Danny bought them back from Netherford, he has made a chicken run in Skinner's yard and...' He stopped to take a breath. 'Meggie Skinner said they had plenty, so would you and Angus like these?' Then he added, 'They're only sixpence each.'

'A proper little entrepreneur, I must say.' Connie was amazed.

'I don't know what one o' them is, but a bloke's got to make a living.' Bobby nodded proudly.

'So, why were you sneaking them under the bar?' she asked, thinking he might have got them by some nefarious means to make a few bob for himself.

'Angus said you don't like birds, they might scare you in your condition,' Bobby said with his customary uncomplicated air. 'Seeing as you're not used to the countryside and that...' His voice trailed off.

'Well, I'll have you know I am not scared of birds,' Connie said. 'I'm not scared of anything.'

'Shall I tell Mrs Skinner you'll have them, then?' Bobby asked and Connie nodded.

'Sixpence you say?' She smiled, amused at his audacity. She knew Meggie Skinner had never asked a soul for money in her life. In fact, apart from Evie Kilgaren, she had never met a woman more independent.

'What about threepence each, then? One shilling, six pence? That's fair, and I'll come over and feed them, every day if you like.' Bobby breathed a sigh of relief when she nodded. 'You drive a hard bargain, Connie. Angus was going to give me a tanner each *and* you get eggs.'

'You'd better put them out in our back yard,' Connie said, putting three silver shillings on the bar, giving Bobby the amount of money he wanted in the first place, and was rewarded when he graced her with one of his charming smiles.

'You'll break a few hearts you will Bobby Harris.'

'See, I knew you'd understand, Connie,' Bobby said, tying up the sack to take out to the yard before pocketing the money.

* * *

The Skinners' front room, although more spacious than most houses round about, was reduced to standing room only. Henry wanted everybody gathered together so there would be no confusion when word got out that Danny now owned the business.

Mr Swann, the solicitor who had looked after Skinner's family business for the past forty years, took his seat behind the lace-covered table in the bay, so the sunlight from the windows could warm his rheumatic neck and shoulders.

Evie had meticulously prepared the accounts and was standing beside Danny near the parlour door behind the workers, while Ada sat on a straight-backed chair near the glass-fronted cabinet.

Ada scowled, her mind on her troubled family and she wondered where that waste of space of a husband had traipsed off to. Not that he was much use when he was at home. But he went off a couple of weeks ago, leaving a note to say he would be in touch and nobody had heard a word from him since.

'How is Grace?' Evie whispered and Ada's buxom shoulders visibly shivered.

'Her new chap, Bruce, has taken her away to rest and reciprocate.' Ada answered knowing Evie had done her a kindness the night Grace had 'taken bad', and she must be civil. But there was no time to say more when Henry came into the room.

'I'm sure you are wondering why I have asked you all here today,' Henry said in that deep baritone voice that filled the room and, looking round, he saw his prim cousins, Ada, and Bea who lived across the canal, nod and shift in their seats. To his satisfaction, they looked extremely uncomfortable.

Ada was sitting upright, her legs, thick as newel posts, were folded at the ankle, a bone china cup and saucer in one hand, while gripping black gloves in the other.

'It's bloody summer and she's got her gloves with her,' he'd told Meggie when Ada had arrived, knowing he and his cousin had not been this close for years, even though they lived within walking distance of each other.

Bea, by contrast, was shrivelled under a coat that was two sizes too big. A hungry-looking woman, she owned the lodging house on the other side of the canal and ran it on a shoestring. Nobody lodged at Bea's house if they could find somewhere else. She regarded Henry with suspicion, although that was nothing new, she always looked like she had just sucked a lemon. Henry held himself in check and could not wait to see the contortions that face was going to go through when he broke the news.

'As you all know, I inherited Skinner and Son when my father died, although Ma had the run of the lodging house until she, too, passed on and we inherited that too.' Henry looked over to Meggie, who was standing at the back and he held out his hand, beckoning her over. 'Then, when I had that little heart scare,' he said, retaining the news that he would be fine in the care of his loving wife and giving up his favourite pipe tobacco, 'I knew it was time to put my affairs in order.'

Ada nudged Bea with her elbow, causing a ghost of a smile to flicker across both their faces. Henry went on to talk about the years he and Meggie had worked all the hours God sent to build up the thriving business and it was obvious by the look of boredom on their faces that both cousins thought he should get on with it.

'But sometimes,' he said, savouring every tedious moment, 'you have to stop and take stock, realise that you are not as young as you once were, and enjoy a bit of life, instead of giving most of your brass away.' He saw no sign of life in the eyes of either cousin. 'So, with that in mind, I have decided to let the business go.' There was a small gasp from everybody in the room while Ada and Bea's eyes swiftly showed some interest. 'I will keep the house,' Henry said, 'as I have to rest my head somewhere, and Meggie's only just wallpapered the back room.'

'Is there a point to all this?' Ada asked impatiently.

'Well, that's the thing, you see,' he said. 'I've asked you here because I don't want any confusion about the circumstances. When you hear this from me, be under no illusion of what I want to do with *my* property.' Henry was alluding to the fact that, when his mother died, Ada and Bea were vociferous in their indignation at being left out of her will.

'I have sold the yard to Danny.' Another small gasp went round the room, and the stable hands turned to congratulate the man they admired so much. 'I am sure you will want to join Meg and me in wishing the lad the absolute best of luck in his new venture.'

A ripple of applause filled the room, but there were two faces that looked like they were cast in stone.

'You mean our Danny's bought your yard?' Ada's eyes were as wide as the saucer on her lap. 'But where did he get the money to buy you out?'

'I know you were expecting a good share of my fortune when I popped my clogs,' Henry said, putting his unlit pipe into his mouth, 'but this yard needs a young man at the helm, a man who has the drive and determination I once had when I married my Meg.'

'Bloody hell you don't half go on when you've got a captive audience, Skinner,' Bea moaned while Ada was most indignant at her cousin's forthright manner and shuffled in her seat.

'The business was started by our grandfather. You only got it because your father was the only male, then the same thing happened with the next generation. You were the only male, so as the oldest cousin and by dint of birth, being female, I'm denied what's rightfully mine.'

'That is precisely why I have sold it before I go,' Henry said. 'I didn't want you in any doubt about who gets what – oh, but don't worry, I haven't left you out.' He saw the two women's stiff shoulders relax a little.

'I just meant... well, I didn't mean...' Ada relented. 'I wouldn't want you to think I'm being greedy. I just want what I deserve.'

'You got the lodging house in Reckoner's Row rent-free,' Henry reminded Ada. 'However, there is one more thing I know my mother would have wanted you to have.' He took two square boxes out of his pocket and handed one to Ada, who got up out of the chair and gave him a hug. And he gave an identical one to Bea, who all but snatched it from his hand and returned to her seat.

The two women opened their boxes, and their faces were consumed by a look of disgust when they realised they had been given the top and bottom set of his mother's false teeth.

'Ma always said you two were so busy chewing the fat, you'd wear down your own teeth, so I thought these may come in useful. After all, these were her best set.'

Ada rose from her chair. 'I suppose you think you are clever, making a show of us in front of the workers.'

24

'Evie we've got a visitor,' Lucy called from the hallway a couple of weeks later, and Evie's eyes swept the room. Everything was in its place when the door opened, and Lucy went to get some fresh home-made lemonade out in the back kitchen.

'Hiya, Evie,' Connie came through the door like a ship in full sail, her hand in its usual position supporting her back. 'You don't mind me popping in, do you? I can't take another minute of my mother and Ada dissecting who said what to whom when Grace's fiancé was nabbed for being an international diamond smuggler,' Connie said, waddling into the kitchen.

'Come and sit down, Connie, you look done in.' The news was stale, but she knew in a small street like Reckoner's Row, it would be examined in forensic detail by the residents for many months to come.

'A diamond smuggler,' Evie said, 'who'd have thought it? And he had two wives, greedy sod – and they say my family was crooked. To be fair, though,' Evie added, 'Clifford Brack didn't murder his wife.'

'You're right,' Connie answered. 'And Bert's done a bunk,

nobody knows where he is, so now Ada knows what it feels like to be the centre of attention.'

'I bet your takings have gone down a bit,' Evie said, recalling the day she and Danny went out to Netherford and Danny had a set-to with Bert. But she would keep the information to herself. 'You look worn out, Con.'

'Don't worry about me, Evie, it's this heat, I swear it's getting hotter.' Connie pulled a ladder-backed chair from under the table. 'I'll sit here if it's all right with you. I'll never get up again if I sit on the sofa – I'm sure there's two in here.' She pointed to her large bump that seemed to be straining to break out of her pale blue smock.

'How much longer have you got to go?' Evie asked while Lucy was filling the tray in the back kitchen.

'Another four weeks, so Angus, Fergus and I are going to the Netherford Fete and Mim will stay here and look after the bar.'

'That's good.' Evie was genuinely pleased. The whole street was going on the charabanc the following day for the yearly trip to the horse show and Evie was looking forward to another trip out to the countryside.

'When Auld Henry took bad, everybody thought the outing would be cancelled.'

'I know, but isn't it a good thing Meggie wouldn't hear of it,' Evie answered. 'They both said the show must go on, so Meggie organised it instead.'

'I think Skinner's secretly glad she took over this year,' Connie replied. 'It did her the world of good to step into his shoes and get out among the neighbours again.'

'Here we go,' Lucy said, bringing in a tray holding glasses of home-made lemonade, 'and our Jack said Danny's going to enter Mr Skinner's favourite horse in the Netherford show this year. And we made all the flowers and silk ribbons, didn't we, Evie?' Lucy added, not wanting to be left out of the conversation. 'The horse will look grand, so he will.'

'I feel exhausted just thinking about it all.' Connie sighed as she, Lucy and Evie sat at the table wafting home-made fans, fashioned from the *Evening Echo*, and even though the sash window was pushed right up, there was little breeze entering the kitchen.

'It might be hot, but look at those clouds.' The three females could see the dark clouds looming. 'It looks like a storm is brewing.'

'Let's hope it doesn't rain before the parade,' Evie said.

'Oh I don't know, it'll be more comfortable if the weather's a bit cooler,' Connie said, 'and not just for the horses either.'

* * *

The following morning, Connie brought in a picnic basket to lend Evie, who was packing parcels of ox tongue sandwiches wrapped in greaseproof paper and home-made sausage rolls into her wicker shopping basket, when there was a gentle tap on the door and Danny popped his head in the kitchen.

'Can I come in?' he asked. 'I did call up the lobby, but nobody heard me,' he explained, looking a bit sheepish in his new dark brown suit. He had been a regular visitor of late, calling in most days on some excuse or other. Usually to have a word with their Jack. As if they didn't share enough words at the yard. But everybody, except Evie, knew why he liked coming here.

'Come and have some lemonade, Danny!' Lucy said, her eyes shining, loving the fact that Danny or Connie would pop in for a natter at any time of the day or night. This house wasn't just a house any more, she thought, it was a home. Heart-warming, safe, welcoming and all thanks to her wonderful big sister, Evie.

'You're looking very smart, Danny,' Evie said. 'Is that a new suit?'

'Aye,' Danny said, 'me mam bought it for the parade, I told her not to, but you know what she's like'

'She'll be paying for that suit until the cows come home,' Connie said. 'It's a nice bit of cloth.'

'Winter-weight-wool,' Danny said, shaking his head. 'In the height of summer, she buys winter-weight-wool. I'll end up a puddle on the floor and I don't think the tie will last the day either. I'm melting already and it's not yet nine o' clock.' He had got up at the crack of dawn to check on the horses, only to find Henry already in the stables. A gentle admonishment was like water off Henry's back. Nothing was going to stop him enjoying his big day. He then went home, lugged the tin bath from the six-inch nail in the back- yard wall and had a cool soak before anybody else was out of bed.

'Oh you do look handsome,' Evie said in her usual friendly manner, and he beamed a smile that could have lit up the room. She passed him the cold lemonade and he put it on his forehead and went to stand by the window, but it was no good.

'There's no air.'

'That's just what you said before, wasn't it, Evie?' Connie had a mischievous gleam in her dark eyes and Evie gave her a silent caution.

'This'll have to go,' Danny said, putting his drink on the table and removing his jacket. Taking off his tie, he opened the top two buttons of his shirt and Evie felt a bit light-headed and giddy all at the same time to see him in a crisp white shirt under his waistcoat.

'You don't look a bit comfy,' Connie said, and Danny pulled a face.

'Nor you,' he said, an incredulous gleam in his eyes and his usual cheeky smile that made Evie feel as if they were the only two in the room. 'I didn't even know you could get winter-weight wool; it'll see me through the ice age and I'll still have to take off me vest.'

Evie could not contain the laughter bubbling up inside her, so much so tears ran down her face. He was so funny; she could listen to him for hours. She was going to have the most perfect day.

'Oh, before I forget, I brought these for Lucy,' Danny said and handed her a white triangular paper bag of humbugs. Her sweet tooth was legendary, and she longed for the day when sweets came off ration. 'I got some for our Bobby as well, so that should keep you both quiet on the journey.'

'We're not five, you know,' Lucy said good-naturedly, and offered the bag around. But Evie noticed her younger sister seemed visibly relieved when nobody took a sweet. 'I'll just have one now,' she said, popping a humbug into her mouth, 'and I'll save the rest for the coach.'

'I bet there won't be many left when the coach gets here,' Evie said.

Moments later, Jack came into the kitchen from the yard, he was going down to the stables to check on the horses and put down straw bedding. Maybe give them another brush before they went to the fete. He had checked, and double-checked, that everything was ready before he and Danny and the other stable lads set off.

'I'll come down and give you a hand, Jack,' Danny said, and Evie felt a momentary dip in her happy heart.

'Don't get your new suit dirty,' Evie said, and Danny smiled.

'It's going back in the wardrobe until Christmas,' he responded.

———

25

'Good morning, Postie,' Meggie said as the postman trundled up the path next to the yard.

'Nice day for it, Megs,' the postman said, taking off his dark Royal Mail cap with its red piping round the peak and wiped his damp brow.

'It is, indeed, Postie, as long as the rain keeps off we'll have a grand time.'

She took the bundle of letters he held towards her and, hopping back on his Royal Mail-issue bicycle, he whistled his way along the street as Meggie saw the large green charabanc manoeuvring round the tight corner at the top of Summer Settle and edge its way down the street. She waved and went back inside the house as the coach came to a halt opposite the yard, knowing that very soon the place would be swarming with excited adults and children.

Leaving the front door open, Meggie was more than ready for their yearly excursion. She and Henry had looked forward to this outing, as they did every year, and they intended to enjoy the day even more knowing they could have a lie-in tomorrow.

The annual Netherford Fete had been their chance to relax with people of the dockside, and it never ceased to amuse either of them that the butties would come out as soon as the bus pulled out of the street.

She picked up the top envelope and immediately recognised the writing, and her hands trembled. The wording looked like a spider had crawled over it with a fine tipped pen.

'Oh, not again,' she whispered. She had seen Henry look more casual and happy in the last few weeks than he had been for months, and she knew why. He didn't have to worry about being blackmailed any more. Danny, God bless him, had let it be known that he got the yard at a knock-down price, although he didn't say exactly how much. So it did not matter one iota what the blackmailer threatened. There was no money in the pot as far as they were concerned.

She knew, before she even opened the dreaded letter what the contents would say.

'Hello Meggie, all set?' Evie asked when she saw Meggie in her garden. Leaning on the gate, Evie could tell immediately there was something wrong by the worried look in Meggie's eyes.

'I won't be long,' Meggie answered cheerfully, trying her hardest not to spoil Evie's day with worry and long faces. 'Henry has gone on ahead with Danny and Jack.'

'I didn't think he would go on the coach,' Evie said, 'but never mind, we can all be together, it will be a fabulous day if this weather holds out.' Evie noticed that Meggie didn't answer, seemingly preoccupied with something else. 'Meg, is something wrong?' Evie recognised the glisten of an unshed tear immediately, 'And don't fob me off, I can see you're upset.'

'It's another one of these,' Meggie said, 'and, because they didn't get last month's money when you and Danny went out to Netherford, the letters are coming in my name.'

'If I were you, I'd burn it,' Evie said, 'or report them to the police. But, trust me, Meg, forget about them. This person cannot hurt you. We'll stand by you. Don't let the buggers get you down. I'll have a word with Danny.' Evie knew that Meggie would not go to the police to tell them what had been going on. It wasn't the done thing round the dockside to involve the police. They would much rather sort it out themselves, unless you were an international diamond smuggler that is. That was different.

But hounding people for hard-earned money was wicked and when people found out who was behind it, Bert Harris would get what was coming to him. So Evie was content in the knowledge that Bert would not be crawling out of his hiding speck any time soon. He might be a despicable excuse for a human being, but he would not chance the wrath of the inhabitants of Reckoner's Row if they got wind of his shenanigans. Evie took the letter, ripped it into tiny pieces and handed them to Meggie who threw them in the bin and dusted her hands.

'You're right, Evie.' Meggie's shoulders dropped and she sighed. 'I'm going to enjoy this day, for Henry's sake.'

'That's the spirit,' Evie replied, 'I'll see you on the coach.' As she headed back home, Evie felt a new determination begin to grow inside her like a warm light, and spread throughout her body.

Lucy stretched across Evie's knee as they both looked out of the wide window of the charabanc to get a better look at the surrounding countryside. The glorious summer day was bright, and everybody was in good spirits as the charabanc crawled down the narrow country lane, with ditches on one side and free-growing blackberry bushes, heavily laden with an abundance of fat juicy berries on the other.

'D'you thing the farmer will let us pick some blackberries,

Evie?' Lucy asked, her eyes gleaming. 'It's been ages since I've tasted the tang of a delicious apple and blackberry tart.' Lucy closed her eyes and joined her hands, savouring the memory. 'Or even home-made jam.' She licked her lips at the thought.

'I don't see why not, they're growing wild at the roadside,' Evie answered, feeling relaxed already. The country air lifted her spirits bringing back thoughts of the day she and Danny came out here. And although Danny was disgusted when he discovered his father had been extorting hush-money from Mr Skinner, he confided in her that he wasn't surprised, saying his old man would do anything for money. The proof was in full view when Bert lay in bed all morning while Ada went out cleaning to put bread on the table. No, Danny had said, not going into detail, Bert Harris would not be hurrying back to Reckoner's Row if he knew what was good for him.

This was Evie's first visit to the Fete, even though she had been to Netherford with Danny. Having worked the years before, she could never afford to take a day off without pay, but this year was different. Danny had closed the yard, giving the staff a day's holiday – with pay, making him extremely popular with the workers, although not with Susie who was sitting at the back of the chara-banc with Ada.

'We're nearly there!' Lucy's voice raised with excitement as she gazed out of the window. 'I can see the tents on that field over there, Evie. Look!'

Evie's spirits rose even higher when she saw the red and yellow bunting fluttering in the breeze between the large tents as the coach finally turned into the huge field, after what seemed an age crawling down the narrow lane.

Evie inhaled deeply as they got off the coach and her senses were dominated by the scent of fresh-cut grass that reminded her of sharp green apples. This was the smell of the countryside, she thought. Not a whiff of chimney smoke. And could that vast, pale blue, cloudless sky be the same one that drifted over Reckoner's Row? She doubted it, because this sky was wide, and high, and there was acre upon acre of it. The dockside was a squashed gathering of roofs and chimneys and machinery from the docks. This... she took another deep breath... this place was something quite different. This is what she imagined heaven to look like. And the colours! Verdant green, pale blue, golds and pinks – so many shades. Nobody should be sad on a day like this.

Evie was in awe of majestic oaks in the distance, standing stately beside towering beech trees that seemed to stretch to the sky and went on forever. Also mesmerised by the billowing elms and sycamores that the dockside lads made a beeline for in the summer sunshine: probably in the hope of finding early 'whirlybirds' that were only produced in the autumn months by the sycamores and which spread over the countryside like indefatigable wardens offering shade and shelter. She had read about them in one of Lucy's school books borrowed from the library and read up on all the native trees.

'Hey! Evie. Have you got your deaf ones on?' Jack called, walking across the field with Danny. 'I've been calling you for ages!'

Evie's heart lurched unexpectedly when she saw Danny's long strides eating up the ground, his handsome features, bronzed and glowing in the heat, sending a jolt of electricity through her, and, by the look of it, attracting admiring attention from many girls who were milling around, chatting or sitting on benches at the wooden tables round the large tents. He reminded her of the mighty oak, tall and strong.

He gave Susie, who was standing nearby, a nod of greeting but she did not return his friendly smile; her eyes were cold, and her crimson lips were twisted like she had just eaten something rancid.

She said something unintelligible before turning, arms folded and strode off.

Considering she had stalked Danny like a big game hunter, Evie knew the reason for Susie's icy glare. Hell hath no fury like Susie Blackthorn scorned and she probably thought Danny would fight her corner, plead to get Susie's job back. But he would not do that, knowing she contributed nothing to the business, and everybody needed to pull together to make it as successful as it had once been.

When the parade of horses was about to begin, Meggie corralled the people of the dockside together, even going to the beer tent to remind the hard-working men who were enjoying some respite from the afternoon sun – or at least that's what they told their equally hard-working wives who had made the sandwiches, flasks of tea, saved the sweet coupons for little treats and made sure their children enjoyed themselves in the countryside.

Meggie wanted as much support as she could get when Henry's favourite horse, a huge black Clydesdale called Thunder, took part in the Working Horse Parade.

'He looks magnificent,' Meggie said proudly as the women grouped together and the men stood in the shade of the beer tent.

'Those silk ribbons and flowers that we spent hours making will win the competition,' Lucy said proudly, while Henry, Jack and Danny gave one last examination to the polished horse brasses, giving them a final buff until they gleamed.

They could almost see their faces in Thunder's glossy, ebony coat and the women beamed when Jack, looking proud, walked the Clydesdale out into the huge arena.

Thunder, loving the attention held his head high, his mane and tail as smooth as silk and Evie smiled to Meg, her heart bursting with pride knowing the best hairdresser in the North West would not have made Thunder's mane and tail shine any better than their Jack had.

* * *

Henry, Danny and Jack collected the silver cup to deafening applause, whistles and whoops of delight when Thunder won Best in Show. They held the huge coveted silver cup aloft, striding proudly across the arena – cordoned off with long ropes – and placing the winner's rosette amid the abundance of colourful silk flowers on the horse's bridle.

Evie knew the cup would stand proudly in the window of Skinner and Son every day for the next year.

'Go an' fill the cup in the beer tent,' Danny said, passing the huge cup to Jack, 'and pass it round, so everybody can join in the celebration!' Then he gave Henry a manly hug, both of them laughing and crying, not giving two hoots who saw them.

'I'm that proud of you, lad!' Henry said, while they slapped each other on the back and shook hands. Evie was thrilled to see both men so happy. But the moment was fleeting when she noticed Ada in the crowd.

Standing square, her shoulders rigid, Ada's arms were folded, and her fists clenched like a call to war, she glared at the happy group, her veins oozing vinegar.

Look at them all, she thought, *enjoying themselves. Not a thought for me.* Danny went straight to Henry and Meggie and Ada's quick sharp eyes swept the happy group of revellers. When did she get to be second best? After all she had done, she should have been the first person who shared in Danny's glory. Well, if he wanted to hug Meggie and Henry Skinner before her he could stay with them, Ada thought turning and heading towards the tea tent, wanting nothing more to do with the celebrations.

'Well done, the pair of you!' Meggie said proudly to Danny and Jack, her eyes glassy with delight as a small quiver betrayed the utter joy she was feeling. 'This is a perfect day.' When her beloved

Henry had put his arms round her, hugging her close, Meggie had felt today was the most wonderful of perfect days.

'We are so proud of the way you are handling the business,' Meggie said lightly touching Danny's cheek, 'you have grown into such a thoughtful, loving young man.'

In spite of, not *because* of Ada, she thought. Ada could not wait for Danny to go into the army and be off her hands. But to stop herself from getting maudlin she said in a brisk, no-nonsense tone, 'where's that husband of mine got to?'

'If I know anything about Mr Skinner,' Jack whispered to Danny, unable to wipe the beaming smile from his lips, 'he'll be in that beer tent having a few celebratory scoops.'

'And I'll be right behind him,' Meggie laughed, hearing every word, and marching to the beer tent. If Henry was going to celebrate then so was she.

'Congratulations to the both of you!' Evie clapped her hands like an excited five-year-old at a birthday party.

'Evie, we won! Did you see it?' Danny lifted her in the air like she weighed nothing and circled around the field.

'Put me down, I'm dizzy.' Evie laughed, delighted that he headed straight for her to share his elation. And when Danny gently lowered her to the ground, she staggered. He caught her in a strong embrace and took Evie's breath away when he kissed her, full on the lips, in front of everybody.

Evie melted into the unyielding strength of his formidable physique. His kiss left a lingering imprint she would revisit for the rest of her days. The air stilled and the sound of children's laughter, stallholders hollering and cattle lowing in the next field hushed into nothingness, and Evie felt herself falling into the deep gaze of Danny's denim blue eyes.

They seemed to be searching, assessing, questioning, and for a hair's breadth of a second, she flinched. She hadn't meant to.

Danny's hungry contemplation had taken her by surprise and she was wide open to the thousands of megawatts buzzing through her like an electric shock. Her armour slipped away and her carefully protected heart was defenceless. All notions of being a self-supporting, one-woman-island suddenly disappeared like ice in a heatwave.

Danny leant down and, cupping her chin with his finger, his smooth sweet kiss lingered, leaving her trembling. He let her go too soon, and pushing his hands into his pockets, he strode off across the field without a word.

Transfixed by the power in his long stride, Danny's departure left Evie with a feeling akin to the shock of a hit-and-run. His pace was relentless, as if he had to get away, ignoring the congratulatory backslapping. Then it dawned on her. He did not want a relationship with a girl like her. He was obviously looking for someone with a bit of class. Someone who didn't have her history. Someone he could be proud of...

What was she thinking? Danny had not meant to kiss *her*. He was so happy he would have kissed anybody. That was obvious by the way he moved off quicker than a man with a rocket up his arse.

And, watching him disappear across the field she felt her face grow hot when she noticed what a tight peachy arse it was, too. Nevertheless, she thought with a hint of regret, she wasn't going to chain herself to a man just because she loved him.

Loved him? Who said anything about love?

'Don't take it personal,' a voice behind her said and Evie swung round, her face hot and clammy. 'He told me he is not the marrying kind.'

'It's just as well,' Evie retaliated, 'because neither am I!' Susie Blackthorn had a bloody cheek.

* * *

'Well, well, well?' Ada's smile didn't reach the fury in her eyes when she found Meggie sitting at a table in the beer tent. 'Look who's here. Let Henry off the leash for a while, hey?' she asked. The drinks she'd had earlier, combined with the heat of the afternoon sun, went some way to loosen her usually tightly guarded tongue where her family were concerned.

'I think you might need a cup of tea, or a glass of water might be better,' Meggie said.

Ada could not ignore the red mist that enveloped her and all she wanted to do was hurt Meggie, a common kitchen maid who not only walked into the family business and took over without so much as a how-do-you-do, fooling her aunt, but took up residence and had a life of luxury, while Ada had to scrimp and scrape by. And not content with all of that, Meggie had Danny eating out of her hand.

* * *

'Danny's not going to look twice at you,' Susie goaded Evie during the next parade. Her arrogance was obvious in the way she stood tall, her chin up, her head high, but she was no threat to Evie. Not any more. Her elderly parents' only offspring, Susie expected and had been given everything she wanted.

'You can't stomach the fact you were fired, can you Susie?'

'Your nothing but an upstart, with ideas above your station,' Susie replied, obviously scrabbling for the most hurtful words. 'Danny will take me back on, and he will give you your marching orders too.' Susie's face was turning a livid red. 'He pities you. It's me he wants. And I will make sure it is me he gets.'

'You didn't say you loved him,' Evie answered, 'nor that you cared for him.'

'Don't be so ridiculous. I expect him to care for me,' Susie scoffed. 'He's the one with the business. He'll be rolling in money.' She stood with her hands on the hips of her pale blue peddle pusher slacks, which she had copied from a pair Grace had worn. 'I've waited three years for Danny to show me the kind of attention he gives you.' Susie's voice lowered and for a moment Evie felt sorry for her. 'But I am not prepared to wait any longer.'

'I always knew you were the impatient type, if you don't get what you want straight away, you usually lose interest.'

'Well, not this time, if you think I'm going to give up without a fight, you can think again.'

'I'd hate to jump into your shoes,' Evie said, 'I would be bored rigid.'

'If he's going to marry anybody it is going to be me.' Susie countered like a five-year-old having a tit-for-tat in the playground.

'He's not ready to marry anybody.' Evie's eyes flashed, and she leaned forward. 'But I do intend to be alongside him, supporting him, boosting his business, with every ounce of energy I possess.' Evie could see by the horrified look on Susie's face that her words had hit home.

'I know things that would change your mind about being so loyal.'

'Nothing you say would make me change my mind about Danny,' Evie said in a low, determined voice.

'Even if I told you that Ada is not his mother?' Susie's face was wreathed in an expression of satisfaction and Evie felt her heart miss a beat while trying to conceal a sharp intake of breath with a small cough. What was Susie talking about? 'Would he still be so loving towards Meggie if he knew she had given him away when he was just a baby?'

'If I hear any more poison from you, Susie Blackthorn, I will not hold back. You will be the one who has to scrub floors to earn money.' Evie would not allow her to continue, but Susie would not be silenced.

'You can't...' Susie countered, but Evie cut her off mid-sentence.

'I can.' Evie leaned forward, determined. 'And I will. So do not test me. You have had your chance, and you blew it. Now step aside and let the big girls take over.' Evie's heart thundered against her ribs and she drew deep calming gasps of air into her lungs when Susie stormed off across the field. She could hardly take it in. Meggie was Danny's mother? But why...? What could possibly have happened to...? Evie could not imagine Meggie would, could ever deny her own flesh and blood. Susie was just trying to cause trouble. As usual.

But Susie's revelation unsettled Evie who had taken many years to find the courage to say her piece and today she made it clear to Susie, who had always looked down on her, that she had the right to stand tall. She proved she was as good as any of them. Not better, that was not her way, but at least she was no longer bottom of the pile.

Taking another calming deep breath, her heartbeat slowed, and Evie was about to go and find Meggie when she heard a noise. It was a cross between a growl and a groan, and she wondered if it was a wounded animal. Would it attack? She had heard that injured creatures could strike when cornered.

Edging forward, Evie reached the gap between two tents, feeling more than a little apprehensive when she pulled back the flap, she was horrified to see her good friend doubled up gasping for breath.

'Connie! What's happened? Did you fall?' Moving quicker than she had ever done before, Evie hurried to help, dropping down to her knees and trying to prise Connie's fingers from the guy ropes.

'My waters have gone!' Connie gasped when the first wave of contractions subsided. Panting slightly, she said, 'I threw a ball at the cocoanut shy and, whoosh, all over my shoes. I'd have died on the spot if anybody saw me, but the old fella was serving somebody else.'

Evie noticed the wet stain on Connie's white leather peep-toe sandals and knew there wasn't much time. 'Where's Angus?' she asked quickly, and Connie's beautiful face contorted when another contraction gripped her. The pains were coming quicker than either of them expected.

Connie motioned to the beer tent, unable to speak.

'Stay there, I'll go and get him!' Evie said, getting up, and realised what she had just said. Of course, Connie was going nowhere. She couldn't. 'There's a 'phone box by the post office, I'll ring an ambulance.'

Evie didn't wait for Connie to respond and tore off to the beer tent which, thankfully, wasn't far. Nevertheless, getting through the burgeoning merrymakers was another matter altogether.

Elbowing her way towards the bar, Evie realised she was wasting precious time. Angus was at the front of the crowd and, due to the singing from the Tram Tavern crowd, it would be impossible to hear her calling. Grabbing a chair, Evie climbed aboard and put her hands either side of her mouth and through sheer force and determination she opened her mouth and shouted louder than she had ever shouted in her life. 'Anguuuus! Connie's having her baby!'

Her voice reverberated round the tent and a sudden hush descended when all faces moved from her to Angus like spectators in a game of tennis.

'She's over there,' Evie stabbed her forefinger to the coconut shy and the rush of excitement was palpable when the crowd parted like the Red Sea. Angus dropped his pint and was gone in the blink of an eye when Evie noticed Susie talking to Danny. And by the look of it, even though she could not hear Susie's words, Danny was not pleased.

26

'At least I know who my mam and dad are,' Susie's lip curled into a sneer, 'but you, Danny boy, you are a nobody. A foundling. Nobody's child.'

'What are you talking about? You scatty mare.' Danny didn't trust a word Susie said any more.

'Scatty am I?' She goaded. 'You go and ask Ada what I'm talking about. She'll put you straight.' Susie said, before storming off across the field.

By the time Danny got back to the fete after a long walk to mull things over, the ambulance had been, and Connie was taken off to the cottage hospital on the outskirts of the village.

His head was swimming, trying to come to terms with what Susie had told him before he sent her packing. Her words seared into his brain, he tried to dismiss them knowing that Susie was a born troublemaker.

If Ada wasn't his mother, then who was? The only glimmer was the knowledge that if Ada wasn't his mother, then that snake-in-the-grass, Bert was not his father either. That, at least, would be some consolation.

He went into the beer tent and ordered a neat Scotch that burned the back of his throat as he downed it in one. In no mood to socialise he was sickened when Susie had the gall to sidle up to him and ask if he was going to buy her a drink.

Her obvious sense of entitlement repulsed him and turning to face her, his eyes blazing, he viewed her with a loathing that matched the feeling he had for Bert Harris.

'Buy you a drink?' Danny replied. 'Certainly.' He ordered a pint and a half of beer and as Evie watched from only feet away, standing with Meggie, she saw Danny pick up the half pint glass full of beer.

'No, don't,' Evie said, hurrying to his side, suspecting Danny was about to do something out of character, which he would remember and regret for the rest of his life. 'Don't let yourself down.' For a moment, there was a look of confusion in Danny's usually peaceful eyes. And taking the glass from his hand, she turned.

'Let me,' Evie said pouring the glass of beer over Susie Blackthorns platinum bouffant, which gave Evie the biggest surge of satisfaction she had felt in a long time.

'You were warned,' Evie told Susie, who stood by the bar, hands outstretched, dripping.

* * *

'It's a girl!' someone called in the tent. 'Princess Elizabeth has had a little girl.' A loud cheer went up inside the beer tent and somebody began to sing Land of Hope and Glory.

'We may have our very own royal baby in Reckoner's Row by the end of the day,' Ada's voice could be heard over everybody else's at the next table, as Evie brought a pot of tea and some delicious light-as-air scones slathered in jam and fresh clotted cream for her, Meggie and Danny. A rare treat indeed in the days when there was still rationing in force. 'I remember when I had mine,' Ada told anyone who'd listen, 'I was in labour for two full days.'

'Come and sit down, Lad,' Meggie whispered when Danny brought a tray of drinks and put it on the yellow gingham cloth covering the trestle table and took the seat next to Meggie, who gave a subdued smile at Ada's words cutting through the low murmur of chatter.

'I'll let Henry know we are here,' Evie said, rising from her seat knowing Meggie had something especially important to tell her son.

'I couldn't help meself, Meg,' Danny said, 'I would have poured the whole lot over her scheming head if Evie hadn't done it for me,' If the truth be told, Susie brought out feelings he was ashamed of. Dark feelings he had never addressed. And he realised they were the same feelings he had for the man he had called 'father' for as long as he could remember.

'Keep your powder dry, Lad,' Meggie's words were as soft as swan down. She had seen the troubled expression on Danny's face and realised it was time he knew the truth.

Evie stayed out of the way, talking to Mr Skinner by the bar knowing Meggie needed the time to tell Danny she was his mother and knowing Meggie would not have given him up easily. She was a natural mother. All the stable lads and carters' lads called her, 'Ma', because she looked after them, even when the business was in dire straits she made sure the lads had a steady job to do. Evie recalled how, when Meggie showed her the blackmailer's letter, her eyes had glistened as she took Evie into her confidence, telling her about her beloved baby, and why she had to give him up.

Talking to Danny now, she told him in a low voice: 'I paid most of my wages every week of my working life for your upbringing.' 'I lived in fear of you finding out before I could explain.' Meggie reached for her son's hand and was relieved when he did not pull away. 'I prayed you would not hate me for giving you up, knowing you have every right not to forgive me.'

'I could never do that.' Danny reassured her. 'But the decision was yours to make. Not Susie Blackthorn's'

'I never meant for Ada to keep you,' Meggie said. 'The arrangement was only ever meant to be temporary until Henry's mother died, but even the grim reaper got fed up waiting.' She gave a little half-laugh. 'By then the war came and I felt you would not want to get that kind of news when you're fighting the enemy.'

'I understand.' Danny said knowing it could not have been easy for this wonderful woman, who had never said a wrong word to him, and supported him in everything he did, to watch another woman bring him up in a way she saw fit, having no say in the matter because her family's livelihood depended on her keeping quiet.

'Do you really?' Meggie lifted her head, craving reassurance, and Danny nodded.

'I'll be back in a minute,' Danny said, when he saw Ada getting up from the table and followed her outside the tent.

'Enjoying the fete, Danny?' Ada asked, her face pink through spending time out in the sunshine and a few sly gins in the beer tent.

'It's wonderful,' Danny answered, 'I've learned a lot.'

'Always learning, hey. A right little ray of knowledge. You've come a long way, Lad.'

'Aye,' Danny, appearing relaxed, was seething inside. 'I've always been quick on the uptake.'

'Like meself. And why not.'

'Why not?' Danny said, wondering if Ada had an inkling about where her husband got his money from, while Meggie had to dip into her life savings to keep their business afloat, trying to survive astronomical demands.

'Were you ever going to tell me, Ada?' Danny's tone was steel tipped and he saw the colour drain from her face.

'I beg your pardon!' Ada said, her eyes wide at being addressed by name.

'You heard right.' Danny's expressionless face sent a shard of apprehension through Ada's body. 'Were you ever going to tell me that Meggie is my mother – who paid you every penny she possessed to make sure I was cared for? Were you ever going to tell me you raised me, not because you loved me or felt a maternal obligation – but because you were being paid to do so? While your husband, that no-good scheming drunk bleeds you and everybody else dry?'

Ada's mouth opened, but no sound came. Then she closed it, but it opened again, reminding Danny of the goldfish Bobby had won earlier and Danny realised he had gone too far. Ada was not to blame for any of this.

'I haven't seen that snake in the grass for weeks, and if he did have money I never saw it,' Ada replied. 'If it weren't for me and you, we would never have had enough money to live on. Bert was out of work more than he was in it...'

'He could have got a job in a bed factory testing mattresses.' Danny could not help himself. He wanted Ada to know how torn he felt. 'After all, Bert had plenty of practice, and not only that, he has been blackmailing Uncle Henry, nearly killing him and for what? So he could drink himself silly and spend money on illegal street bookies.'

'We had nothing.' Ada's plaintive tone was like a sword in his heart. 'The Skinners had the house. The business. The money. The lot. But I knew nothing about Bert's devious shenanigans.' Ada's voice trembled and Danny, confused, wanted to put his arms round her and tell her everything would be fine. But he could not be sure of that.

'You mean to tell me when Bert came home with pockets full of money, you didn't ask him where he got it from?' Danny was in bits and he needed to understand.

'Bert Harris? Have money in his pocket?' Ada scoffed. 'If he had money I didn't see any of it,' Ada said again. 'That was my penance for having a loving heart, and a hasty marriage to a man who loved his ale more than he loved his family.'

'Bert was a crook and you should have slung him out years ago.' He watched Ada's shoulders slump and she looked beaten and said in a small voice.

'I didn't live round here when Henry came to me that night with a bundle in his arms. I was already pregnant with Grace and my husband was out of work. We were penniless and badly needed the money Henry offered for taking care of the child. And then my aunt died, I was left the house in Reckoner's Row and after we moved in it paid for gas and food for us all.'

'Well, I don't know if I see it quite the same way.' Danny answered knowing he had spent his life supporting his moth... Ada. He did not regret bolstering the woman who he now knew was his aunt, but at what price?

'I gave you away for your own sake,' Meggie told Danny as they sat at the table, their tea had grown cold, 'not because I didn't want you or love you. Nothing could be further from the truth.' Tears burned her eyes, but Meggie held fast, not letting them fall until Danny reached for her hand and it was all too much. Twenty-five years of heartache welled up inside her and overflowed down her cheeks.

'I used to watch you playing in the street.' Meggie had a catch in her voice. 'I never tired of watching you play football or cricket, always determined to win, urging your team to do well.'

'I'm not a good loser,' Danny smiled.

'Did you have a happy childhood, Danny?' Meggie asked and he nodded, watching Meggie pour the dark red tea, just the way he liked it, not too strong you could stand a spoon in, or so weak it crawled out of the pot, exhausted.

'You don't have sugar?' she said recalling every little thing about him.

'No thanks,' Danny answered with a slight shake of his head, 'Ma never allowed us to have sugar.'

'Wise,' Meggie said, the quiet smile did not quite reach her tear-stained eyes.

'She did her best, I suppose,' Danny said, feeling awkward calling Ada 'Ma' in front of Meggie. 'I never went without if she could manage it. I always had good leather shoes and warm clothes, and I never went hungry.'

'I'm glad to hear it,' Meggie said, knowing every Friday since Danny was born she had put her wages into a small envelope and passed it over to Ada, so her child would be well cared for. Even when he joined the army at seventeen, she continued to provide for him and was glad to do so.

The money was the only link to the boy she had regretfully abandoned into the arms of another woman. And that woman's hand was always open, even if she wasn't the one who had been blackmailing her husband. Ada took credit for the good shoes, the warm clothes, and his full stomach. She smiled when Danny got up and said he had to find Evie.

* * *

'Henry asked me to look after the baby. Meggie needed the work and she could not look after him while she was earning,' Ada told Evie, glad the secret was finally out. 'I needed the money.

Bert couldn't get work on the docks or anywhere else, so I said yes.'

'Why didn't you give Danny back?' Evie asked knowing how heart-breaking it was for someone else to look after the children you love so much, when her own siblings had spent seven years in Ireland during and after the war. She scraped and saved every penny she could to bring them back. So Meggie must have felt the same way.

'None of us knew Henry's mother would live as long as she did.' Ada explained. 'She was getting on for seventy when Meggie turned up that night with a babe in arms and no place to go. By the time she died, Danny was seventeen – he couldn't get into the army fast enough.'

Danny overheard his mother. But she wasn't his mother in the way he thought Meggie would have been. Meggie, wonderful, kind, supportive Meggie who had always been there for him. Who hid him when he got into a scrape and Ada was on the warpath. She was his mother. Danny's heart sang. But he must contain his joy. Ada had done her best, and had made a good fist of it given the slimy little toad of a husband she had been forced to put up with. He decided to let Evie and Ada talk.

* * *

'Are you my father?' Danny asked Henry later, as he sat down next to the man he had always looked up to, 'is that the reason you sold me the business for a pound?'

'No, Lad, I'm not. But you have always been like a son to me.' Henry wished he had been given the opportunity to be Danny's father. 'I did it to put right the wrong I did to my Meggie, because I loved her so very much,' Henry said. 'I denied her the chance to raise you, her own son because I was selfish. Love makes you do

things like that, and I have to be honest, if I could ever have a son...
I would want one just like you.'

'Times were hard back then, and they were different,' Meggie
said when Henry reached for her hand, the gesture was as natural
to both of them as breathing, 'but we both watched you, all your
life. I even signed your forms to go into the army after you came to
tell me how much you needed to get away from Reckoner's Row.'

'Away from Bert and Ada,' Danny said. 'I couldn't discuss their
bitter feuds.' Because he did not want Meggie to feel any worse than
she did already. He was in awe of Meggie and Henry and hoped
that when his time came, he would be as happily married as they
were.

'I loved you like a son,' Henry said, 'and I had to keep the business going for your sake. My mother would have sold the yard from
under me out of spite if she knew about you. And it was only right
that you have it. You deserve it. You kept it going when I couldn't.
The men look up to you.'

'You're the man I aspire to be,' Danny said, knowing Henry and
Meggie had given him the things he always wanted: a business of
his own to build upon, and the motherly love he had always felt
from her. 'You're two of the best people I have ever known.'

'You don't know how much those words mean to me, my boy,'
Henry said. 'I am so proud of you.'

'We both are,' Meggie said, and, without warning, she felt the
burning sensation rise inside and her heart swelled with more
love than she ever dared dream possible. She had longed to tell
Danny she was his mother. But could not bear to see the disappointment in his eyes. She believed, wrongly, that his natural
sparkle would be snuffed out if he were to find out the truth. But,
by the look of it, the revelation had done the opposite when
Danny said:

'I will not only keep the business going, I will build it up.'

'This is the right time,' Henry said. 'The business won't stop thriving because I'm no longer in it.'

'I was hoping you would like to stay close, in an advisory capacity,' Danny said.

'I thought you'd never ask,' Henry replied.

'Having you around gives me strength. So don't go upsetting that ticker of yours.'

'You go down each morning and open those gates, my love,' Meggie told her husband, 'while Danny is building his empire.'

'Glad to be of service, Mam,' Danny said, unaware of the joy that last word brought to Meggie. But her reflection was short-lived when Angus came into the tent and caused a bit of a commotion...

'It's another girl!' Angus was jubilant. 'The baby has been born and she's eight stone eight pounds.'

'Poor Connie. Evie laughed as she joined them and was thrilled when she felt Danny slip his hand into hers. 'Eight stone?'

'I mean pounds,' Angus laughed. 'Eight pounds eight ounces.'

'Congratulations, Angus, well done!'

'I think you find, Connie did all the work,' Evie laughed, delighted when she saw the look of wonder on Danny's face.

'Come on Evie,' Danny said, 'let's wet the baby's head. Connie's baby, not the new princess's. That would be treason, I imagine.'

'I can't see Connie being too chuffed either,' Evie said.

27

Danny took off his cap and had a whip-round for the driver. He would speak to his mother... Ada tomorrow. It was too late in the day to rake up the past. But he knew he could never turn his back on the woman who had reared him, knowing she had never had it easy with that rogue, Bert. She had done her best with what little she had, even if she did give the impression she was Lady Bountiful, he knew differently. Or at least he thought he did. But at least Ada would get the peace she deserved. And would no longer be bled dry by a leeching husband.

Everybody was in friendly spirits, singing songs on the journey back to Reckoner's Row, where the coach pulled up outside The Tram Tavern, all eager to join the revelry, which was obviously going on inside when they heard singing.

'Is that our Grace singing?' Danny asked.

'It certainly sounds like Grace,' Evie answered, and Jack told them he would just pop in and have a look, closely followed by Lucy who had no intentions of missing out. Everybody was relaxed and the mood was mellow when Lucy reminded Bobby that they, too, could enjoy the party if they collected empty glasses.

When they entered the bar the revelry was in full swing and Angus, euphoric having held the most angelic little girl in his arms for the first time, went behind the bar to help Mim who rang the bell to a pub full of moans.

'Are 'ey, Mim, we've just travelled miles to get back here and fill the coffers.'

'Fill you bellies with my good ale,' Mim replied taking no lip from any of the smart-mouthed customers, 'and I'm not ringing for last orders. There is someone here who wants to make an announcement.' Mim nodded to Grace Harris who linked her arm through Bruce's arm and beaming, she said:

'Mam, Danny, everybody, I'd like you to meet my new husband.' A roar went up and Danny shook Bruce's hand before lifting Grace and twirling her round the floor, while Ada, standing back, her mouth open wide, was speechless. But rest assured, she thought as soon as she got her voice back there would be words. Plenty of words.

'Don't worry Mam,' Grace said, giving her mother a hug, 'you can still buy a hat. We are having the formal service next month.'

'Well,' Ada suddenly found her voice, 'I'll have to go and see Father MacManus in Saint Patrick's. And we will have to book the church hall and the cake. Have you had time to look at the wedding dresses, how many bridesmaids will you want? I've got a few bob put by. This wedding won't be shabby.'

'Mam,' Grace could not hide her delight, 'you do not have to worry about a thing. Everything is sorted. After the wedding, we will be going to the country house for the reception. Everybody will be welcome. Money is no object.'

Bruce told her only after their onboard wedding that his father had died, and he owned one of the most exclusive shipping lines in the world.

'Oh, Lad,' Ada said hugging Bruce to her motherly bosom, 'I'm so sorry to hear your sad news.'

'Thank you, Mrs Harris,' Bruce answered when he could speak.

'No not Mrs Harris, you call me Mam – everybody does,' Ada said knowing there was a lot to discuss with her only daughter and this was not the time or the place.

'A new hat, Mim.' Ada was more delighted than she could imagine. Her daughter was married to a millionaire and the reception was going to be held in his country house that could sleep everybody in Reckoner's Row.

Put that in your pipe and smoke it Mim! Ada thought raising her sherry glass to Mim, each wondering how they could outdo each other in the wedding hat department.

'It's been a bit of a day, one way or the other,' Danny said, 'first Connie has a baby on the same day as our future Queen, then our Grace marries a millionaire – if you please.'

'And Mister Skinner won the Netherford cup, don't forget,' Evie reminded him as they finished their drinks and made their way out of the Tavern with Lucy, Bobby and Jack. 'Good news comes in threes, they say.'

'It might even come in fours and fives,' Danny said, glad that the man Ada Harris married was not his father. 'But one thing's for sure, I doubt we will ever have a repeat of this day for a long time – if ever.'

'And you taking over Skinner's yard, don't forget,' Jack added, and they all laughed.

Danny didn't mind the yard being known as Skinner's; it had an excellent reputation and everybody in the business knew that the workforce were reliable and value for money.

'I've had a smashing day,' Lucy was glowing and tired as the heat of the day cooled only a little, and the pink and gold sun dipped down over the horizon of the river Mersey.

'Me too,' Meggie and Evie said in unison, and laughed.

Evie looked to her younger sister, who was getting taller than she was, even though Lucy wouldn't be fourteen until November. 'I'll tell you what, why don't I make us all a nice plate of chips and egg?'

'Eggs, real eggs, not powdered ones?' Lucy asked, wide awake. She could think of nothing better to finish her wonderful day out than a nice plate of crispy chips, just the thing to dip into a delicious, frilly-edged fried egg.

'And,' Evie said with a gleam in her eyes, 'I bought some fresh bread and a packet of best butter from the farmer's wife, too.'

'You never did!' Lucy's mouth was already drooling. 'What are we waiting for?'

'Can I tempt you both?' Evie asked Meggie and Mr Skinner.

'Not for me,' Meggie said, unable to suppress a tired but happy yawn. 'I'm off to my bed and I'll take this fellow with me,' she said, lifting the heavy trophy.

'I'll put it on my side of the bed,' Henry said with a twinkle in his tired eyes.

'See you bright and early in the morning, young whipper-snapper!' Meggie called, heading down Reckoner's Row towards their own house in Summer Settle. She could not remember when she had enjoyed herself so much.

Danny, Evie's constant companion, gave Meggie cause to suspect the girl was more than glad to keep him company – for a long time. Well, there was nothing wrong with that, she thought.

'I'll walk you home,' Danny said making Evie laugh as they reached her gate. Lucy and Jack carried on ahead inside the house.

'I only live six feet away.' Evie laughed looking to her own front door. 'But you can come in for a chip butty if you peel the spuds.' Evie said, overjoyed when Danny agreed. She liked that in a man, she thought. They could be just as equal as women when they put their mind to it.

'I'll have you know when I was in the army I was a champion spud basher,' Danny's eyes twinkled as he spoke. 'You could read The Evening Express through my peelings.'

'There you go, then,' Evie said, 'you've got a job for life. Some girl is going to be extremely lucky to get you.' She smiled, a little surprised when Danny stopped and turned her round to face him, unprepared for what he did next. In a voice more solemn than she had ever heard him speak before, he said:

'How would you like me to be your life-long spud peeler?'

'Will you have time?' Evie could not help but smile, gazing into his warm, loving eyes. 'What with having an empire to build, I mean.'

'An empire?' Danny's brows creased momentarily, then he realised what she meant. 'If I'm going to build an empire, I will need a strong woman to help me. Do you think you would like to join me?'

'I would like that very much.' Evie melted in his arms when he lowered his head to kiss her.

'I've loved you from that moment, when I saw you carrying little Lucy on your hip to the dockyard, while holding young Jack's hand. Taking them to be evacuated to Ireland. I wanted to put my arms round you and tell you everything would be all right.' Danny's voice was raw with pent-up emotion, and he drew Evie to him once more. 'But none of us knew that back then.'

'We know now,' Evie answered.

'Our future will be strong because of our past. Me and you can build a whole new world, together.' He paused and his voice softened when he continued, 'There has only ever been one girl for me, Evie Kilgaren, and that girl is you.'

'And you for me, Danny Harris,' she answered, her heart bursting with love for this wonderful man.

'So what are we waiting for?' Danny's eyes glistened, full of promise. 'I can't give you the life Grace has. Not yet. But one day...'

'Let's build our empire first,' Evie said placing her finger on his lips, 'until then I have all the riches I could possibly need.'

ACKNOWLEDGMENTS

As always to Tony, Nicki, Lee, Abi, Daniel, and Hollie

Kevin, Gina, Emily and Jack

Alan, for all that you are: determined and never giving up.

My brothers, sisters, their wives and husbands and my gorgeous nephews and nieces.

A special mention for our Chris. Stay strong. Know you are loved.

Love, Sheila xx

MORE FROM SHEILA RILEY

We hope you enjoyed reading *The Mersey Girls*. If you did, please leave a review.

If you'd like to gift a copy, this book is also available as an ebook, digital audio download and audiobook CD.

Sign up to Sheila Riley's mailing list for news, competitions and updates on future books.

http://bit.ly/SheilaRileyNewsletter

The first book in the Reckoner's Row series, *The Mersey Orphan*, is available now.

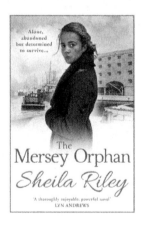

ABOUT THE AUTHOR

Sheila Riley wrote four #1 bestselling novels under the pseudonym Annie Groves and is now writing a saga trilogy under her own name. She has set it around the River Mersey and its docklands near to where she spent her early years. She still lives in Liverpool.

Visit Sheila's website: http://my-writing-ladder.blogspot.com/

Follow Sheila on social media:

- facebook.com/SheilaRileyAuthor
- twitter.com/1sheilariley
- instagram.com/sheilarileynovelist
- bookbub.com/authors/sheila-riley

ABOUT BOLDWOOD BOOKS

Boldwood Books is a fiction publishing company seeking out the best stories from around the world.

Find out more at www.boldwoodbooks.com

Sign up to the Book and Tonic newsletter for news, offers and competitions from Boldwood Books!

http://www.bit.ly/bookandtonic

We'd love to hear from you, follow us on social media:

facebook.com/BookandTonic

twitter.com/BoldwoodBooks

instagram.com/BookandTonic

Printed in Great Britain
by Amazon